Enjoy the journey.
Its a wonderful life !
Gaelyn Whitley Keith

NOT ALONE

GAELYN WHITLEY KEITH

NOT ALONE

TATE PUBLISHING
AND ENTERPRISES, LLC

Unless otherwise indicated, all Scripture quotations are from the New King James Bible. Other scripture identified in chapter 15 is from The Everyday Life Bible: The Power of God's Word for Everyday Living and is used with permission.

Cover Image Credits: idfonline/5615747708, gerlos/3119891607.

"' represents statements one says when one talks to oneself.

Published by Tate Publishing & Enterprises, LLC
127 E. Trade Center Terrace | Mustang, Oklahoma 73064 USA
1.888.361.9473 | www.tatepublishing.com

Tate Publishing is committed to excellence in the publishing industry. The company reflects the philosophy established by the founders, based on Psalm 68:11,
"The Lord gave the word and great was the company of those who published it."

Book design copyright © 2015 by Tate Publishing, LLC. All rights reserved.
Cover design by Ivan Charlem Igot
Interior design by Gram Telen

Published in the United States of America

ISBN: 978-1-68028-433-1
1. Fiction / Religious
2. Fiction / Christian / General
15.06.03

To anyone who is looking for truth.

Acknowledgements

I owe a debt of gratitude to many precious people whose support and wise counsel assisted in the creation of this unique project.

Tiffeny the jack of all trades, who kept me on track and insured that I kept things simple and easy to understand.

Michaela the wise grammarian, who knows invaluable sources of academic writing guidelines and was helpful in pointing out my many shortcomings.

Randy my amazing husband, who created a new punctuation mark "', it gives the reader a glimpse at other's hidden thoughts—what people say when they talk to themselves.

And finally to my many friends who shared invaluable knowledge and showed extraordinary patience as I pursued my journey in the search for Truth.

Author's Note

The Keith punctuation mark "' indicates thoughts that are spoken in the mind. It is a new form of punctuation that helps explain to the reader why things happen. This novel is a creative work of fiction that imparts wisdom and truth about the affects of what happens when one talks to one's self.

Introduction

Has any of you suffered an injustice, been overlooked, ignored, rejected? Has anyone been denied, repudiated, negated, humiliated, devastated, infuriated, frustrated, or transgressed upon?

You're a good person. So why have people disrespected, slighted, wounded, snubbed, oppressed, held down, discriminated against, beaten down, distressed, tortured, haunted, bullied, teased, tormented, or talked smack about you? Why?

And when it was over, did you think, "'I don't deserve this! Why me? I'm a good person!'"

If someone is going to get divorced, have a heart attack, be mugged or raped, blown up by a terrorist, lose a limb in an accident, be swindled, slandered, foreclosed on or fired, don't you think it should happen to someone who deserves it?

"'It should never happen to me! I'm a good person!'"

Well if any of this has happened to you, I just want you to know that Joseph Michael Moretti has found the answer!

1

I wanted to make it so that young people would begin to ask questions about the mystery. Not having enough interest in the mysteries of life to ask the question, "Is there a God or is there not a God"—that is for me the worst thing that can happen.

—George Lucas

Joseph Michael Moretti awakened to the muffled crying coming from the guest room. Grace's sobbing echoed in his mind. Quickly dressing, he slipped on a pair of flip-flops and headed downstairs for a cup of coffee.

After hitting the button on the coffeemaker, he got his favorite lucky mug and the bottle of vanilla creamer. Desiring to avoid Grace, he softly called Hershey, their chocolate-brown Lab, for a walk on the Strand.

"'It will be good to feel the fresh ocean breeze.'"

As soon as he picked up the leash, Hershey was at his side. After pouring coffee into his mug, he headed out the front door.

"'Why does she have to cry all the time? I can stand anything but crying. Yelling would be better.'"

Joe strolled his way along the Strand, his flip-flops echoing on the pavement. He watched the gulls diving for their breakfasts. He spotted a dog, paddling out into the waves after a red ball as his owner stood at the shore, laughing and yelling encouragements. When he retrieved the ball, he paddled to shore. Shaking like a wild thing, he showered his owner with water. His bark was full of immense joy when the ball was thrown again out into the waves, and he leaped back in the water to repeat his trick.

Seeing a couple of guys surfing in the distance, Joe craved to have the energy to join them. If only he could muster the strength. Not anymore. He just couldn't. Once he had thought of himself as unstoppable—a shrewd businessman, stylish, even sexy when he wanted to be. But his face seemed too careworn now, his cheekbones too protruding, and the gloominess too deep. The restless nights had taken their toll leaving his brown eyes heavily sunken. Sitting like a stagnant pond clouded by fear, he wondered what evil lurked below the surface, what unbearable pain might soon unfold?

A cool breeze blew across his face, smelling of the ocean, clean and fresh. Walking close to the shoreline, a wave caught him by surprise. Wet and clammy sand oozed between his feet and toes. Arriving at his favorite spot, he sat in the sand sipping his coffee, while Hershey curled up next to him taking his morning nap.

His mind rambled about without a clear-cut purpose. Most of his important decisions in life had been made here, but for the first time he had no spot to place his pain and nowhere to turn to for help. Joe was heartbroken. He wondered what force had led him to this place. There seemed to be no magic healing, no easy step to get him back to where he once was happy.

Over the last few days, Joe's emotions twisted and plummeted, sending him on an uncontrollable roller-coaster ride. He felt weak and lifeless, and there was a strange chill in the pit of his stomach. His feelings of injustice and anger let him know that something wasn't right in the universe. A heavy cloak of anxiety hung around his shoulders, "'Why has this happened to my family? When will it stop? The pain! I can't take it anymore! Why can't someone, anyone help me?'"

Bewildered, he sat puzzling over the past events one more time. He felt alone, disconnected, and alienated even from Grace. His life no longer had rules, boundaries, or protocols. His grief stripped him of everything he understood. His life used to be so blissful, so free of worry, so free of pain. Of course things had changed. The fates are so cruel. Everything switched around, and his life took such dark turns, knocking him into the abyss of uncontrollable suffering and despair.

He had lost them—forever. He never got to say goodbye. They were everything to him. Tears streaked down his pale cheeks. So what if men weren't suppose to cry? He ached to hug them one more time. His surroundings had taken on an uncommon tone; the shadows of nightfall emerged more dismal, his mornings were less optimistic, his walks along the beach less enthusiastic, and there were moments at work in the late afternoon when a kind of panic overtook him.

Before he had his first child, he anticipated battles ahead, knowing his children would test and possibly defy him in their teenage years. But surely he had never anticipated this. The moment that he heard Christopher's first cry, he found within his heart this unexpectedly raw capacity for love. All at once he was a protector, a nurturer, a defender of innocence, a storyteller, a kisser of boo-boos, and a coach until the end of time. It was a special club he joined that day, one he was humbled and grateful to be a part of. How had everything gone so wrong?

"'I'm spiraling out of control being pulled down a narrow drain, headed for the garbage disposal of life. I feel like I'm trapped in a never-ending maze with dead ends and traps in front of me. How will I ever end this nightmare? I can't handle things any more. Do I know what I'm doing? Why am I the only one whose life is in shambles? It seems to me everyone—yes—everyone I know has got their life more together than I do. Can I survive this? Do I even want to? Wouldn't death be better?'"

Tears flow down Joe's cheeks. Overtaken by his feelings, Joe longs to pull things apart into small pieces so that he can manage his life. Sweet Hershey nozzles closer. Joe is relieved he is alone. No one should see him in this state.

"'Will this ever stop? Good people aren't supposed to be punished by God. Or are they? How could this possibly be a lesson you need to teach me? I haven't learned a thing. Was I wrong to think that there is love and truth in this world? What did I do to deserve this? My children may not have been angels, but how could a loving God let this happen? God, I'm desperate, help me! I want to be free of this. Free from it all. Why is love so unbearable? I've made such a mess of things. How can I rest in your peace when you let everything be taken from me? Nothing is left. God, I need your help. Please send someone with the answer. Please, stop the pain. I can't work like this. I'm afraid we'll lose our house too. Where are you? Damn it. I didn't do anything to deserve this! How can I ever trust that you won't let this happen again?'"

So unwilling to continue crying, he sat there distressed, panicked, and storming. It was as though his own words were eating him alive. Joe needed to think. He wasn't certain who he was, not any longer. Was he incredibly stupid to think that bad things could not happen to good people?

"'Why can't I find anyone with the answers? Everyone avoids me. Even you, God. Are you on vacation or something? I'm grieving and out of my mind. Why don't you talk to me? Why don't you comfort me? Please take this mountain off my back. What I wouldn't do for a warm hug or an encouraging word. Why does everyone look at me as though I'm dying of cancer? I don't need their pity. I just need an answer to the pain. God please help me! Where are you? Why did you let this happen to my family?

I'm entitled to feel intense sorrow and fear, all of which I'm sure any person in my position would feel. Nothing is off the table, nothing is wrong. From now on, if I want to cry I will do it. I can't imagine how anyone would get over a loss like mine. No, I will never get over it. I won't ever be able to move forward. I feel so numb like the world is going on without me. Nothing seems to bring me happiness. Time heals all wounds. I wonder who thought up that meaningless cliché. Why do all my friends just think I should get over it? I feel frozen in time. I can't go backward to fix anything, and I can't move forward either.

But God, you know what I hate most is the sudden grief of outbursts that erupt just when it seems I'm doing better. Sometimes I understand why—like an identifiable trigger set things in motion and at other times—the times that disturb me the most are when they come from out of the blue. Why do you let this happen to me? I fear I will never be able to handle a baby crying without longing for my children's tender hugs?

God, you know I've tried everything. I've questioned my friends and family. We tried reasoning together. This morning I didn't want to get out of bed. I felt profound sadness, hearing Grace's muffled crying. If you've given up on me, couldn't you at least help her? She didn't do anything to deserve this. I wanted to walk into the living room this morning and find them there on the couch, sipping a latte after a jog on the beach. Only this morning they weren't there. They weren't anywhere. They are lost. I keep telling myself it will be okay, but how? God, I've always trusted you. So today, for the first time in months I'm asking one last time. The only prayer that comes to mind is the prayer my granny taught me as a child.'"

Clasping his hands together while bowing his head, Joe quietly begins his prayer: "Lord bless and keep me. Lord make your face shine upon me and be gracious to me. Lord lift up your countenance upon me and give me peace. Amen."

Joe hungered for familiar things. His mind began to wander, to daydream searching for relieve from the pain. He pictured himself standing on the deck, overlooking the ocean, with hamburgers and hot dogs on the grill and a Sam Adams in his hand. Clouds serenely floated across the sky while his children's voices echoed from the tables. Music resonate from his sound system. Joe's vision surrounded him with familiar feelings, smells, and sounds. Wrapped in a blanket of happy memories, Joe felt momentarily safe in its glow.

A moment later, Joe's attention was abruptly drawn to a tall muscular blond-headed surfer who appeared, yeah appeared, like he came out of a wave and then walked on to the sandy shore. The powerful morning sun illuminated his body, presenting a shower of diamonds in such a way that he appeared to be some type of supernatural being. From the distance, he appeared to have a glow around him.

Then returning to his thoughts, he gave no more notice to the man.

"'If only I could turn back the hands of time. I'm so sorry; I should have been there to protect you. If only I had put my foot down and forbidden you to go. You might not have spoken to me for a few days, but in time you would have forgiven me. I was so preoccupied with upcoming business. Now it's too late! Why do I keep playing these what ifs over and over again in my mind? I'm going to drive myself insane.'"

Yelling over the roar of the ocean's waves, the man approached Joe and asked, "Wow, did you see that? Look about a half mile out past the pier, there is a school of whales. Just look! I'm sure they'll surface again in a minute."

He quickly slid the pair of binoculars from around his neck and handed them to Joe. Looking into the horizon, a moment later, they saw a pair of gray whales rise from the water, twirling as they flew through the air—a better act than anyone could have seen at SeaWorld. The two men stayed transfixed for some time.

In the distance, Joe saw more giants, their tails and spray announcing their presence. At one point, the largest whale breathed through his blowhole, spewing a rainbow mist across the horizon. In the silence, tranquility filled their surroundings.

Joe was surprised by the peaceful feelings that came over him when the man sat down next to him. His Tommy Bahama shirt, cargo pants, and OluKai flip-flops appeared dry.

"'Wasn't that the guy I just saw minutes before come out of the surf? Maybe this is a side effect from the experimental medication MK-1313 I've been taking. Of course, like any drug, the doctor had warned that there may be crazy side effects. I think

I remember reading it could cause dizziness, tiredness, or chest tightness. I'll have to call the doctor when I get home. Hope the doctor won't think I'm losing my mind.'"

Stretching out his hand, "Hi, I'm Joshua."

"Hi. I'm Joe."

"Wasn't that just the most amazing sight? Was that your first whale spotting?"

"I just live a block or so down on the Strand, but I've never seen anything so spectacular before. I've lived here all my life except when I went to UC Berkeley. How about you?"

"Oh, I'm just here on an assignment for work. It's been a challenging project, but I know that everything will work out. After seeing those whales, don't you think it's a sign? If God takes care of those magnificent creatures, surely he can make things work out for us. I just know things will change for the better. It's like the changing tide. First it has to go out until at last it stops; then before long, it comes back in. Give things time to turn around and things will change for the better."

Joshua's reassuring words persuaded Joe that somehow things would work out for him too. As Joshua rose to leave, a wave of peace swept over Joe, and for the first time in months, he felt life stir in him again. Turning to say goodbye, he was startled to find that Joshua was gone. He jumped to his feet in amazement and looked in every direction, but he had vanished. Looking down at his hands, he saw he was still holding Joshua's binoculars. "'Too bad Joshua forgot them. Wonder if I'll ever see him again.'"

Suddenly the sun came out from behind the foggy haze, surprising Joe who hadn't expected the sun to arrive so early. His eyes squinted; the glare from the water seemed incredibly intense. Everything reflected amazingly bright colors—the water turned from gray to blue. As his eyes adjusted, he sat, listening to the roar of the waves as they crashed upon the shore. A gull cried high overhead, searching for its breakfast. The beach was very serene.

2

My words fly up, my thoughts remain below:
Words without thoughts never to heaven go.

—William Shakespeare

Joe could no longer see Joshua, but he was still standing there. Joshua yearned to tell Joe everything. If he only understood the entire story, he could change things so easily, but the laws of the kingdom had been set up before time.

In most trials, it always seemed the home team had the advantage, but Joshua had firmly stated, "It ain't over until it's over." He could see the picture Joe had hanging on the wall in his office. It portrayed a frog partway in a crane's open mouth holding on to the crane's neck for dear life. The smile that crossed Joshua's face was soon accompanied by a small chuckle. Placing a thought of the picture in Joe's mind, he said, "Remember, it ain't over until it's over."

Joshua's liquid-blue eyes flashed as he pondered these things, "'Somehow I must get Joe to realize that there is another world that exists right at this very moment in a parallel plane. But since I promised I would not interfere, this has become a very difficult task. Joe must be finding things more complex now that he is in charge of his own journey. So many things are invisible to Joe's eyes, but that still doesn't negate the fact that they are just as real as the world Joe sees. This invisible world influences everything. Will Joe ever be able to see his story as anything other than unspeakable pain. Truthfully, there are many new and delightful stories waiting to be written. Joe it is up to you! I know what you think; I hear it just as if we were speaking to each other.'"

What was visible to Joe's eyes was only a very minute part of what science knows exists.

Looking intently at Joe he discerned that Joe didn't want to keep having negative things come to pass. But doesn't he believe that they will? Doesn't he keep whining they will? Thanks to processes started when Joe was just a child, he finds it all but impossible to believe in the unknown while the familiar is before his eyes.

From the teachers he'd studied under, and even the religious leaders of his church, Joe had learned to believe only what he could see. Joe hadn't given much thought to the other world. As the old saying goes, "seeing is believing." Joe had learned to only trust his five senses. If it wasn't spelled out right in front of his nose, to Joe, it was hocus-pocus.

Oh, I guess it would be good for me to fill you in on some important facts about the events that are bothering Joe. Without them you would be as lost as he is. Most people forget that the Devil is in the details. A cliché that rings truer than most.

Thinking back, Joshua remembers Joe on his first day at UC Berkeley. Joe was an attractive impressive figure, with a rough rugged look, the sweetest smile, and just a little bit over six feet tall. His shoulder-length auburn hair was curly, and his bellbottom pants were ragged because they dragged across the ground as he walked.

Some thought Joe should try out for the school musical *Jesus Christ Super Star*. Not only did he look like Jesus most of the time, but he acted like him too. There weren't many other college students who attended Mass on Sunday. Joe was irreproachable and respectable. Attending Berkeley did not change him a bit. Everyone knew Joe's character was genuine, yet no one thought of him as a Jesus freak.

Having attended American Martyrs Parochial School as a child, he had developed the habit of praying every morning as he awoke. He couldn't think of a better way to start his day than saying, "Hi, Father, what do you have planned for me today? Hope the day includes lots of crispy bacon and some chocolate chip pancakes. With you on my side, I know it will be a great day."

His actions spoke more than his words. Attending the early Mass each Sunday gave him more time to play. After all, God didn't expect him to become a monk. When he graduated from Berkeley, he wanted to participate in the stream of community life, sharing the joys and sorrows within it.

Some of his college buddies did foolish things doing it their own ways and getting themselves into trouble. Drugs and rampant sex were everywhere. Abortion and rehab followed. Then they would complain to Joe, "Why did God do this to me?" Joe's answer was always, "Are you kidding? God didn't shove the drugs in your mouth!"

"What am I going to do?" they'd ask.

"You're smart. You should know you got what you deserved. Tomorrow is a new day. Just take a better path and things will change."

He wondered why he was so much wiser than them. He guessed it was because he willingly used his intellectual mind in choosing right and wrong. To him, holiness was not a removal from a prosperous life, but rather a rejection of evil temptations. Joe's life was full of love, friendships, success; and on Sunday morning, even God had his place. His life was full of endless possibilities and bright tomorrows.

I guess now would be a good time to introduce you to Grace. She plays a pivotal spot in the story too.

Why should Joe ever feel tempted when he had such a foxy girlfriend? Joe's friendship with Grace began when they attended preschool together. They had both grown up in Manhattan Beach. In their high school days, they would occasionally run into each other at local downtown spots or while jogging on the beach.

Grace had an enchanting even-featured face. Grinning as she talked deepened the dimples in her cheeks, and her bright blue eyes twinkled as she quickly gave Joe the once-over. Grace usually wore shorts, a pale blue T-shirt with her shoulder length sandy, sun-streaked blonde hair pulled back in a pony tail. She had a warm golden tan that came from the beautiful California sun. They would say hello and head on their way, but Joe couldn't help but say to himself: "Wow, that Grace Ross is a fox!"

There was something about her that pulled his gaze back: panache. Though she wore beach attire, she had it. Confidence gave Grace her own brand of style. It appealed to him as much—well, nearly as much—as a good football game. Seeing her made his heart race a million miles a minute. Yes, indeed, she had endless possibilities.

Grace's parents were both lawyers. When Grace was turning two, they both decided one child was enough. How could any child be better? They enjoyed being parents, but her mother refused to give up her career. More than one child would make it too complicated. Additionally, they both cherished their freedom to travel and ability to afford a beach front home. Back then, their choice was rare.

As an only child, Grace thought of her bestfriend as someone who was better than a sister could ever be. They seldom argued, and they shared the same interests. Despite being a little self-centered, Grace was extremely loyal—her friends were everything. Thankfully, most of the time, when she told people she was an only child, they skeptically looked her up and down before saying something cryptically critical and carelessly cheeky like "Hmm, really? You don't seem like an only child." What Grace hoped they were implying, believed they were implying, was that she possessed a strong independent spirit that remained calm under pressure.

Grace possessed many of her grandfather's endearing traits. His Scottish heritage imbued him with a most feisty nature, yet he was strangely calm most the time. His principles were impeccable, and his integrity had enabled him to prosper in all he put his hands to.

If you got him talking on anything Scottish, you never knew when the conversation would end. He was a descendant of George Ross, and his family had come to America for religious freedom. He took great pride in telling anyone who would listen that his great-great-great, and then he would stop and say, "Oh you know, way back during the Revolutionary War, had affixed his signature to the Declaration of Independence."

But perhaps what Grace remembers most about him is his favorite saying, "The right thing isn't always popular and the popular thing isn't always right." Since both Grace's parents worked full time, her grandfather was greatly involved in her life. He was the kind of grandfather every kid wants to have. When she needed a playmate, he was up for endless games of Clue, Life, or Monopoly. As she grew older, he's been a listening ear whenever she needed to talk about anything—from boys to gossiping girls. He was continuously interested in anything she undertook and constantly encouraged her to pursue her dreams.

But perhaps what Grace remembers most is her grandfather's special smell. It is hard to describe it in relation to other scents because it is unlike anything else that ever existed. She could only explain it by the memories it brought forth when she breathed it in: peppermint, Christmas, old spice, fresh brewed coffee, and sun tan lotion. This scent instantly evokes the exhilarating sensations of a day spent at the beach, or an evening curled up on the couch, listening to him read aloud her favorite stories.

After attending Graces's high school graduation, he developed a few health concerns and as a result, he began using a cane. Late one summer evening, he became dizzy and staggered to the bathroom. The next day, Grace's mother found him, laying cold and stiff on the bathroom floor.

The death of her grandfather left Grace feeling like a piece of her heart was missing. She wondered if anyone could possibly understand how she felt. Tears, bewilderment—how would she ever find peace again? The world seemed so difficult. Thankfully, the fall semester was about to begin.

The first person to catch Joe's eye at freshmen orientation was Grace. He spotted her across the room and wondered if she would go out with him. Walking across the room, he immediately struck up a conversation, "Hi Grace. How was your summer? I didn't know you got into Berkeley. What's your major?"

She was surprised that his full-on stare had made her heart beat faster. She flipped her hair back, shifted her angle so her gaze was locked in on his face. "Journalism. Someday I want to write a book that will change the course of the world. How about you?" she replied.

Her smile and friendly body language seemed to indicate her interest in him. Now it was time to make his move. He remembered that he had often seen her family eating at Old Venice. There was a good chance she liked Italian food. He tried to focus on her eyes. He didn't want her to see him staring at other parts of her body; she might think twice about going out with him. The best kind of first date is one where it is easy to talk, get to know each other, and have fun. Trying to act casual and confident, he flashed his earmark smile at her.

Just standing near Grace made it happen. Joe's heart raced, it was hard to breathe. He could still talk around her, but he was incapable of feeling normal. It had never happened like this. It was such a strong attraction. His brain was telling him, "'Hey, bro, wake up. This girl is perfect for you. Ask her out before someone else does.'"

"I'm following in my dad's footsteps as a business marketing major. I hear there will be a concert tonight in the gym. Would you like to go? Some friends from the dorm are going, and we thought we would go for pizza after it's over."

"Sounds good. Can I bring my roommate Annie?"

"Sure we'll stop by your dorm room at about three, and we can all walk over together."

Laughing and having fun came so easily to them. Ironically, it was their first fight that made Joe realize they were meant for each other. One night, Grace was not her usual perky self. Shades of sorrow from her grandfather's death lingered. Everything Joe said seemed to rub her the wrong way. Then they had a dilly of an argument over whether a women's place was in the home raising the kids. After all, the 70s had ushered in so many changes. Feeling frustrated, Joe stood to leave. Grabbing his arm, Grace yelled, "You can't go. I won't be able to sleep if we don't come to some mutual agreement."

Instantly they both said, "Never go to sleep angry."

So instead of leaving, Joe stayed and talked with Grace for two more hours until they worked through it. There was no point in dating Grace if such an important issue was not resolved. Joe wanted the woman he married to be the person who raised his children, no ifs, ands, or buts. He didn't want his wife to feel she has to do it all. Joe felt that many women were often pressured into feeling that they must be both a mother and a career woman to be successful. This isn't true in Joe's opinion. Being a parent is a huge responsibility, one that gives parents the privilege of influencing their children's lives in so many ways.

"Surely you don't want our children to ride the school bus home, unlock the door to an empty house, and fix their own milk and cookies." Joe lamented. "Everyone will think I'm not capable of taking care of my family. My mom never worked a day in her life, and she says the thing that brought her the most happiness was her five children. She couldn't imagine any job that was more important. I just figured that when I got married, my wife would want to be home with our kids just as my mother had done."

"I'd like to work, at least part-time, because it's interesting and stimulating and part of my identity, because it will make me, I hope, a better mother. Writing is like a piece of my soul. It takes me on a journey to new amazing places, without it I would be lost." Grace sighed.

Eventually, a compromise plan emerged; other than journaling, Grace would put her writing on hold. They decided that Grace would stay home while the children were small, perhaps until the youngest one was in kindergarten. Then, if Grace still wanted a career, they would readdress the issue at that time.

Three warriors had been at their post watching, hovering above, nestled in the corner, bold and brilliant. Joe and Grace didn't notice them. Most humans were unaware of their presence. Nothing was said, but you could tell they were thinking, pondering the effects this event might hold on the future.

"'Compromise: a word that doesn't usually work as well as people publicize it will. Grace is the sort of woman who lives for others. I wish I could warn her that her blind commitment to Joe is setting her up for a potential trap. This trap most likely will appear when the excitement of this new romance has worn off. Yes, courtship was a time when young lovers often sow seeds, which can grow up in ten to twenty years later into domestic hatred. Would she remain happy looking back over her life, or would she feel cheated? Time would tell, but as they mature we will have to try to help them resolve this issue in a peaceful manner.'"

Still Grace had another possibility. In her spare time she could pen an article for *Vogue* or a bestselling novel. After all, how much work could children be? As much as Grace longed for a career, she also craved a large family: something she felt she had missed out on in her own childhood.

By spring semester, Joe caught an incurable case of the love bug. To be in love for the first time was a unique feeling that introduced Joe to a new and mesmerizing array of emotions. It was the most enchanting sensation that left a deep mark on Joe's heart. They sang songs together, went to the movies, they enjoyed a simple friendship that sprang from truly liking each other. They never ran out of words and talked about everything. They laughed, they giggled, and their eyes twinkled from the joy of being together. The way he looked at her—well, he was definitely starstruck.

After graduating from UC Berkeley with his MBA in business and proposing to the love of his life, Grace Emily Ross, the only thing left to determine was where they would live.

Yes, he had done it the proper way. Joe was a man of tradition; so before proposing to Grace, he went to Robert, Grace's father, to ask his permission for her hand in marriage. He expressed his desire to spend the rest of his life with Grace. He would honor, respect, and take care of her for the rest of their lives. Robert was pleased and quickly gave his blessing.

Grace had always dreamed of a romantic proposal, and she definitely got it from Joe. Easter was Grace's favorite holiday, probably because of all the jellybeans and candy her family gave out at the annual Easter egg hunt. Having purchased a giant hot pink Easter egg, he placed it in the garden of his parent's home. He invited Grace out on the deck for a cup of morning coffee. Grace noticed the egg of course. How could she miss something hot pink?

Joe picked it up while Grace was saying, "Open it up. I wonder what's inside."

So Joe did. Nestled inside was a classic Tiffany & Company 1ct emerald-cut diamond engagement ring. It twinkled in the bright sunlight, just as it had when his great grandmother, Mary Ellen Moretti, wore it. The face of the classic Tiffany ring was surrounded by a row of glittering round stones. The band was white gold—delicate and elegant. It was a traditional style that Grace adored.

"It's so pretty," Grace whispered.

"Do you like it?"

"It's beautiful!" She stared into his eyes for a long minute.

Joe reached for her hand and slid the ring into place on her finger. He held her hand out, and they both examined the sun-drenched ring, sparkling against her skin. It was magnificent to see it there.

"A perfect fit," he said confidently. "That's nice. It saves us a trip to the jeweler."

Grace could hear some strong emotion burning under the casual tone of Joe's voice, and she stared into his face. The love he had for her, it was there in his eyes. Joe was glowing—his angelic face brilliant with joy.

Joe struggled, trying to find the right words. His heart was fluttering like pistons in a race car.

Joe got down on one knee and proposed, "Grace Ross"—he looked at her with his impossibly long lashes and hazel eyes—"when I think about you, I know that no one else will ever hold my heart the way you do. I promise to love you forever, every day of my life. Will you marry me?"

There were many things Grace wanted to say, something romantic; but with a teary smile, the only word that came was a heartfelt, "Yes!" She knew she would remember this moment for the rest of her life. She couldn't wait to tell her parents and friends about Joe's sweet proposal.

While the proposal was a big deal, Grace's reaction was just as important. "Halleluiah!" he said. He took her left hand, eyeing the ring one more time, and then he kissed her.

3

Coming together is a beginning; keeping together is
progress; working together is success.

—Henry Ford

Grace knew what she wanted out of life. She yearned to be loved,
to have a magical fairy tale wedding, a large home that would
be filled with laughter and children, and if she was lucky, her
home would have a magnificent view of the ocean. She smiled
delighted with her dreams of a happy future. Everything seemed
to be falling into place. And in time she would also have a career
as a bestselling author.

"'Why are there so many concerns in my head? Why do I
worry so much about things ? I didn't use to. I guess growing up
and being totally responsible is harder than I anticipated. In the
entire world, only one thing matters to me, and that is marrying
Joe. When I'm with him, my world is complete. He is my best
friend. I'm the maker of my life. Joe is the one person I can tell
my honest feelings. He always listens and is there for me. I know
he will bring joy into my life.'"

Joe and Grace decided that their June wedding would be
held at the American Martyrs Catholic Church. It was just four
blocks from their home, dominating the skyline of Manhattan
Beach. It was a church set on a hill. Sometime in the early 1900s,
an adventurous nun, St. Francis Xavier Cabrini, had prophetically
chosen the site when she climbed the high sand dune that
overlooked the Santa Monica Bay and declared, "Here is where
a church should be built, on this hill, a beacon for the villager or
sailor. And it shall be."

The church, with its tall stained-glass windows, tapestry,
and stone, was a model of purity. The litanies and creeds of the
Catholic Church helped them experience a closer relationship

with God. Life's rituals. Grace loved the way the church had sacramental ceremonies for all the big moments of life: baptisms, confirmations, weddings, and even funerals.

Fortunately, June's drab foggy haze burned off by noon, making their special day fabulous. The dusk-to-nighttime wedding was officiated by Father O'Brian, who made the ceremony very personal and a special treat. The most striking moment of the ceremony was when Joe and Grace recited their vows.

Joe went first, smiling and looking into Grace's eyes, "I come freely and without reservation to give myself to you in marriage. I will honor you as my wife for the rest of my life. I will lovingly accept all the children that the Lord gives us and bring them up according to the law of Christ and the Church. I promise to be true to you in good times and in bad, in sickness and in health, to love you and honor you all the days of my life."

They had memorized the vows instead of repeating them after the priest. This seemingly small touch had a great impact, allowing them to speak directly to one another as though they were the only two in the room. Emotions soared, eyes filled with tears, and hearts united—their bond to last an eternity.

As a young child, Joe listened to records by the Beach Boys. He and his friends used to hang out at the wide, friendly beach in front of his parent's ocean view home. They came there because Manhattan Beach had some of the best surfing around. Clearly, Manhattan Beach had been a wonderful place to grow up as a child.

Even in the 70s, it was synonymous with the California beach culture. Joe and Grace's childhoods were filled with surfing, beach volleyball, Strand bicycling, and plain old sun-worshipping. They knew that was where they wanted to raise their family. It was the ideal spot for Joe's exclusive business deals. In the evening, it afforded a place to unwind with a glass of wine and watch the sunset.

After an amazing honeymoon in Hawaii and hours of lovemaking, Grace had hoped to find out that she was pregnant before the escrow on their first home had closed. A little disappointed, Grace attempted to convince herself that it might be easier to get the home fixed up without a baby in the mix.

Grace only needed to buy a few things for their new home. The towels, sheets, and kitchen supplies had been covered by wedding gifts. It was a big step to buy a fixer-upper, but there seemed no other way to afford a home at the beach.

Her first morning alone in the house felt overwhelming. Grace knew that Joe would be working twelve hour days; there were so many bills to be paid. But although her mind could rationalize that this was a good thing, her heart felt troubled. Grace stood silently, looking at the view from the home's massive windows, letting her thoughts run uncontrollably through her mind.

"'Was this too big of a step too soon? What if we can't afford it? God, I annoy myself. Maybe, I should put off starting a family and have a career for a short time to help with the bills. Joe will just feel he is a failure if I do that. Why is he so determined that he has to be the man of the house and do this by himself? Why is he so stubborn? My mother worked, and I'm fine!'"

Grace took a deep breath, struck a yoga pose, and made an attempt to calm herself.

"'What-ifs are for tomorrow. Being here with Joe and, hopefully soon, a baby on the way were all that mattered. Maybe if I start writing a list of everything that needs to be done, this won't be so bad. Writing usually helps me get a better perspective of things. After all, I want to live here.'"

And at that moment she decided everything would work out fine.

The 1922 tile-roofed Mediterranean home had windows in every direction, generous ones, which offered views of the ocean and the sound of the surf. In the evening, the light in the west often streaked the sky with pink and gold and then spread over the ocean until the distant waters glowed like a quiet fire. There were four bedrooms that supplied plenty of room for their growing family. Grace envisioned the home the way she would make it: spacious, well-lit, with hardwood floors.

Over the next few months, all their free time was spent on the house. The kitchen would have loads of counter space in gorgeous tones of bronzes and coppers. Double ovens were a must, along with a Sub-Zero fridge and a Vulcan range. But the high-efficiency kitchen also needed a warm-family feel. She would place blooming bulbs on the windowsill. The air would be filed with the perfumes of fresh breads and chocolate chip cookies.

They worked on the house every weekend. While their friends were off surfing and playing volleyball, they were home scraping off old wallpaper and painting. They learned that their real resources came from within; to change their world, they only had to press to the finish line.

Grace's favorite day was Saturday because they could sleep in late, and she could slowly awaken to the scent of his cologne and see his dark head on the pillow beside her. She knew the overtone of his voice: low and ever so faintly peaceful. She knew his taste, how he kissed, and the softness of his lips.

This Saturday was different. Grace hoped that she and Joe would soon have something special to celebrate. Rising early so that she would not disturb him, she went into the bathroom to take the pregnancy test. The hardest part was waiting for the ten minutes to pass. Then to her joy, she saw a pale purple line appear on the right-hand side, which clearly signified that she was pregnant.

"'I feel so overwhelmed. What should I do? How will Joe react? I need to call the doctor for an appointment. What should I eat? I hope it's a boy. Then we'll have a girl. I always wanted a big brother. I'm so blessed!'"

Barely believing how happy she was, she quickly decided that she would tell Joe the exciting news over breakfast at the Coffee Cart.

"Joe." She reached across the table and cradled his hands in hers. "We're having a baby!"

Joe squeezed her hands affectionately, "I knew it!" Joe yelled.

"How did you know? I just found out this morning."

"Well, I saw the test in the trash. I just wondered why you hadn't told me, but then I figured you wanted it to be at a special spot, to make a special memory."

"You were right. I will remember this day for the rest of my life!"

Inside, her stomach fluttered with excitement, and Joe just stared at her with the biggest grin painted across his face. The chatter flew between them as they finished their omelets and coffee. Their walk home along the Strand was peaceful and filled with dreams of their future child.

4

"I think he has always been there…God is a logical outgrowth of the fact that life fits together as well as it does, but that doesn't mean that we know God's mind."

—Stephen King

Nothing seemed to notice when he began his decent from the second heaven. He moved across vast physical distances in a matter of seconds. As he approached Joe's home, he tried to hide his gargoylian features in the shadows, hoping that nothing would notice him. He was the smallest of them, unseen and immaterial to the humans that abided in the physical world. He drifted over to the house guided by the darkness, his churning wings quivered in a reddish-gray blur as they thrust him to his destination. He remained floating and carefully watching while sizing up his next assignment: the baby boy who had just been born. Satan wasn't leaving anything to chance; the best time to ensnare a person was when they were only a babe.

Named Smug due to his highly self-satisfied ego, this wicked menacing evil spirit appeared bat-like, acting as the guard dog of all things evil. His dragonish body had leathery wings, a long neck and piercing red pug-eyes that bulged out of his face. Smug was edgy and would panic at the least irritation. When enraged, he would spout obscenities; and when in battle, fiery words spewed from his mouth.

Christopher Ryan Moretti was born on July 13, 1980 at 3:55 a.m. It was a long and difficult labor. He weighed in at nine pounds, eight ounces and was twenty-two inches long. He was a fair-haired, blue-eyed baby. Harassed unseeingly by Smug, Christopher cried every evening for hours at a time.

Joe and Grace were worn down to the point that joining in Christopher's cry fest seemed like their only alternative.

Fortunately, Grandma Ross came to the rescue. Sitting in the old rocker she had refurbished from when Grace was a baby, she would cuddle Christopher and sing him her favorite children's hymn.

> Sleep, my child, and peace attend thee
> All through the night
> Guardian angels God will send thee
> All through the night
> Soft the drowsy hours are creeping
> Hill and vale in slumber sleeping
> Love alone its watch is keeping
> All through the night
> Angels watching ever round thee
> All through the night
> In thy slumbers close around thee
> All through the night
> They will of all fears disarm thee
> No forebodings should alarm thee
> They will let no peril harm thee
> All through the night

Smug covered his ears and cowered in the corner. Minutes later, a peaceful baby slept in Grandma's arms. Grace was a quick-learner and soon had her household under control.

In the next four years, Joe and Grace were blessed with two more sons, William and Luke, and twins, Sara and Jennifer. They loved their children deeply. You would see them offering gentle cuddles, words of encouragement, approval with a smile; they even avoided comparing their children to one another. They set aside a time every evening just before bedtime to talk individually with each child. It was a sacred time without every day distractions. It would be difficult to imagine two more loving parents.

All the children inherited the family's good looks. The boys were blessed with broad shoulders, big bones, and a heavy jaw, while the twins were petite, like Grace.

Their children had varied personalities. Joe and Grace celebrated their children's differences and instill in each child the desire to pursue their own interests and dreams. Christopher was somewhat haughty. William was full of life, while Luke was extremely bright and somewhat aggressive. The twins, Sara and Jennifer, were very mischievous and were always playing pranks on their brothers.

Joe and Grace were extremely permissive parents who basically let their children do pretty much whatever they wanted. Love abounded. Rather than disciplining her children, Grace preferred to use bribery, gifts, and trips to the Joe's Candy Cottage (no, Joe was not the owner) and Manhattan Toy and Variety Store to motivate them. Without any boundaries, their children were always getting into trouble. They never asked permission to do anything. As an only child, Grace never experienced the challenges of managing young children and found herself completely overwhelmed. Why hadn't Berkeley offered classes on this most important job?

"'How could I ever think there would be any free time to write? Joe and I were crazy when we thought raising kids was so simple. I'd be lucky to have time to write a want AD for the paper. I'm amazed if I take a shower. Luckily my hair looks okay in a pony tail. About the only good thing about being run ragged is it has been easy to take off all the weight I gained while being pregnant. Why did I think being a mother would be easier than having a career? I'll have to give my parents credit for only having me. Why are my children so difficult to manage? Where do their mischievous thoughts come from? They just seem to come out of the blue.'"

Instead of being managed by their parents, the twins were left to the suggestions of any number of demon's evil suggestions. Smug had invited a few of his friends to live with him. Prankster and Chaos set up shop in the dark recesses of the Moretti home.

To help in their mischievous fun, they often held parties to which they invited Disorder, Havoc, and Chao's little cousin, Mess.

The twins were always doing something playful. Just the other day, Disorder had suggested to Sara that she should drag a chair over to the kitchen counter and help herself to the cookies that were cooling there. Sara effortlessly climbed onto the chair and retrieved some cookies. While she shoved one into her mouth, Jennifer encouraged her to share the rest of the plate with the neighborhood kids.

Returning home, they wiped their chocolate-smudged hands on clean kitchen towels Grace had hung there just minutes before. Entering the kitchen, Grace exclaimed, "Why do I even bother?"

Thinking for a moment, Grace suddenly realized this was just one of the trials of having five active young children. "Oh well, that's what washers were made for. Next time, girls, remember to ask before you take the cookies. They were supposed to be for tonight's book club meeting."

She sighed, realizing there was no point in being angry. Overly tired and wanting to avoid any additional conflict or outburst of tears, Grace called Joe. Of course, because he felt somewhat guilty for working such long hours and helping so little around the house, Joe always agreed to the little demands Grace placed on him. Now that they were more financially settled, he had hired a cleaning lady who came once a week, a gardener, and a babysitter who let Grace spend Friday afternoon going out to lunch and shopping with her friends. After all, that is what he promised her—a life of ease. It really wasn't that much out of the way for him to stop at Becker's Bakery and get some cookies for her evening meeting.

"'If I add some appetizers and wine from Manhattan Grocers, maybe I can earn some bonus points—even score big when we go to bed.'"

He would leave work a little earlier than usual, but the book club would allow him some time to work in his office while the girls critiqued the book. Problem solved, at least in Joe's mind.

The antics of their children grew and became legendary. Joe was often absent attending to business when the children were young. Thus Grace played a key role in the children's upbringing. At times, she would criticize Joe for being too demanding on his sons and too permissive with the twins.

"Grace you have to understand boys are different from girls. They need more discipline or they will get into trouble. At times, I worry about their mischievous ways."

Scowling, with a few tears welling in her eyes, Grace howls, "It appears to me you are wearing blinders. Your daughters seem to get into more trouble than your sons. But how would you know? You are always off working!"

"'He used to say I was the first thing he thought of when he woke up. When we would hold hands, it seemed as if our blood flowed together. Spending time with him was like playing at the doorway of heaven. I was in love and I thought it would last forever.'"

Joe stared out the window at the ocean, arms crossed, face set. Then he laughed his smirky laugh. "Don't you know how much your criticizing hurts me? I'm working all the time for us. Why do you have to be so negative about this? We agreed before we were married that my responsibility was providing for the family, and yours was the children. When they get a little older you will have your turn."

"'Why does she think I will come home earlier if she demands it? If she would just say, "Please, come home early tonight," I would. Sometimes she acts like a tyrant. Why does she always make me feel guilty for doing what I know needs to be done? I'm only human. I can't do everything.'"

Grace answered, "I don't hate your work. I just hate the fact that I feel so little love and support coming from you. Instead of coming home from work and listening about my day, you always turn on the TV while we are talking."

Joe replied, "Welcome to the real world of marriage! I guess our desires are different. I want sex, and you are too tired. You would like to visit your parents more, but I don't like wasting so much time. I've so much work to complete. I wish it was just easier. I want it all, but I also want you to be happy. I'll try harder. Maybe your parents could watch the kids for the weekend. Some time off together is just what we need."

This intentional action of love ended the bickering. Just knowing that Joe wanted to look out for her interests brought Grace the peace she needed. Joe's love for her had elicited the appropriate response. With her love tank full, Grace felt secure in Joe's love. The whole world looked brighter, and she was able to deal with the antics of her family.

The children were all good-natured, rambunctious hooligans and daredevils who loved to have fun. Whenever possible, you would find them wrestling with one another. They were active combative athletes, "little warriors," looking for their next adventure. Spending their summers at the beach, they were fabulous swimmers, but even better surfers. They raced in on waves cutting each other off, knocking each other over, and were often tossed about in the undertow.

"Are you all right? That looked rather grueling." one of them would call. They set such high standards for their recklessness that, eventually, Joe would put his foot down and have them stop before someone got seriously hurt.

"If you don't take it down a notch there will be no video games or television when we get home."

Indoor life with them was no less vigorous. The savagery of pillow-fighting would leave them all breathless. Every activity they participated in was competitive, and without a doubt, it irked the twins that they were usually the losers.

Star Wars offered a different difficultly. There was only one heroine, and Jennifer and Sara spent more time arguing over who would be Princess Leah than actually playing. Their number one favorite indoor game was hide-and-seek.

But most importantly, they all loved each other and late at night when they were all in bed, Joe and Grace would hear them calling down the halls with plans for the next day's adventures. Each would dream of the exhausting contests they would encounter the next day.

Breakfast was one of the few times Joe was able to eat a meal with his family. Throughout the meal, Joe was able to chat about how everyone was doing and discover who needed his help. Finding a time to have a conversation with his children was a difficult task, especially with their different attention spans and passions. Consistently gathering for meals and intentionally using this time would have made it easier, but Joe found his business demands overwhelming. He was often up and off to work before everyone was awake. In reality, he spent little time with them. He counted on his prayers to keep them safe, but sometimes, he worried that the prayer wasn't enough.

Sitting at his keyboard, Joe reached for the phone to call Grace. As he expected, his daughter answered the phone on the first ring, "Hey, Pop! Can I wear lipstick to the football game tonight? All my friends are. Please?"

"'I'm not surprised. She is almost thirteen and in junior high. I'm sure that Grace wore lipstick at that age, but there is no way I want my daughters to start so young. I know the thoughts that run through the minds of young men. Not yet thirteen and already it's lipstick at football games.'"

"What did your mother say?" Joe asked.

"She said she'd think about it."

"Then I'll think about it too."

"Oh, Pop!"

"Put your mom on, Jenny."

"Can't you come home so we can talk? I don't want everyone to think I'm a baby."

"'God save me.'"

"I have to work late; put your mom on now."

Joe could tell that the conversation had annoyed his daughter, and he wished it hadn't. But he had to put his foot down sometimes.

"Mom! Pop's on the phone. He has to work late."

"Thanks for the bulletin," Joe added.

Sounding cheerful as usual, Joe wondered, like always, how she could manage their five teenage children.

"I was hoping you would be home for dinner," Grace said.

"Stuck at the office for a while. Can't say how long. Why does Jenny need lipstick?"

"Gloss," Grace corrected, "lip gloss, you know it's a basic female tool."

"Next thing she'll be wanting is a tattoo. And the answer is no. No tattoos."

"I think you are jumping a little ahead of things. Relax. We have good kids. I'll save you some leftovers for dinner. We can unwind with some wine and talk about this when you get home."

Joe sat for a few minutes in the quiet, drinking his coffee and thinking of Grace and their five children. He didn't want his baby wearing makeup, but he knew she would wear him down. The twins were already beginning to develop a sex appeal, a tomboyish type. They had athletic bodies, clear skin, solid curves, and taunting eyes with a dangerous-looking intelligence—and now lip gloss.

He was pleased that his daughters were going to be beautiful young women like their mother. As little girls, the most noticeable thing about them had been their angelic blue eyes surrounded by a mass of blond curls. But now the curls had become striking locks that fell thickly below their shoulders. Boys were starting to turn and look just as he had when he was a teen.

With a sigh, he booted up his computer to study the details of the project his new business partner had proposed. He spent another hour reading and taking notes. Crew costs had skyrocket the last few years, and they were trying to find additional ways to increase their bottom line. At a cost of $3,299 a day, it was accounting for about 44 percent of their total operating expenses. Even though all the information looked good, he felt apprehensive. Would they compromise the quality of their services and potentially lose business? Sometimes he felt William Martin wanted to take potentially high risks that did not merit the savings received.

Hidden in the shadows, Dishonesty lingered in the corner. He was on a covert mission and hoped to come and go unnoticed. Spewing whispers from his drooling mouth, an invisible red fog floated toward Joe.

"'Why am I worrying so much? The bottom line is much better than I had anticipated. William is really a magician with numbers. That's why I hired him. I'm just tired and longing to see Grace. It should be a great night. She already said she would have a glass of wine waiting when I got home. I work too much. I think I'll just go home and enjoy my wife.'"

Dismissing his concerns as exhaustion and foolish suspicion, he stored the information on his computer and left the office a little before nine.

Joe had started his business career in an office next to his father. Eager to learn he'd received an education that few ever receive in a lifetime. Some of what he learned came from books and some from college lectures. But mostly he learned from his mentors.

Chief among them were his father and grandfather. Rule number one: be in the office by seven; there were deals to be made.

Yet part of what he learned came through the cold hard knocks of experience. To learn, he developed a set of guidelines: the Moretti rules. The rules were shaped by his larger strategy, simply put, to make the world a better place. Most people would have found it hard to accomplish such a vision. He never wanted to waste, he preferred to create. He figured if he was smart, worked hard, and honored the law there was nothing he could not accomplish. There was no part of the transportation industry that he hadn't mastered. His father often remarked that everything Joe touched would turn to gold; he had the Midas touch. Joe built his business with little more than thrift and creativity. Without a doubt, Joe was a young idealist, who, with basic tools and some sound management skills, was shaping the world around himself.

Joe's business ventures continued to grow over the years until he needed to hire a vast array of employees. He was the classic definition of the American success story. His increasing reputation, his widening circle of acquaintances, his sense of importance, and the growing pressures built up in him a false sense of finally arriving. Prosperity had built a false self-assuring net around him.

He continually set new standards of excellence while expanding his interest nationally and internationally. He was more than happy to be part of the $375 billion shipping industry that carried 90 percent of world trade. If all the work wasn't enough, he also was an ardent philanthropist. Joe was personally involved in everything he put his name on. This commitment made him a preeminent developer around the world but not the best dad or husband.

5

When a man arrives at great prosperity God did it;
when he falls into disaster he did it himself.

—Mark Twain

Late on a waning crescent moon night, two figures appeared on the Strand approaching Manhattan Beach. One was blond and strongly built with soft features, and the other was dark-haired and mighty. They were tall, at least seven feet, rugged, and extremely handsome.

They spotted the house and heard laughter and sounds of music flowing through the open windows. It was time for the Morreti's yearly family summer birthday bash, which was jam-packed with amusement, pleasure and all sorts of foolishness. It was a wild time, a chance for his sons to drink a little too much, and if the stars were aligned right in the sky, they might even get lucky with a couple of pretty girls.

In June, Joe's oldest son had graduated from college and bought his first home. Wanting to impress his friends, he decided to host the annual party. He was over twenty-one and would be able to buy more booze than they could possibly consume. All their friends were invited, and to keep the cost down, they started the party with salsa and chips. Christopher had also marinated meat overnight and cooked it to perfection on a backyard grill. Along with it, he served veggie skewers and corn on the cob. Barbecue was Christopher's passion, and he made it clear with a backyard spread destined to be a home run.

The twins were celebrating their sixteenth birthday, and Joe, being the ever-indulgent father had purchased each of them a new beamer. They were everything he hoped and dreaded they would be; just what any young man would want: funny, optimistic, bright, athletic, outgoing, but more than that, they were adorably cute. Joe was worried they would get into trouble, but Christopher assured him he would be their guardian for the night. Besides, all his friends knew they were off limits.

Joe and Grace decided to leave the party early just as the dancing started. Grace said she felt out-of-place and preferred to go home to watch her favorite television show. At Joe's reluctance to leave, she told him, "Let the kids have some fun, and stop being such a worrywart. We'll be able to hear all about it at lunch tomorrow."

The two mysterious visitors had entered the house unnoticed. Standing in the middle of it all, they patiently watched Joe's children, aware that at any moment the battle would begin. Suddenly they could feel it—an uncontrolable, powerful, growing, very deliberate, purposeful, and sensual kind of evil.

Then they spotted Lustapher, hiding in the shadows. Hunchbacked, he began to weave through the crowd. The shadow had a shape—an animated, beastly shape—and was placing suggestive thoughts in the partygoers' minds. He suggested to a group of beautiful young girls that dancing would make the occasion even more joyous. In the wee hours of the night, the dancers' flowing, continuous, sinuous movements caused crazed thoughts to pass through the men's minds. As Lustapher planted sexual thoughts into Christopher Moretti's mind, he began to make a move on a beautiful blond, who seemed to be the center of everyone's attention.

Suddenly, as if colliding with a speeding wall, Lustapher was knocked backward and into a spiraling tumble onto the floor, his glowing red breaths spewing in the air. With an eerie cry of rage and indignation, he gathered himself up off the floor and stared at the two tall strangers who blocked his path. The snarling creature screamed in pain as a powerful hand lifted it from the floor and tossed it through the open window.

Together, the strangers forcefully spoke, "Go to hell." The wings on Lustapher's back began to unfold as he flew with a rush of wind toward the highlands to tell Satan about the attack.

Christopher staggered, drunk with beer. His brothers suggested he sit down and stop making a fool of himself.

When the partying for that summer was over, or in other words, when all of the children returned to school, Joe went to confession telling Father O'Brian of his concerns for his children's behavior over the summer. Joe's fear was turning into a phobia. As Joe knelt and prayed at the altar, a creature with bulbous eyes looked over his shoulders. The gnarled head sat on deformed shoulders and gasps of decayed, red breaths spewed in labored hisses through rows of spiky fangs. He and Joe had been acquainted for years, but as with all humans, things had become easier as their relationship solidified. The spirit of harassment placed its talons around Joe's chest, and he began to think that perhaps his children had sinned in their drunken spree. His spirit felt troubled.

Up until this day, Joe had always trusted that God was in charge, and things would work out to his advantage. Sure, over the years he had concerns for his children's behavior, but he knew they were good kids. Bad things did not happen to good people. Now he was having trouble letting go and believing that God had his children in his hands. Continuing to hold onto these cares, he held them tightly in his heart. He was sure if he pondered the problem long enough, his intellectual mind, his superior intelligence would stumble on the answer.

"'Sure, I've been working long hours over the years, but haven't I sent them to private school to ensure their moral character? It isn't as though work is all that enjoyable. I've been doing it for them. I want them to have the best money can buy. Doesn't every parent want that for their children? I don't know any successful man who doesn't spend long hours at work. Plus, I refuse to go golfing on Sunday with my business associates. It is the day I go to church and spend time with my family. Quality time. I'm sure in God's eyes, I'm a better parent than most. I've sacrificed my entire life for them. I'm sure I can figure this out— I've always done it in the past.'"

6

I shall be telling this with a sigh
Somewhere ages and ages hence;
Two roads diverged in a woods, I—
I took the one less traveled by,
And that has made all the difference.

—Robert Frost

One day, a battalion of angels met together to discuss events of the world. They were dressed in linen, with belts of the finest gold around their waists. Their bodies resembled translucent chrysolite, their eyes glistened with a fiery light from the altars of God, their arms and legs like the gleam of burnished bronze. They were huge, muscular angels, towering twelve to fifteen feet tall and were as wide as four or five of the biggest linebackers on any NFL team. Their faces were distinctive as though carefully chiseled. None of them had shaved heads, but some of them had beards. They look to be about thirty years old in human age. It appeared the largest of them had a thirty-foot wing span. Their massive power made it evident that no demonic force would want to fight them. Just one of them could destroy an entire army.

These angelic beings were the armies of God. They were standing right where they had been positioned by God when he first created them for His purposes. They would leave their post to come down to fight battles for men. Then they would come back to wait until they were needed again. Some had swords and some did not. The swords they carried were flames of fire, and the ground shook as they walked. They carried huge shields, a broad piece of armor, which was carried on their left arm as a defense from demonic blows. These were supernatural weapons. Some of them could speak words and cause whole nations to crumble and fall into the sea. They were armed, some with words, some with swords, some with spears that had special purposes, but all had the power of God. They knew their jobs—highly specialized jobs. Nobody had to tell them how to do their work. God just told them where to go. Some of them were clothed with the power to move the earth, and others were clothed with power to bring judgment; they all had power to defend and keep God's children.

Their words, clothed with power, were ready at any moment to come and do battle against the powers of Satan. They were released to fight the minute men would pray the Father's words in the name of Jesus. Oh, the power of God that is there and available for man when he speaks the right words and stops putting his foot in his mouth. If only man could discern how valuable the angels were in achieving their victory against Satan, things would be subsequently different.

Satan slowly paced along the back of the battalion, having transformed himself into an angel of light, with his arms and legs resembling polished precious stones, and his face with a flickering glow. Sinister and diabolical as ever, he hoped to remain unnoticed. Satan knew he was most effective when he was not acknowledged or believed in. It is almost impossible to defeat an enemy that you refuse to admit exists. That was why Joe and Grace had become such easy prey for Satan and his demon armies.

Michael, whose countenance was like lightning, and his garments white as snow, spotted Satan and cried with a loud voice, as when a lion roared, "Where have you come from?"

Satan hated Michael because he had stolen his job, and now he was better at it. Satan realized there would be a final war in heaven, one in which Michael and his angels would cast him out of heaven for all time. Reluctantly he answered, "I've been wandering around the world, going back and forth across it. I never hear anyone say anything good about God. Everyone is just complaining and griping about how awful life is. I hear everyone whine at least fifteen to thirty times a day. As much as you try to tell me that everyone loves God, the truth is that everyone is guilty of being a complainer with little respect for their master. Just a lot of God damit or Jesus Christ why did that happen!"

Then Michael said to Satan, "Have you noticed Joe? There is no other man like him; he is chaste and honest, and everything he puts his hand to is prosperous. He continually sings praises to God. God thinks highly of him."

"Why shouldn't Joe love him? God gives him his heart's desires!" Satan retorted. "Haven't God's blessings protected his family and his businesses? He has made him prosperous in every endeavor. But if you would let me destroy everything he has, surely he will curse God to his face. If you will only let me test Joe, I will expose him and all so-called righteous people for the frauds they are."

A weird muffled laugh escaped as he tried to hide his excitement. It was not as though Satan hadn't been working on Joe for years, but this new plan could bring the job to completion. Satan expected with one crafty blow both to assault God's beloved and make him a fool. At last he felt he had found a way to alienate humans and destroy their faith in their creator. His all-consuming passion was to drive an irremovable wedge between them, one that couldn't be reconciled. Who could love a God that caused bad things to happen to them? Only a fool would.

Satan was incapable of contending with God hand-to-hand, power pitted against power, so instead he was bent on destroying Joe by opening the doors of hell with uncontrollable fear. Then he was sure that Joe would want nothing more than to curse God. How could Joe continue to love him if he saw how unjust he was, punishing those who did not deserve it? Wasn't Satan thrilled that humans blamed everything on God? No one liked to think that evil might be lurking just around the corner.

Chuckling, he said, "I'm so grateful everyone would rather blame Mother Nature or fate for the evil in the world. It's even better when they blame God! People are so stupid, fearful, and weak."

The celestial challenge that came on fiery words of hate, once raised, could not be ignored. Michael said to Satan, "Very well, then, you know the terms of the covenant. You can influence everything he has, but do not lay a finger on Joe."

Joe's fear had breached a hole in God's protective hedge. He continually said things like, "This just kills me. I'm afraid something bad will happen to my children. I'm scared to death. That just blows me away." He had no idea of the impact of his words. He was saying what he felt, unfiltered in the stress of the moment. When you live long enough, most of us begin to sing the blues, a song that tells how it is for us on a bad day.

It seemed he felt better when he said these clichés. Undeniably, it was tempting to Joe—almost a reflex now—to spit out an always or a never. "You never come home when you are supposed to, and we are worried you're up to no good. You always forget to call when you are running late, so we sit home and worry. It is like you never listen to a word we say. Why do you never listen to us?" Joe was offended that his children weren't living by the few rules he placed on them. He hadn't expected them to be perfect, but how hard was it to be home on time? The problem with this was he was giving labels to his children that would stick for life. His kids were becoming what he said they were. So telling them that they "always forget to call" made them more likely to be the kid who, you guessed it, who never called. Too bad he didn't understand the impact of his words.

The mood of the gathering shifted and became somber. Everyone continued to look at Michael with the same serious expression, driving the gravity of the situation home. Michael felt the others staring at him. He suddenly turned and looked directly at them. His expression softened, and the look he directed at them was pure love. It was plain he thought the same as all of them.

"'We can't fight or even offer any assistance if Joe uses the covenant principles incorrectly. Unfortunately we are inexperienced in this type of battle. It would make such a difference if at least one of us could help Joe's family. Why do humans always find ways to water it down—dilute it until it is ineffective? They have even been warned to study and seek the truth. The problem is Joe never took it upon himself to learn anything but intellectual knowledge. He lacks God's wisdom. That's what makes this situation so difficult. Without God's miraculous intervention, things aren't looking good. Joe's life is in for some sharp turns. I hope he can hadle them.'"

Thinking to himself Gabriel pondered, "'Why can't Joe just believe the Truth?'"

Michael's thoughts told it all, "'We will have to wait until Joe understands and uses the weapons God has provided.'"

Standing next to Michael was Raphael, one of the chief princes. He was often dispatched by God to answer Joe's prayers. Raphael had a deep, strong voice and the sight of him brought terror to the eyes of the enemy.

Alongside Michael and Raphael was Gabriel whose piercing war cry and fierce countenance would often send demons flying even before the onslaught began. Next to him were Joel whose mighty domain was the wind and waves, Nigel who had an ability to take fiery blows and shield many from Satan's turbulent wordy attacks and Lionel who was sent to bring assistance and security to Grace.

How poignant it was to see them stand at rest, acquiescing to this peculiar command. There was an eerie grimness in their eyes. Everyone could sense the ominous effect of the appalling news. There would be no skirmishes or confrontations. They would no longer be the aggressors, but rather, the guardians sent to see that Joe himself was not harmed.

Michael and his assistant, Manuel, immediately left for their positions silently without saying a word. Joe remained secure. Joe was to be protected from any direct onslaught. Tonight they would stand by and keep watch but aside from that, do nothing else.

With similar qualities to men, the angels were used to wielding swords and waging verbal combat. They had feelings, passions, and desires. They had minds to think with and the ability to communicate. Yet, they were not natural beings; they were supernatural. Even the strongest of natural creatures needs sleep and rest, but angels do not. When they run, they had the appearance of a flash of lightning. Even though they have appeared visibly and interacted with men on several occasions, this time it seemed these ministering spirits would remain unseen to the material world.

7

"The compensations of calamity are made apparent to the understanding also, after long intervals of time. A fever, a mutilation, a cruel disappointment, a loss of wealth, a loss of friends, seems the moment unpaid loss, and unplayable. But the sure years reveal the deep remedial force that underlies all the facts."

—Ralph Waldo Emerson

As Satan turned to leave, their presence made his appearance transformed into a gigantic demon with a wild predator-like face, fierce eyes, incredibly powerful-built body, and expansive black wings that draped behind him like the robe of an emperor. His raven-black hair hung in shiny ringlets to his shoulders, and on each wrist, he wore a gold armlet studded with sparkling black diamonds. His index finger displayed the death ring—a stellar-cut precious stone gem, offset by the subtly doom-laden symbols of mortality. Wearing the ring on this finger represented his desire to have power and show off his strong ego. A ruby-red belt glistened on his waist. His voice gargled up from deep within his chest and sprayed out in fiery red vapors as he yelled, "Let the fiendish competition begin, and may the wicked prevail!"

Some of the happiness faded from his smile. Satan glanced distractedly at the many rows of angels, attempting to gather his courage. Overcome by anxiety, hate oozed from his being. His tongue felt as if it had sunk into a pit of quicksand, and he was beginning to doubt if he'd be able to utter a single sensible word. His eyes snapped with impatience as he screamed, "I hate God and his creation!"

After the rebellion, Satan had been fortunate that a third of the angels had followed him, but his small numbers had left him at a disadvantage. This time things would be different. He would not have to contend with the heavenly host. He now had rulership over Joe. Satan was the puppet master and Joe was his puppet as long as he would tolerate his dictatorship, Joe would remain subject to him. It would be up to Joe to rid himself of every demonic relationship.

Feeling the pressure of this ultimate challenge, Satan escaped to his highly organized empire of evil. Behind the façade of everyday life, there had been a spiritual battle raging, and now it appeared that Satan had the advantage he desired. He was sure he had found an opening to accomplish his purpose. Humans were totally dependent on God for their very lives and well-being. That fact could give rise to one of humankind's greatest temptations: to love the gifts rather than the Giver.

Satan appeared suddenly in a violent, boiling mood that crashed and thundered around his lair like a hurricane. The demons bellowed air-piercing shrieks of praise and adoration as they were swept about screaming in anticipation of their new orders. For a moment he stood there, glaring at them with sinister, smoldering eyes, studying them until he was greeted by Forboden, the fallen archangel of death, better known as "The Fatalities Friend." He was the prince of over three infernal realms of the earth and was responsible for the scorching wind of the desert.

The stirrings in the evil realm indicated something monumental was in the making. The catacomb was gloomy and depressing. Everything—walls, ceiling, and floors—were dingy taupe, and light was limited, which suited Satan and his tribe just fine. They preferred the darkness, and there seemed to be even more than usual that day. A smoke, as that of a great furnace, encompassed the vile pit, and the air was darkened by it.

Satan was unquestionably the one in charge. He maintained an imposing stance, his fists clenched and ready to strike. Many demons coveted his rank, and he knew it. He trusted no one and suspected everyone. His first conference was with a small huddle of other power players, going over the next strategies for the destruction of Joe.

Many others had arrived before Smug floated in to the cauldron of percolating evil. The room was dark, but the darkness seemed more a presence than a physical condition, a convulsive force, an atmosphere that floated and skulked about the tomb. Out of the darkness angrily stared many pairs of red demonic eyes belonging to a hideous array of gruesome faces. The various faces were silhouetted by a red glow permeating from Satan. Red vapor hung heavily in the room and filled the air with its disgusting stench, as the many spirits carried on their raspy muted discussions there in the dark.

Satan walked with heavy, ponderous steps up and down the line of demons, giving them each a closer look. In the front of the horde, spewing lethal words, were two slithery creatures with darting and shifty eyes. They were experts in suggesting, infuriating, and spreading hate and fear. They used their crushing words, massive arms, and venomous quills to constrict and poison the love out of people.

Back near the corner was Dishonesty. He was pompous— the haughtiest demon of them all. He boasted of his supposedly superior knowledge of how to control man's soulish minds. His appearance was far less frightening than most demons; he almost looked human. His weapon, he bragged, was always a convincing, believable argument in which he cleverly had woven hidden lies.

Many others were there: Envy, a suspicious and difficult demon to work with; Mayhem, his talons still dripping with slim; and Strife, his fists sharpened into spike like protrusions and his hide gelatinous and rubbery.

Smug was excited enough to violate Satan's idea of protocol and shoved his way to the front. Satan glared at him, surprised by the rude interruption. "My Prince," Smug pleaded, "I must have a word with you."

Satan's eyes narrowed. Who was this little imp to interrupt him in the middle of a conference, to violate decorum in front of others?

"How dare you speak out of order! What do you want?" he growled.

"I must speak with you!"

"You must never speak to me without first being addressed. Is that understood?"

"Yes, I humbly beg your pardon, but this is vitally important. I've been with Joe's family for over twenty years, and I know the one way to stop Joe's faith! Over the years we have been planting seeds of concern. Joe has seen things that have happened to his church friends, and he is beginning to have a lack of trust in God's word. Negative events have piled up over the past years, things we designed to erode away Joe's hope and zeal. Joe just recently began to have sleepless nights, dreaming about his children. Now that God's protection is distant, and we have power over Joe, it will be an easy task to get him to go from legitimate concerns to paralyzing fear. Joe will be terrified of failing. Fear or, as I prefer to call it, 'false evidence appearing real' is the mighty force that will lead to his destruction."

Satan, who lacked any spiritual discernment, suddenly realized the dangerous parapet that Joe was on. He immediately became a violent volcano, spewing forth horrible curses and wrath that would lead to the destruction of Joe's family. Sinister laughter echoed off the walls surrounding him, coming from everywhere at the same time.

8

Even with all our technology and the inventions that
make modern life so much easier than it once was, it
takes just one big natural disaster to wipe all that away
and remind us that, here on Earth, we're still at the mercy
of nature.

—Neil deGrasse Tyson

It was midnight, and overcome by disturbing personal issues
racing through his mind Joe found it difficult to sleep. He had
a troubled spirit after spending the afternoon lecturing his
oldest son.

"You are setting a bad example for your brothers and sisters. I
know you think life is just one big party, but I don't want to be a
grandfather yet. Do you want other guys to follow your example
and treat your sisters like sluts? Don't turn your back on me.
Come back here!"

Looking over his shoulder Christopher shouted, "Do you
really think I'm that evil? Have you forgotten I go to church with
you every Sunday? I may not be a saint, but I'm not the devil."

Joe wondered why their conversation had blackened so
quickly. All he was trying to do was protect Christopher from
making a life-altering mistake. Where had such thoughts come
from? Perhaps because the alienation had developed slowly, he
never saw the crisis coming.

Strife had found it so easy to plant thoughts in Joe's mind.
Years ago he thought before he spoke, but with continual years
of demonic harassment, he now spewed out whatever thought
popped into his mind. His ears were still ringing from the
conversation. His mind kept playing it over and over until every
bitter comment poisoned his heart. From their hiding place

across the room, Joe's hideous opponents were whispering vile words into the air.

"Good, he seems very disturbed by all this. We have him right where we want him for tonight's attack," Satan quipped.

Joe worried that his children were getting themselves into unpardonable trouble. Eyes began to glow in the steadily thickening darkness. Satan's taloned fingers continued to tap his knees, his brow furrowed with an obsessive scowl. Behind him, a host of demons were positioned, spellbound with anticipation, waiting for Satan's orders.

Sleep eventually did come, but it was accompanied by dour dreams fed to him by Forbodden. Joe dreamt he was outside in a storm, the wind blowing all about him. He stood at the end of the pier, trying to understand the quickly moving shapes; he could only dimly see in the darkness of the crashing waves. At first, there was nothing but sets of red piercing eyes, darting toward each other. And then the moon suddenly broke from the clouds; Joe could see everything. Chaotic and frantic images rushed at him. He could hear screams; there was a sensation of death, and the sight and taste of blood.

Joe broke into a run but found himself moving in the frustrating slow motion of nightmares. Joe was constantly fighting and struggling for his life; insurmountable fear and danger surrounded him. He tried to call for help, to tell the creatures to stop, but his voice was stolen by fear, and he could make no sound. He waved his arms hoping to catch someone's attention. Something flashed in his hand, and Joe cringed as he saw the gun. There, lying dead in front of him was a dark demon with her bright red beaming eyes, staring right at him. She had wild grayish-blue hair and was wearing a long sheer gown with black twisted marks tattooed on her face.

Joe's eyes snapped open to the silent darkness of his room. The first thing he realized was that he did not feel like he was alone.

He looked all about the room and saw nothing. But the hair on his arms warned him; something was not right.

Satan sat and waited as his own breathing began to deepen and rush out of his nostrils like a rancid red steam. His eyes narrowed and his talons uncurled. Time stood still.

Laying there in a state of stupor halfway between sleep and consciousness, he suddenly noticed his heavy breathing. His pulse began to pound in his ears. The horrible fear racing through his mind was so real. Fear seemed so close that he could almost smell it. Hovering over him midair was the hideous face of Strife, who spewed out vicious words of terror and mayhem. Planting these thoughts in Joe's mind was an easy task now that the angels of God were at bay.

Joe lay there drenched in sweat, waiting for his heart to calm down, for the stark fear to go away, but nothing seemed to change, and he couldn't seem to make it go away. He kept telling himself it was only a nightmare. Looking around the room, he saw nothing out of the ordinary, but he still could feel an evil presence. Even the now-silent room seemed sinister.

Darkness deepened over Manhattan Beach. The messenger departed, a filthy black nightmare of a creature, borne on scabby wings; he departed to take word to the others that it was time for the attack. "Go!" he shouted and hundreds of demons shot into the sky like a thunderous flock of bats, rushing along a straight and level route eastward to Christopher's house.

"Look," said an angelic warrior, and Michael and his host all saw what looked like a black swarm silhouetted against the night sky. Frustrated by their lack of power, they watched as the squadron approached Christopher's house. Raphael was assigned to get a closer look but was admonished that no help could be offered.

Ignoring Joe's warning, Christopher had decided to have a party that night that would be like no other. Joe had threatened that if anything happened to Jenny and Sara he would disinherit him. The tension had become so intense that Joe refused to attend the party. "Your mother and I will sit this one out! We can celebrate Jennifer and Sara's birthday at lunch tomorrow after church. Well at least I hope we can if all of you aren't too hungover."

"'What's wrong with my old man anyway? Does he really think it would work saying, "Because he said so!"? I'm not a kid anymore. "Because I said so" only makes me want to do it more. Why is he such a jerk? Has he forgotten what it's like to be young?"'

Grumbling to himself, he began to marinate the meat. He could still hear his father say, "I wish you didn't hang out with Dan, I don't like the way he looks at your sisters."

"'Yeah, a lot of people don't like Dan for that reason, but doesn't he realize Dan knows better than go after my sisters. I wish he had a little more faith in us! Sara and Jenny would be furious if they knew he had threatened to ground them their entire senior year if they came to my party. Stop being a jerk, Dad!"'

Joe awakened from his nightmare and paced the house waiting, anger spewing from him. Over the last year, their partying had seemed to escalate in frivolity, or at least in his mind it had. The house was jam-packed with young men.

Having ignored their father's advice, Jenny and Sara were out dancing when the first song played. Their favorite songs were being played by a DJ in the corner. A girl who was dancing in the middle of a crowd acted as though she was the hottest thing.

An ugly little imp with piercing, needle-sharp words called erotic thoughts that went into the dancers' minds. Feeling the power of his intoxicating words, one girl slowly began to remove her clothes while dancing in a most suggestive way. Men began to sweat. Beer flowed. Blackness like blindness seemed to invade the heart of each partygoer.

The demons arrived in arrogant brashness, descending on the party in the dead of night to ravage them all. Their ghastly red eyes full of lust circled the room planting immoral thoughts. The two most evil ones slipped through the front doors and into the living room. People passed on all sides of them, and sometimes right through them, but that of course was of no consequence.

Within moments, an evil wind blew through the room: hot, repulsive, and oppressive. At least a hundred demons swooped like deadly bats playing havoc with their bodies, minds, and spirits. They screamed dirty sexual thoughts and wickedness playing with the party goers' corruptible souls. There could be no doubt that Satan had sent Lustapher to direct them. Around 2:00 a.m., the party began to die down as the last party-goer left. William and Luke had passed out in the upstairs bedrooms, and Jennifer and Sara were asleep on the couch.

Jennifer and Sara knew Damien from school. He'd been expelled right before spring break. Riggins, Damien's only friend, left school shortly after the incident to be homeschooled. As with their rebellion against their parents, their perfidy, their world was filled with ritualistic violence. They had been seduced in to following the precepts of a newly formed satanic cult. All they had to do was perform one ritualistic killing. To prepare for the murders, they had practiced killing and mutilating a dog and a cat. Originally they had planned to kill only one girl, but they hoped that killing twins would elevate them to a higher position.

The Satanic cult had offered them unlimited sex and drugs and the promise of power over others. Their world was filled with ritualistic violence, perverse sexual activity and abuse. Heavy Metal music and the use of illegal hallucinogenic drugs heightened the experience. They had been inspired to follow the precepts of Anton LaVey's *Satanic Bible*.

Sara and Jennifer had been randomly selected as targets because they were identical twins. Damien plotted their murders for more than a week. Obsessed with being accepted by the cult, he spent hours playing with demonic powers and taking drugs. Anticipating the big event, Damien and Riggins exchanged text messages. Damien's first messaged to Riggins read, "I feel electrified. Can't wait to get started. Meet me at Hennessey's Tavern."

That night the police of Manhattan Beach were overly busy. Satan was making sure that no one would interfere with his plans. Fights broke out at the bar on the pier, slogans were spray-painted on the city hall, and some cars were stolen and driven on a joyride through Polliwog Park.

Assasin, a huge coal-black malicious creature, whose hellish looks are set off by the errie glow of his crimsom eyes carefully stocked his prey. He felt provoked, and his eyes flickered from yellow to green. He is the harbinger of death, and those who are unfortunate enough to meet him soon encounter calamity or death. He prefers to hunt alone, intending to deliver as many souls as possible to his dark master. Although he has never actually harmed anyone, eyewitnesses are usually never the same after they encounter him. His presence sends a terrifying chill through the bodies of those who hear him. He usually disappears completely after an encounter and lives in an abandoned graveyard until his master beckons him once more.

Assasin had been handpicked to coordinate the attack. With him was the Massacre and Slaughter, two of the most destructive demons in Satans forces. There targets were two young men whose minds were easy to manipulate.

"'The Moretti girls are making a mockery of you. Don't fail us!. You have to stop them or you will die. And why not do it right? Kill their friends and family; none of them have treated you right. They all deserve to die. Listen to me, I would never mislead you. I'm your friend.'"

Grabbing his claymore, he could feel the yearning, a terribly strong impulse to finish them all off. He had planned it to the last detail.

Assasin whispered in a high pitched shrill, "'Kill them, kill them, kill them. The master will be pleased, you will be rewarded.'"

Flattered by the demons' approval, his answer was automatic; "I won't fail you."

In a few minutes, Damien and Riggins were seated at a table, served water and a bowl of popcorn. Riggins grabbed a handful and popped it into his mouth. He ate another and then another before he noticed that Damien hadn't had even a single kernel. He raised his eyes to him and stopped chewing, his mouth was full.

Damien apparently read the question in his eyes. "I won't eat before a job. I want to be at the top of my game!"

Riggins swallowed and nodded, "Oh."

A moment of silence passed before the waitress came back to the table to take their order. The bar food at Hennessey's wasn't bad, especially when washed down with a pint. Damien was pleased at how easily the waitress had accepted his fake ID. But most important to Damien was the fact that he was sitting there with Riggins, finalizing their plans. It was a strange place for the two of them to meet, one that had a traditional cozy feel indigenous to an Irish pub.

Their table afforded them a view of the ocean. There were Bud and Guinness on draft, and the world's largest pint served in a gigantic fifty-ounce souvenir-glass filled with premium draft. Other options were Harp if you were female, or a pansy, in Riggin's opinion. The crowded display of liquor behind the bar was laced heavily with whiskeys. Downing several drinks and a few pills, they finally decided it was time to give the twins a visit. Rumor had it that their older brother was having the party of parties that evening to which, due to their having been outcast, no one had invited them. The bar would be closing in five minutes, so they headed to Damien's house to get their weapons.

As they walked up the walkstreet, they spotted Christopher Moretti, sleeping on a couch on the porch. With a baseball bat

Damien found in the yard, he bludgeoned Christopher to death. The thrill of the kill exponentially increased the taunts of demons.

"'Kill them all, kill them all. History will record this. I'm a master. I'm even more powerful than Ford. I will make Riggins second in command when we return from our victory. Maybe we will even form our own cult. This is amazing!'"

At gunpoint, they bound the rest of the Morreti family and locked them in respective bedrooms throughout the house.

These practitioners of Satan became extremely cruel and vicious, temporarily losing control. Their behavior became emotionally-charged with little or no thought to the consequences of their actions. Substance abuse added to the mix of this improvised ritual and the pulsating music they played, coupled with the euphoric excitement of primal lust caused these frenzied pseudo-Satanists to indulge in behavior closely resembling madmen. Their preys, the Moretti children, were hapless victims of a bloodthirsty ritual. They suffered pain as helpless sacrificial lambs.

With his rough hand, he grabbed a fistful of Sara's hair. With a violent sideways jerk, he tore her clothes. Throwing her to the floor, her body was reeling. He stared at her with a blurred hate-filled face. She whimpered laying limp on the floor. A black boot blotted out her vision, driven into her face as her skull thudded on the floor. She went numb. Her body was twitching, and she kept hitting him. Both men then took turns sexually assaulting her.

Jennifer was next. The force of the first blow knocked her out of the chair, but she held on to Riggins's leg firmly. Her head sank, and she began to cry in very short shallow gasps of terror. Riggins, like a possessed man, stood above her and boasted over her limp and trembling body. "What you don't realize is that we are actually doing you a favor. Perhaps in your next life, you will remember to treat others better and have more fun."

Then he grabbed her wrist and held them behind her body; she heard a click and felt the cold steel of the handcuffs. Sara heard her ear-piercing scream. All the while, they filmed it on their video camera. There was blood upon the floor, and broken glass was scattered about the hardwood floor.

The demons moved very little, mumbling back and forth in different languages, their sulfurous breath forming a horrific atmosphere. Forbodden screeched.

"'Faster, faster, murder them. They have wronged you. They deserve to die. Kill them. Torture them.'"

Riggins and Damien were getting more electrified and anxious like caged animals. They fed the girls' ecstasy and tied belts around their necks "to make it easier to stab Jennifer and Sara," and offered them up as the "ultimate sin against God." They selected and stalked them believing that a virgin sacrifice of identical twins would earn them a "ticket to hell. In an agitated frenzy they strangled both girls, and then doused their lifeless bodies with gasoline.

Running from one room to another, they played Russian roulette with the Morreti brothers. Holding his gun in the center of the pillow, Riggins placed it against Luke's head and pulled the trigger. Nothing. Crying and trembling, they begged for mercy. None was given. William was the first to be shot in the head. No one survived.

Envy shrieked.

"'Finish it quickly. Don't let the police get you. Stop playing around.'"

After two more clicks of the gun, Damien grabbed his clamor and chopped off Luke's head.

The teenage murderers fled the scene, yelling profanities and laughing hysterically. The noise awoke the neighbor who called the police.

But no sooner had Joel stepped into the narrow and rutted alley behind the house to see what Damien and Riggins were up to than he felt a sharp pain in his leg. His bellowing shout flashed out in an instant, and in one quick word, he beheaded a small spirit that had been clinging to him. It dissolved in a puff of blood-red vapors. Joel wished he could release his fighting power with full force, but he had his orders. Thus he had to deal with this cluster of angry spirits one by one.

Another spirit clamped onto his back. He yelled, "Away with you. Go to a dry place!" Another demon landed on his back, then another on his leg, and if that wasn't enough, two more came with slashing words and nipping remarks.

Growing tired of their game, with piercing words he vanquished them all to the abyss. A large, laughing spirit flew in close for a look at Joel, and then shot straight into the sky. Why start a fight when he had already won his battle? At last, Joel was free of demons.

The demons were exhilarated by the murders, and at first continued to flock and circle about the house; but then they realized that they should return to Satan to receive their reward. Their numbers quickly dwindled, their cries faded, and soon they were nowhere to be seen.

The first policeman to arrive at the scene stopped at the front gate.

"Police," he assertively said.

No response. Getting closer, he could see that the couch was already soaked red with blood. There was nothing anyone could do. Looking through the front window, he saw total chaos inside; the house had been ransacked. Waiting for backup to arrive, the first officer on the scene began to devise a plan on how best to enter the home.

Drawing their guns, and yelling "police" as they entered the home, they stepped into the once-quaint beach cottage, now a pitiful shambles. The furniture was thrown everywhere, the cushions on the sofa were slashed open, the coffee table had been chopped in several pieces and broken, and everything was out of place. In the middle of the floor were papers, books, small boxes, several items of clothing, and dead bodies. What type of animals would do this?

Someone had taken red paint. Or was it blood? They would have to check it out. A sickening feeling flooded the room. It was blood! Scrawled on the mirror was an obscene message of hate—a very clear message. They were young and beautiful but dead—violently dead. The expression on their faces were blank, the eyes dry and staring. Each body was a crumbled mess. Their necks were broken and twisted into strange angles; a pool of blood had formed in front of their opened mouths. The spirits of these once cheerful and beautiful girls were gone; they were far, far away in heaven.

The police would have to check every room in the house to determine the damage. They checked the whole house, upstairs and downstairs. There were terrible discoveries in each room. The investigation team felt concerned, nervous, and depressed. As they took a second look around, they tried to think of the criminal connections that might be involved. Why was the Moretti family a target for such a brutal attack? This was way more than your typical vengeance-seeking vandalism.

The neighbor who called the police was questioned. "Christopher Moretti was such a nice young man," she said, her face full of grief and surprise. She gave a nervous chuckle as she shook her head. "He always said hello and smiled. We enjoyed having him as a neighbor. He was clean, responsible, and happy. Why would anyone want to hurt him?"

The policeman wrote it all in his report. "Can you think of anyone who might have had some kind of grievance or grudge against the Morettis?"

"No, I can't imagine anyone doing this."

"Well, it's been quite an evening. We've had a real tragedy here. We have your statement. If you think of anything else give us a call." With that the officer handed her his card.

Meanwhile, Riggins and Demien attempted to flee the scene using Christopher Morreti's sports car. They drove down the alley, panting, crying, terrified, and looking possessed. Three cruel spirits rode on each of their backs, with their talons deeply rooted in fleshy tissue. The demons hissed and spit foul suggestions into their minds.

The young men and their demons came to a corner and were about to turn left when they were spotted by police surveillance. Pursued by police, Riggins immediately opened fire. Assisted by his fiendish companions, Riggins quickly pinpointed his target. The first shot struck the forehead of the officer behind the wheel. He was instantly killed; the car careened into a neighbor's garage. As back up arrived, gun shots were fired. Spurred on by an immense number of demons, a battle ensued in which both of the fugitives were killed at the site. These guys were not like most criminals the police encountered. This was not a robbery gone wrong. This was out-and-out mayhem. Sergeant Scott shook his head.

"'It always happens to the good people.'"

The culprits appeared to be completely unprepared. They had no identifiable plan. They were improvising all the way. They even had to steal their getaway vehicle. Why? Murders like this didn't happen in Manhattan Beach.

During the grim investigation, the policemen did not smell the order of sulfur, or see the red eyes staring at them from the ceiling. Neither did they hear the evil sneering, nor the sudden rush of black leathery wings as the demons soared away.

A sea breeze fluttered around them. Details were crystal clear to Michael, but he felt oddly detached. From his vantage point, he could count thirty pairs of shifting red eyes staring at him. Time was moving on around him, yet he felt like he was in a bubble where time stood still. ""Joe just has to figure out why all this has happened! I hope he isn't foolish enough to blame God. Satan is, and always has been, man's adversary. You would think they would have a clue from his name. The word *Satan* means adversary.'" Michael looked into Nigel's eyes, so full of the white fire for battle, and yet so tender toward God's commands.

"'Good friend, we all have compassion for Joe. We can only do as God commands. All this is in Joe's hands. It is up to him to find the answer.'"

"'May Joe's revelation come soon,'"

Nigel thoughts flooded Michaels mind.

Manuel started to quote God, but Nigel held him back.

"'Bridle your word-sword. Joe must go through this by himself. It is now time to test Joe's faith; it will be a real trying of his soul,'" Michael commanded.

9

We can decide to let our trials crush us,
or we can convert them to new forces of good.

—Helen Keller

Satan began to chant unrelenting curses that droned on mechanically. On cue, all the other demons did the same. The echoing choruses filled the air of the Pacific Ocean along the coast of Japan with crimson smoke that danced about the advancing ship. An armed ring of demons were stationed to block any attempt at interference. Satan glared at his opponent with burning hatred that made his red eyes bulge, and his sulfurous breath spew out through widely gaping nostrils. He toyed with the words he shouted, watching to see if any of the angels would make the slightest move. They only watched him, not moving at all.

With piercing accuracy, Satan sent a word-laser blow in Michael's direction. The resounding clang of the blow connecting with his word-shield rang out as Michael staggered backward. Cheers and laughter came from the crowd of demons. Returning his attention to the ship, he poised himself for the ensuing fight. He stood strong, with his wings flared. Satan had already increased the frequency and intensity of the upcoming earthquake. Joe Moretti's natural gas supertanker was their target.

The sky was a searing cauldron of black ghouls, their tribe forming a swarming, living haze over the battle scene. The sounds of their chants formed a constant, low-pitched hum that echoed back upon itself from the rocky shores below. The demons were very disturbed like angry bees in a hive. The demonic cloud continued to thicken and swirl, and from his vantage point, Michael saw the glimmer of millions of pairs of red eyes.

With cries and wails of rage, demons scattered everywhere. Murder's chin-length dark-hair framed his face, which was a pale shade of onyx. It was hard to tell his features because they were twisted by his rage and thirst for death. His feral red eyes were dominant, difficult to look at. He glared viciously, shuddering and writhing every few seconds with vile words spewing from his lips. He bellowed forward, growing darker with each move.

With a clang like thunder, the earth began to move. The first jolt of stress coming out of the ocean floor sends a shock wave hurtling like a tornado. Over several tons worth of water surged toward the tanker. At 3:13 p.m. a massive 9.1 magnitude earthquake struck just off the coast of Tokyo, Japan. The seismic waves it created on the Pacific Ocean floor set off tsunami waves that traveled at the speed of a jet plane. Waves forty-five feet high pounded the ship. It was tossed like a tiny matchbox toy.

On impact, an explosion of loud noise and shock waves rang through the air. Windows shattered and black clouds of smoke and balls of flame shot into the sky. For a few stunned drivers on the roads in predawn gloom, the pulse of energy that tears through the ground looks dimly like a twenty-mile snake slithering across a pasture. Telephone poles whip back and forth as if caught in a tempest. Power lines are ripped loose in a shower of blue and yellow sparks. Lights go out, and the telephone system goes down. The destructive force of Satan had been unleashed upon world.

There were several phases to the devastation: the original shock wave blast of the explosion; the flying shrapnel of the exploding tanker, which carried such parts as walls, roof, floors, doors, windows and ceiling. When the shock waves of the blast rose up between the sky scrapers of Tokyo, a vacuum-effect created an implosion. Atmospheric pressure that was inside nearby buildings collapsed glass and parapet walls back onto the sidewalk and street. The explosion generated massive amounts of heat that caused secondary fires and structural collapse. Ground shock waves broke gas, water, electric and sewer pipes. Subway tunnels and building foundations were affected.

There was nowhere to run when you have something like that happening. Japan was completely unprepared for this. All of a sudden—bam—it just hit. You could tell this was different instantly from other little tremors they had before. It just picked up in intensity. In downtown Tokyo, large buildings shook violently, and workers poured into the street for safety. Large buildings were on fire and bellowing smoke poured from the Odaiba district of Tokyo. In central Tokyo, trains were stopped and passengers walked along the tracks to platforms. Thirty minutes after the quake, tall buildings were still swaying in Tokyo and mobile phone networks were not working.

The death toll was estimated to be in the neighborhood of twenty-five thousand, of which the entire crew of Joe's tanker was a part. This was one of the most devastating major natural catastrophe in modern history.

Their answering screams were ear-piercing; their bodies arched stiffly into distorted, unnatural positions. The dark shapes came closer, separating themselves into groups, solidifying their positions. Men, women, and children had been condemned to misery and death. Their cries intensified, becoming a mad echoing drone of savage fury that rang over Tokyo like a thousand firing weapons, spreading shrapnel filled with grumbling, whining, and yelping. Demonic forces shrieked confusing ideas into the mind of anyone willing to listen. In the ensuing melee over the next few weeks, many more would die from their injuries. Finally, there was quiet.

"You did an excellent job," Satan burbled to Confusion, who had just returned from the battle. He stood on the other side of the cavern, near the exit. Demons didn't like getting too close to each other. It was always wise to leave an avenue of escape in case the meeting turned sour. Demons that were wary of Satan tended to fare better than those who trusted him.

Confusion gave off a creepy appearance the way he never seemed to blink. Smug had seen him before, and at this meeting, he made it obvious that he disliked this demon's presence. Confusion leveled his flat unblinking gaze at Smug for so long that he began wondering if he made it a practice to eliminate his competition. Smug thought of him as one of Satan's assassins, but in fact he wasn't one of his regular crew. He was more of a free agent, doing whatever he pleased and very difficult to control.

When Confusion did not reply, didn't rush to assure Satan that he was honored to work for him the way others had, Satan's fingers drummed impatiently on his thigh. It was a nervous habit he had when he wasn't comfortable, a telling little gesture. He wasn't exactly afraid, but he too was being wary, which meant there were two powerful demons in the room.

Confusion suddenly looked at Satan, his dark gaze cool and assessing. He sucked in a breath and was actually considering the idea, weighing the cost of continuing to remain silent. Seeing no better alternative, he bowed silently in Satan's direction and snickered "Thank you, my Lord."

Joe heard a mad pounding and a disturbing commotion at his front door. William Martin, his business partner, screamed, "Turn on the TV. Our ship has blown up! The largest earthquake in history just struck off the coast of Tokyo. The powerful tsunami that followed tossed the tanker like a football onto the shore. The explosion it caused has leveled parts of the city."

Entering the family room, Joe clicked on the television and switched the channel to the news. "Don't worry so much, the insurance will cover this."

"I don't even know how to tell you this, but I decided to self-insure the ship and cargo. I was hedging on the money we would make. I had no idea this would ever happen. This is horrible. I can't image the lawsuits that will be filed against your company. I don't even want to estimate how much we've lost: the ship, the cargo, the crew, and the damage the explosion caused. It seemed like everything you did turned to gold. I just thought I would capitalize on this to help you make more. You know I always like to play on the edge."

A piercing groan escaped from deep inside his chest as he collapsed onto Joe's couch. Both men's eyes were glued to the television screen.

The Bloomberg reporter sat with a concerned look on her face, "The epicenter of the earthquake today was fifteen miles off the coast of Tokyo in the center of Japan, and it generated a tsunami wave up to five miles inland. The tremor was felt across Japan. The waves were mixed with mud, with ships and cars smashing and exploding into high rise buildings in the business district bashing them to pieces. The initial 9.1 magnitude earthquake was followed by aftershocks measuring 7.3 in magnitude. Tsunami warnings are in effect for much of the Pacific Rim. One natural gas supertanker went up in flames adding additional destruction to the city. Eleven nuclear plants were shut down."

Just having awakened from a terrifying dream, Joe steeled his thoughts probing his feelings, almost avoiding the gaze of William's blue eyes. He thought back to the night he had stayed late at the office years ago. He felt that same uneasiness now. "'Why have I been so careless? I usually go over every contract with a fine-tooth comb. Why have I been so nervous and worried about everything, while missing the most important issues? I'll need to call my lawyers in the morning. Why did I ever hire William? I should have given Christopher the job, or, at best, if he were interning for me, he might have caught this mistake. What is wrong with me? What has happened to my common sense?'"

As soon as the first earthquake ended, a swarm of demons left for Joe's ranch. Right behind them, so dangerously close, was a brilliant, fiery meteor carrying the force of the sun itself. The black creatures and the meteor shot into the sky, zigzagging, shooting this way and that like wild fireworks. Satan and his hordes descended on the ranch, a blizzard of screeching fiends. The storm exploded out of the sky, raining a glittering inferno in all directions. You could feel the heat of the warrior's words. The buildings, cattle, and land were consumed by them.

On the right, a long, slithering spirit yelled one more curse over the prairie before curling tightly and rising to watch the destruction. Sodom and Gomorrah once again.

On his left, a loud-mouthed boasting imp cursed, filling the air with blasphemies. He was quick and confident, knowing that he would prevail. His face wore a proud sneer. And then it was over. The demons were gone, but not before Joe's ranch was decimated.

"Are you sure you have destroyed it?" asked Satan.

Forbodden had made sure. "Everything is dead, if that's what you mean."

Mayhem added, "Only one employee remains alive, and he is injured and frightened."

Satan replied, "Then the end is near, and there is no stopping it!"

While he was still thinking, his cell phone rang. Joe listened as his face filled with horror. "Joe, I've some horrible news. A large flash of light, a huge detonating fireball streaked across the sky. I've never seen anything like it. This massive meteor shower appeared as a shooting star lighting the entire sky. As it grew closer to the ground, it shed glowing material in its wake. Fire fell from the sky and burned up your cattle ranch in Texas. Hundreds of people and cattle are dead and injured. I'm your only surviving employee."

Joe tried to calm himself and said he would try to be there tomorrow to sort through things. At least his children were safe. "'Why is all this happening? A meteor from nowhere! Why hadn't I heard of its approach on the news? I would have thought it would be there. It's like it just happened miraculously. Wrong word. It's not a miracle; more like an antimiracle if there is such a thing. What am I going to do?'"

Michael heard a distinctive whistle. It was Raphael, signaling trouble. He shot down the length of the attic, out the end of the house and into the concealing branches of a large pepper tree.

And then there was trouble! The demons appeared first, whirling and soaring in a flock of at least one thousand. They weren't too large, probably not frontliners, but deadly nevertheless. Michael had to wince, just gazing at those flashing fangs and hearing their piercing razor-sharp words. He needed to avoid assailing that bunch for the time being; more important business was at hand.

Then a second band appeared; all cackling and chattering, some sitting on the neighbor's roofs, some just flitting about the front deck looking for mischief.

"Lord, help us!" Joel exclaimed.

Raphael hadn't seen these two yet. From inside the police car, like huge hulking monsters, two demons emerged and watched with their red eyes darting about with great guardedness. They were searching the area for intruders. These were vicious characters, indeed. There was something about them that Raphael could sense, something more sinister and wicked than most.

Oh no! Beyond the shore, just out where the waves began to break, another large detachment of demons approached like a swarm of hornets, appearing as a long, thin charcoal smudge across the horizon.

While he was still speaking, he could hear footsteps—urgent, thumping footsteps—of several sets of feet. Out of the corner of his eye, he saw police officers approaching his front door. The sharp rap on the seldom-used door made him jump. He saw the outlines of two men and a woman dressed in uniforms. Flinging the door open he heard the lead officer say, "We're looking for Joseph Moretti. We were told that he lives here."

"Yes, I'm Joseph Moretti."

The officer's face wore a placid smile, and he could smell the faint scent of her perfume. Her hair was tied back in a bun. Her brownish-amber eyes reminded Joe of a cage panther in search of solace. They were watchful and somewhat sad. She took out a notebook.

"There's been a home invasion at your son Christopher's home. We're sorry to inform you that we believe all of your children have all been killed. Once you have had some time to process this we will need you to either provide DNA samples or come in to make a positive ID in person."

Joe felt light-headed with grief. A moment of silence passed. The preliminaries were brief: the time of the incident and the believed names of the deceased.

"I understand how distressed you must be, so we will leave you to contact other family members. If you have any further questions you can call us at any time. Here is my card. Also if it is alright with you we will be sending over a grievence councelor to help you process everything. She will be here shortly."

With that, the officer handed Joe her card, closed her notebook, and then she turned and walked out.

Then Joe took a deep breath and turned slowly to find Grace. She was standing near the family room doorway with her back against the wall, and she boldly met Joe's look.

"Grace," he said, his voice nearly inaudible. "They are saying that they believe all our children are dead."

She saw Joe's agony, the torture in his face.

"What?" she screamed abhorring his expression. "What happened?" she asked, though of course, she already knew the answer.

It took Joe a moment to answer her.

"This can't be happening. Our children, all of them, are dead," he whispered.

His eyes were as guarded as if she were another enemy. More than guarded, they were afraid. Joe stood frozen. Tears poured down his cheeks, and they cast a dark shadow over him.

Grace's mind was panicky, stunned, and useless as her body. She stared at Joe in bewilderment.

Sorrow exploded in her skull, mental fireworks that obliterated both thought and action. She didn't react, she couldn't. She stood there, violently trembling, because she was incapable of doing more. Then she sat on the couch as everything went black.

"Oh, Grace," Joe sighed in grief. Grace was first aware of cool hands touching her forehead.

"Joe," she whispered.

"Yes, I'm here."

She got her eyes to open and stare off in unbelief.

Joe watched her eyes carefully for some sign that she would be okay.

Grace struggled trying to sit up. Her body shook in a frenzied fear. Joe realized what she was doing and helped her. She stared at the television. Then she was aware of the voices around her. They were buzzing at first and then they grew in volume, but she did not want to listen. Her mind needed protection. It was trapped in the knowledge of what had just happened. Her pain was now part of the blackness that filled the room. She felt totally disconnected from her body. She couldn't think. Her mind felt simultaneously imprisoned and out of control. But she could do nothing about it. The agony was too strong for her soul to process. There was no escape from it.

"Joe," she sobbed. "No, no, no, no!"

He drew several deep, ragged breaths. His actions were instinctive, given without thought. He tried denying his feelings, but they came automatically. So much pain, peppered with rage and fear. His thoughts raced. "'What will people say? When you lose a spouse, you're a widow. A child who loses his parents is an orphan. But there is no name for me, that's how awful this is! Oh, my God!'"

Then he fell to his knees sobbing, "God has given and God has taken away. God you must have a reason for this. Help me see!"

Joe had never been in fear for his life, but he could imagine how afraid his children had been that night. How they feared their imminent death. Imagining was what he did. He imagined the panic of lying in pain, the abuse, the fear, the confusion. Despair settled in as a permanent guest. Add up all these tragedies and it was too much for one person to handle. He felt mad. He considered taking a gun and killing himself to just stop all the pain.

Yet in all all that had just happened, Joe refused to accuse God with wrongdoing. What infuriated Joe was that he had no one to blame, but perhaps himself. All his illusions had been shattered. They had been destroyed by some unseen force. He accepted each blow as he felt he must, but he could not help asking himself the question "Why?"

""Why have Grace and I been singled out for this bad luck? Why has God alienate himself from us? What have we done wrong? How will we ever be happy again? Why me? Why my businesses? Why Christopher, William, Luke, Sara, and Jennifer? We aren't bad people. We don't deserve this. We went to church. Why didn't God warn us? Why didn't he stop this? Why?'"

Joe couldn't remember a time in his life when he had been dishonest or ruthless. Not once in his adult life had he ever made a decision based on doing what was criminal. Sure he wanted to make a lot of money, but his reputation was more important. He had gone out of his way to help his friends, sacrificed his own material needs for his children and his aged parents, and even gave to local charities. Joe had looked out for everyone—first, last, and always. He hoped in the depths of his heart that his godliness had been authentic and that someday he would be vindicated.

Joe's profound anguish robbed him of his ability to understand how God worked, and therefore, God had become a great enigma to him. Overflowing with anguish, puzzlement, anger, and bitter complaints, he still clung to hope. Yet part of him wanted to turn his back on God, to march off—godless—into the dark night. How could a God of love allow such horrible things? Joe had considered himself a strong person, someone willing to take risks and accept consequences. But after all the news, he could feel himself sinking fast. Taking on whatever had caused this evil required more physical and moral courage than Joe feared he had. His whole being desperately yearned, not so much for the gifts God had given him, but for a sign that He was still there. He felt lost and trapped. It was as if he was stuck in quick sand, sinking fast.

10

There's no tragedy in life like the death of a child.
Things never get back to the way they were.

—Dwight David Eisenhower

When the priest said, "Give courage to those who are bereaved," Joe was already dreading the final hymn; the passing of his children would be complete. When the priest said, "Help us, we pray, in the midst of things we cannot understand," Joe began to sob. Echoing from the foyer of the church, Joe heard the bagpipes begin to play "Amazing Grace" as the coffins were carried down the aisle. "'I feel queasiness hovering over me. I'm so angry. So much pain, I can't bear it. Half of what people are saying about us is true. But half of it is made up of lies, and even though I know the difference, it still eats at me. I know my friends and family are tired of dealing with the complexity of my life. They would be better off if I would just disappear. No one would miss me. Not like they miss Christopher, William, Luke, Sara, and Jennifer. I've lost everything—maybe even the kindness in my heart. I live a poisoned life. God, where are you?'"

The drive to the Pacific Crest Cemetery took about ten minutes. Certainly the burial was even more difficult after that reassuring nonsense Joe received from the priest as to why this had happened. What was left of his family was standing outside, exposed, on a typical summer day, breezy and cool.

"In sure and certain hope of the resurrection to eternal life through our Lord Jesus Christ, we commend to Almighty God Christopher, William, Luke, Jennifer, and Sara, and we commit their bodies to the ground," it was all Father O'Reily could do not to burst into tears. He muttered a quick prayer under his breath and continued, "Earth to earth, ashes to ashes, dust to dust," he continued.

Joe immediately bent down and took some loose dirt in his hand. With a quaking voice he prayed:

"The LORD bless thee,
and keep thee:
The LORD make his face shine upon thee,
and be gracious unto thee:
The LORD lift up his countenance upon thee,
and give thee peace."

He was the first to cast dirt on upon each of his children's coffins. One by one, the mourners threw dirt on the coffins. As Grace passed by, Joe heard her softly say, "I'm sorry." Yet she was not to blame for what had happened.

That evening after their funeral when the last guest had left, sorrow lingered and demanded to be felt. He watched Grace get into her pajamas and brush her teeth. Grace's eyes were sore from crying. She was characteristically subdued by the tragedy. Grace kept saying, "I can't believe they're gone!"

Then Joe tenderly put his arms around her, and they stood in the dark weeping together. The terrible feeling that had been gnawing at her during the funeral came back, with just the same awful, insistent coldness.

"We've done something very wrong," Grace sobbed. "We wouldn't be here tonight, like this, if we didn't do something wrong."

Joe sighed. "Grace."

She closed her eyes but with a defiant expression. "I didn't even get a chance to give them a hug goodbye or tell them how much I love them."

"You're wrong. You told them every day that you love them. They knew."

"Maybe."

There was a truth to what Joe had said, but not enough. Grace needed absolution.

Joe tried to start again, "I want to give you an accurate picture of things, but I really don't understand why all this has happened.

We are in a horrific spot, but it isn't the end of the world. It's possible we can pull through this thing and come out okay. Right now, we just need to give ourselves some time to heal."

But Grace would not let the thought drop. Tall, lean, and athletic, she was no weakling and could be very persistent when it came to fighting for what she thought was the truth. Maybe Joe was right that it wasn't her fault. But then whose fault was it?

Finally, Grace curled up on the living-room couch with her head in Joe's lap; she just lay there without moving, looking into space like a toddler who had lost her lovie. "It doesn't make any sense," she whimpered and then put her head back down on Joe's lap and cried for a while.

Joe got up and began to pace in front of the fireplace in the dark, unable to rest. Thoughts swirled in his mind. He pitifully cried to God for an explanation, putting his human wisdom, understanding, and insight to a test.

"'Why me, God? Why?" Being a good person didn't mean I had to be a saint. I have always felt lucky that it was not a requirement because I don't think I could ever reach that level.'"

All these questions made him anxious and ill-tempered. Rather than hearing from God, Joe felt a black fear cover him, and he broke out in a cold sweat. His head was pounding, swirling with thoughts as he groaned.

"'My children were good people who helped others in need. They were friendly, caring and for the most part decent kids. They might mess up sometimes, but that was life; it was about growning up and becoming an adult. Why them? Why?'"

Joe flopped in the couch, his face like chalk, his hair uncombed. For a moment, he just sat there, trying to think, trying to calm down. Shiny talons pierced his skull as the black and twisted hands of the hideous demon held his thoughts in a viselike grip. The spirit leaned over and whispered words into his mind.

"'God is to blame for this! He destroyed my family. Don't I need them more than he does?'"

Joe had trouble processing all that had happened and was terrified by it. He knew that life as he knew it had ended, and there was no going back for him. He couldn't stand the thought of living without his children.

It took a few more shakes, and Joe's eyes never did really open more than a slit, but Grace managed to get him off the couch. She helped him up the stairs to their bed where he collapsed on top of the quilt, fully dressed in what he had worn at the funeral and started snoring again. It really didn't matter if the suit got wrinkled; he probably would never wear it again anyway. Grace collapsed next to him, but it was more than an hour before she fell into a fitful sleep.

Grace would sit with the *Los Angeles Times* spread out on the bed. She'd paged through it a hundred times, hoping all the details were not true. The front page carried a story of a local political scandal and gas prices going up, but the big headlines read, "Local Family Found Dead." The Los Angeles County Coroner had identified the five victims of the crime as members of the prominent Moretti Family.

It was a ridiculous piece of reporting. Grace couldn't, or rather, wouldn't pull herself away from it. A brainless turkey could have written a better story, maybe even gotten her children's names right. The story was incredibly, shockingly wrong. Why hadn't they portrayed her children as victims? Why did they believe the Moretti Family had done something to deserve this?

Curled in a ball, rocking on the bed, Grace began to sob. "'It's too difficult. I want my children back. I don't know how to get out of this hell. I can't eat. Why am I so useless? So empty? I'm so lonely! What do you want from me? There isn't a thing left. Do you even care that I'm hurting? My heart is broken, and you are silent. Why do you let the nightmares taunt me? I feel so overwhelmed, what am I going to do? Where can I find someone to help me stop this pain? I feel like a spider is spinning its web around my heart and soon it will die. That might be better—at least the aching would stop. I just want Joe to hold me in his arms cradled, and safe away from this nightmare.'"

Trying to make sense of things, she'd spent the afternoon with all of her favorite stationary, just scribbling thoughts down as they came to her. Now as evening called, she sat and leafed through page after page. It made no more sense than the newspaper's article. She had failed to capture her thoughts. There was no accurate way to do it. It was as though she was turning memories of her children's lives from beautiful encounters to dried flowers. And slowly one by one, the petals fell to the floor, lying there waiting to be swept away. She felt even more depressed. At times her writing appeared to be just chaotic scribbles. Grace recalled that she had done that when, in the pit of depression, she couldn't write anything else.

"'Wow, none of this is actually helping. Yeah, I did feel a little better writing it down, but that's it. All it really did was keep me trapped in my thoughts. I feel so powerless over my thoughts, my feelings. I know to most people, it would make sense to feel helpless and not want to participate in life anymore. But I really only have myself to blame, and I can't handle it.'"

She was insecure and aching. She was exhausted and spent. She longed to hear her children's voices, even the arguing that she used to wish would go away. But because rest and truth and hope had vanished, her heart was hazardous. Flick a spark in her direction, and the whole forest could go up in flames. She was in some kind of raging, agonizing battle to remain sane. Her mind had not slipped over the edge, but it was close. There were so many mindless wanderings, so many emotions, and so much fear. With only a little imagination, she could sense the evil lurking in the room ready to pounce on her.

She sat on the bed and tore the first sheet of paper, and it ripped in half. And then, with tears streaming down her cheeks, she picked up another one and did the same thing. And then another. The whole thing was so invigorating, and she realized she would have to find some other way to save herself. But how?

Grace felt sorry for herself every waking minute. It bothered her so much she had added a tablespoon of red pepper to dinner rather than a teaspoon. At first, she thought it was all nonsense, but then she began having thoughts that maybe Joe had hidden things from her. Joe must know why this had happened, but he just wasn't telling her. Slowly she began to have sinister thoughts, almost as if she were hallucinating. The stress and the sorrow were too overwhelming.

Bad enough—horrible that her children were gone—but what about the rest of her family? Grace could not bear it if they were in danger. Her nerves felt tattered and open to the elements. She didn't know how much longer she could restrain the urge to scream out loud.

"'People I loved are going to get hurt because of me. Hurt because of Joe. For the millionth time, I wish my bad luck would focus on someone else, anything else. Why do I feel like yelling out into the ocean? How can I get my bad luck to focus somewhere else? It won't be easy. I will have to wait and bide my time. Maybe Joe is to blame. Maybe if I get away from him, all this will stop.'"

11

If a man has a right to find God in his own way,
he has a right to go to the devil in his own way also.

—Hugh Hefner

Satan stalked around, downcast with angry words streaming from his mouth. In his mind he saw Joe cursing God, defeated. Fearing that God might intervene at any moment, he concocted such a devious plan that he felt success was inevitable. Joe had been lucky; his businesses were crumbling, but he was not completely bankrupt. Satan would be sure he finished the job properly next time. Looking intently, he studied Joe mercilessly. Everyone had faults, and he would use Joe's against him. He was the only one that could.

The next time that the angels gathered, Satan made sure he was there with them. Michael asked, "How are things going with Joe? You've destroyed almost everything he loved, and still he did not change. It appears that he still loves God."

Satan sighed, "Joe will only feel pain if he himself is hurting. He will do anything to save his own life. But if Joe had great pain in his own body, he would not love God. Nor would he obey him. I challenge you to put him in my hands."

"You know the rules of the kingdom. He is already at your mercy!" Michael bellowed.

So Michael agreed that Satan would be allowed to cause Joe pain; that is, unless Joe himself used his faith in God's word to stop him. Love casts out fear. There was one stipulation God had instructed Michael to convey: you can cause Joe as much pain as you want, but his life is to be spared.

His cry of ecstasy and destruction streamed over the expansive earth, on to the shores, and into obscure hovels—for the rays of his power had been sent out to accomplish his desire. With that Satan vanished.

Satan took great pleasure as he afflicted Joe. Joe had tried to shake it off, tried to ignore it, but it was there. His palms were sticky with sweat, he felt nauseated. It was dark in his bedroom, the shadows were very black.

Behind and above him, black leathery wings quietly positioned themselves. Leering red eyes watched Joe's every move. Here, there, and everywhere all over the room, in the corners of the ceiling, upon the furniture, clinging like spiders to the walls were the demons, letting out little snickers, some of them knife-like cursing. Hundreds of red eyes watched Joe's every move. There was an occasional hacking from the throat of a demon, a short burst of red vapor spewing from its mouth.

In his bedroom awaited the most loathsome spirits of all. They watched him lying in bed, never moving from their positions on the ceiling. On command, shrieks rang around the room. Their words exploded like arrows sent straight into Joe's heart. A blinding flash and then another. Spores of red-hot light traced brilliant fiery arcs, a searing edge that cut through Joe like a sword. Painful sores began to appear on his body. Waves of spirits poured down upon Joe in reasonless terror. All strength left his body, and he began to shake uncontrollably.

When Nigel arrived, he could only see the eyes. As he scanned the room, straining to see more, it occurred to him that there were more than twenty pairs facing him. He counted the pairs swiftly in his mind. Nigel went pale and drew a deep breath. He looked directly into the eyes of the tallest, most sinister of them. It was impossible to separate his shape from the darkness. A rumble passed down the shadowy line of demons, a low hissing mutter that echoed about the room.

Satan was in the lead, of course, unbelievably huge, black as midnight, a monster straight out of the abyss. Now Nigel could see them all, match the vastness with each pair of eyes, and it looked like more than twenty. The horde was overwhelming. Out of one corner of his eye, Nigel could see that Satan was watching, carefully evaluating him.

"What are you doing here?" he cried.

"You have been instructed not to kill Joe! Have you forgotten our agreement?" Nigel smiled.

Then suddenly, Joe was surrounded by four heavenly warriors robed in glorious light, their majestic wings unfurled like a canopy over him, their words, swirling sheets of brilliance. The air was filled with the deafening cries of hideous spirits spiraling through the roof, leaving a trail of red vapor as they vanished.

Their words vaulted through the demons as though they were clay pigeons used in target practice. The demons began to shy back; half their numbers were now gone as was half their zeal.

Joe fell into a fitful sleep, waking early in the morning with excruciating pain covering his body.

And then, almost as suddenly as it had begun, Satan's attack was over. Only three little demons remained: ones that might induce continued pain and the spread of the unknown disease, but not death.

Michael alighted back in the hallway as his wings folded and the light around him faded.

"How's Joe?" Joel asked.

Michael was relieved to say, "He's still shaken, but he's all right. He has the will to fight and the pain is endurable."

Returning from the doctor's office, Joe entered the kitchen, giving Grace a sour look. He sighed.

"What's wrong? What did they say?" Grace pried.

Joe replied, "I didn't understand all the verbiage they were using, but it is obvious they have no idea what is wrong with me. They have run more tests than I care to think about, and there are still no answers. All the doctor could suggest was that I seem overly stressed, and that maybe a vacation would do me some good."

Grabbing a mug from the cupboard, Joe filled it with the coffee Grace had just brewed. After adding some vanilla creamer, he headed out to the deck to watch the ocean.

"'Why is this happening? What have I done to cause this? Why can't the doctors figure out what's wrong? Why are sadness and depression such an ever present companion? I know there is a time for sorrow and grief. The pain never seems to go away. It just seems to lie there heavy upon me. Deep and uncontrollable sadness fills my soul. Death of my children is so against the way it is suppose to be. It is so hard to bear. There is no place to put it that makes sense. It just seems that I must endure it. I'm just going through the motions of life. I feel I'm wasting away. This pain does not just visit because my children are dead; everything in my life is dead. My dreams are even broken. I'm powerless to make things better. I don't think I can bear this. My heart is broken, and there isn't a thing to make it go away. It is so hard to even think of happiness, let alone experience it. I've carried this too long. There are too many sleepless nights and tearful prayers. And nothing will make it go away. It is all I can do to get up one more day and put my game face on and go through the motions. All I really want to do is be sad. I just want to shut the world out for awhile as best as I can and just be sad. Friends ask what they can do for me—just be okay that I'm not okay. It's so exhausting to pretend otherwise because I'm not okay. It just hurts.'"

Sadness masked his face. He sat there and removed bad bits of skin from his shoulder. Unseen to Joe, two angelic beings watched. In their unglorified state, they were of little consolation, except that they made sure that Joe remained alive.

Multiple ulcerated skin lesions that were raised and reddish covered his body. His hands appeared more as claws, and if he tried to walk, his left foot dragged. His eyelashes and eyebrow hairs were starting to fall out, and he found it difficult to close his eyelids. With uncontrollable itching, Joe took a small seashell that lay on the table next to him and scraped his arm.

At the end of the pier, on top of the roundhouse, like an enormous black dragon, Satan sat. Other demons attended him, waiting to hear his next command, but Satan was silent. Hour upon hour, a tense scowl on his face; he sat and gazed at Joe with his slowly shifting red eyes.

Standing guard around Joe's house, Michael and his warriors could feel the lull, the silence, and the ominous deafness of the atmosphere. It had always been the same throughout the centuries.

Grace also indulged in self-pity and anger, enlisting anyone who would listen to her tale. She should have kept her mouth shut. There was no way to explain to others how she felt. But she wanted to keep on talking anyway. She was starved for human conversation because Joe just didn't want to talk about it one more time. She was like a broken record, stuck in one spot, continually repeating itself. Soon the town was full of rumors and malicious gossip. Grace vacillated between wanting to be with friends and wanting to be alone. She couldn't sleep and was delirious at times. She had panic attacks.

The attacks seemed to strike out of the blue and without warning. Grace couldn't find any clear reason for the attack. They occurred when she was relaxing or sound asleep. These panic-induced attacks left her feeling endangered and unable to escape. Because of these fears, she began to avoid things. She dreaded the surge of overwhelming anxiety and fear. Her heart would pound, and she couldn't breathe. At time she felt like she was dying or going crazy.

"'I wonder what people think after they talk to me. Actually, they must know my life sucks—life as I know it has fallen apart, and sometimes, I hope I won't wake up in the morning. It's not like I want to kill myself, or do I? No, I just want out of my life and into someone else's.'"

She felt intimidated just while walking down the street or into a room, and she hated when people pointed her out as that poor woman whose children were murdered, or looked at her out of the sides of their eyes as if she might start babbling any second. Everyone seemed to offend her. No one offered her the mercy she so craved. Grace was tired of that, even pissed off at times.

"'I'm tired of it all. How long am I going to keep bitching and moaning? Get over it—you are better than this. I just need to think about something else. About anything but my children! I don't want to fall asleep frightened by continual nightmares. The blackness is so threatening. I feel so alone. I miss my children. They were my world. How can I ever replace them? Love has died. Sorrow surrounds me. I'm overwhelmed. I'm afraid something else more sinister will happen, although I really can't imagine what it could be. My days are drudgery to be lived out with a hollow heart. Even my muscles ache and have no strength. I'm afraid to call on God for what other punishment he might have? All my prayers are in vain. I've had too many losses, and my heart can't bear any more. My heart is closed. I'm afraid of love. I tried it, and it hurts too much.'"

Then her chest would go tight and her breath short. Grace developed the perplexing habit of taking her pulse the way a runner might at the end of race—two fingers at the neck—even though she was sitting on the couch, not crossing a finish line of a marathon. The anxiety just whipped out of nowhere, tightening its grip on her heart. As her head went light with it, she gasped. She did this out of the fear that she might be dying. She'd convinced herself it might happen any time, and feeling the steady beat of her heart made her relax.

"'I can't breathe. Get a grip. Think of some happy times.'"

Then her expression tightened, like something painful was attacking her, yet she saw nothing.

An apparition stepped forward, a ghastly figure. It was tall, cloaked in billowing wings. It moved so smoothly, so silently that it seemed to float right up beside Grace. The other demons in the room stopped talking and bowed slightly.

The thing looked at Grace with calculating eyes. Its face was entirely hideous, especially its bulging eyes. It was pure evil, filled with hate. Forbodden's face mirrored his determination. His eyes tightened, and he looked as if he were trying to decide how to word his next statement.

He spoke portentously, "I want you to torture her tonight and finish her destruction. You all realize we are here to bewilder her. We must make the best of our situation. Both Grace's mental and physical condition are in our favor. Work hard, and then certainly, we will have a celebration in the next few weeks. Once our plan is in motion, we will let them complete their own destruction. And there lies our opportunity. But we must also be aware; there is the danger that either Joe or Grace will discover the truth and change things. We must keep them totally emotional and irrational, and Disappointment must be their constant friend. He will push Grace to feel extreme dissatisfaction with her life! Ever so cleverly, he will sink his deep roots inside of her. After he enters, not only will he torment her terribly with disappointment, but he will open up more doors inside for his others friends to enter."

Sizzling words cut through the air and divided the demons' ranks. The thing stood there motionless again, his eyes burning with anger while his wings slowly came to a standstill.

His low ominous voice was seething with hatred.

"Rumors have spread that we might not win this competition. If our opponent is hard-hitting, so much more of a thrill the challenge will be. We now have the advantage. Grace and Joe are divided. We will keep them busy, criticizing and arguing with each other; then their hearts will be far from praying. Over the years, we have noted the tones of voice and facial expressions they use to irritate one another. Work on that as well. Remind Grace how much she hates Joe's smirky smile, and how it makes her feel that he is treating her like a child. Let her assume that he knows how annoying it is, and that he is doing it to annoy her. And of course never let Grace expect that any of her tones or expressions similarly annoy Joe."

Grace rushed into the kitchen, the sanctuary where she hoped to find a moment of peace. She got out the wine first and then a corkscrew. Her shoulders relaxed a little as she took out a pack of skinless chicken breast from the fridge. Next she reached for the garlic and green onions. The nerves that seemed to dance around her didn't sound or show when she was in this element. She did something quick and easy with the rice. The air was pungent with spices. She stir-fried slices of mushrooms and small trees of broccoli. Her face was now relaxed and a little rosy from the heat and wine. She gave the vegetables one last toss and called for Joe. "Honey it's time for dinner."

Grace fixed herself a plate with considerably smaller portion and came around to sit at the kitchen table beside Joe. Taking another sip of wine from her second glass, she smiled over at him. Taking his first bite, he sat back to consider things. A smirky smile appeared on Joe's face as he was sucked in by the atmosphere. He innocently commented, "You look so tired, maybe you need some help to get through this."

It was Forbodden, standing tall and imposing, his expansive wings just settling at the dinner table. His glowing words were ready to be launched in an attack. A dozen demons accompanied him on either side, almost as malicious as he was. The hot red vapor from their nostrils was already spreading ribbons that drifted around the room.

The black beastly lips pulled back a contemptuous grin, unveiling a long string of obscenities. Forbodden spread his arms with a flourish, and then arrogantly declared, "Grace, it's all Joe's fault. You despise him. Look at his smirky smile. He is hideous-looking. Tell him. Yell at him."

His insane laughter echoed about the room. With that came an explosion of rushing, leathery wings, the demons began whooping and wailing, mocking and spitting, enjoying a moment of victory as every form of love had been vanquished from the room. Under normal circumstances, Joe's words would not have been offensive, but with a smirk on his face and the tone of his voice, such a moment felt like a slap to her face.

"Offense, you must see to it that these two fools keep up this game. They must go away from this quarrel convinced that their marriage is in shambles. In no time, Joe will turn his anger toward God as well," bellowed Forbodden.

In an instant Grace seemed to draw back from him, the moment was over. "You're the one who looks like crap. Leave me alone!"

It was like a blow from the pit of hell. Grace turned away from him. Joe remained motionless. "Is she no longer mine? Is my whole family secretly deserting me? I simply suggested she looked tired. What was wrong with that? Why is Grace so offended?'"

He took a deep breath. He grabbed her wrists and pinned them to her sides. They glowered at each other.

"You asked for it," she flatly said.

His eyes were intent on her face as he struggled to understand what was happening to their marriage. He stared into her eyes for a long minute. There was no sign of compromise, no hint of indecision in them.

"Please," he finally whispered, hopeless. "All I want is to try to find a way through this disaster without letting it destroy us."

But she didn't answer him. He hesitated in disbelief, stunned to hear her breathing was uneven, and she was still angry.

"Please?" he whispered again.

His words tumbled out as he looked at the uncertainty in her eyes.

"You don't have to make me any guarantees. Just try to at least be civil. Just let us try, only try. And I will try to give you what you want," he promised.

"This is unbearable. I can't handle this now," she cried.

Joe didn't respond. He let her go.

Joe wasn't eating. He couldn't even swallow food. He wasn't sleeping. He was down to 150 pounds. At six-foot-two, when he looked in the mirror, he saw his shadow staring back. It felt like ghosts were haunting him big-time, pushing him to the edge of a cliff.

Four spirits were following Joe wherever he went, but not the close companions he wished for. Despair, Fear, Poverty, and Sickness were there to inflict pain and frighten his battered soul. They were there by right, and besides, if Joe only knew the truth, it would set him free. Michael would just have to withhold his power until then.

Joe and Grace did not say another word to each until bedtime.

"Why don't you try to put this whole ordeal out of your head for a while? Take a pill and go to bed," Joe said.

"How would you know I've any pills to take?"

He smirked, "Take an Ambien, and we can talk in the morning."

His fists clenched into angry balls. He flinched.

"'Where did that come from?'"

As much as he worried about Grace being in pain, it was nothing like the panic he felt at the idea of not knowing why all the evil was happening to them. A tear ran down his cheek, and he wiped it off with his sleeve.

"'But how will I erase the stain in my heart. Why is Grace doing this to me? I thought she loved me. All this anger and tears. Should I just give up?'"

Grace continued to stare at him but said nothing more, neither then nor later that night. Whatever she felt, she kept it to herself. Joe hoped it was because she still loved him. But what could he do? There was nothing he could do. He understood her feelings. In many ways, he shared them. She was shocked at the devastation, but so was he.

She lay in her bed in the dark trying to sleep. Replaying the argument she had with Joe. Why was he so mean and insensitive after all they were going through you would think he could just notice she was doing the best she could? Unable to sleep she decided to get up and sleep in the guest room. Maybe a night off would give Joe a clue.

She got to her feet, swaying a little as the wine sloshed in her head as unsteadily as it did in her glass. Depressed and angry, her heavy heart made her think longingly of the sleeping pills in the medicine cabinet. Those and the antianxiety medication were now the threads that made up her security blanket. She prayed that tonight she would be able to sleep without help but was sure it was unlikely. She told herself she was safe. There wasn't going to be a fire. No one was going to break into their home and murder her in the night. She headed to the guest room and curled up on the bed. Covering herself with a quilt she fell into a fitful sleep. Her dreams were now plagued by every fear she had known: fear of dying, fear of loneliness, fear of disasters.

Someone was out there, out in the dark. She could hear him out on the deck, and then the shattering glass.

The pain was so fierce, she couldn't scream. The black force crushed her against the wall so she couldn't breathe, couldn't move. She tried to gasp for air, but the pain was too intense, and her immense fear was even greater. Wild screams, more like feral growls, echoed in her mind. She slapped and kicked at the talons that reached for her.

Her eyes flashed open. The room was pitch black. She could feel her heart racing. Her fingers dug into the quilt, and her own breathless screams echoed in her head. Waking in a sweat, she began to sob. She sat shivering and shaking and hated the person she had become.

She wasn't being held under the wave by an unseen force. She wasn't racing toward certain death. Just a dream, just a panic-dream. Regulating her breathing, she lay very still and tried to reorient herself. Looking at the clock on the wall she saw it was 7 a.m. She turned on the radio, maybe music would get her mind off of things. The radio was playing "Stronger (What Doesn't Kill You)" by Kelly Clarkson.

For a moment, she remembered none of it. When it flooded back, Grace wanted nothing more than to yank the quilt over her head and dive back into oblivion. How would she get through the day? Face anyone? She wanted to slink out of town.

Demons ruthlessly planted evil thoughts in her mind. Exciting her feelings and evil imagination, all kinds of vile and unclean thoughts came to her. They were the kinds that cause divorce, hatred, jealousy, murder, betrayal, and suicide. Their assignment was to frustrate, to conquer, and ultimately, destroy Joe. Grace felt as if she was having something place its hands about her head and force her under a spell. Gargoyling and hissing vicious, filthy, and lustful desires, their ambition was to get Joe's wife to act contrarily to her redemptive nature. Her soul was at their mercy, open to a merciless attack. There was no way that she would be praying today.

Aren't the little cartoons funny that depict little demons putting pictures into human's minds? But really, demon's best work is done by keeping God's promises out. It is an amusing pastime to make humans think that these promises will only come true when they reach their final destination—heaven. Then they remain helpless, trapped in the sludge of hatred, regret, unhappiness, and fear.

Grace propped herself up on an elbow, waited to see if her stomach would hold, then sat up. There was her favorite insulated mug on the nightstand. Baffled, she picked it up, slid back the tab, and sniffed her coffee.

Joe couldn't sleep, so he had gone downstairs to make coffee. He brewed a pot of Irish Cream coffee, Grace's favorite, and left it so it would be close and warm when she woke. If he had recited a Robert Burns poem with a Scottish accent while showering her with red roses, she couldn't have been more touched. She'd said horrible things to him, had behaved like a monster. And Joe had made her coffee.

She sipped it and let it slide down and soothe her abused stomach; too much wine always left her feeling that way. Because she could hear him down in the kitchen, she squeezed her eyes shut to help gather some courage. A little stressed, she got up to face the music.

In the dark corner of the kitchen, the little demon lingered, waiting for Grace's arrival. His drooping face was spread with an unsightly, drooling grin that revealed his fangs, as he cackled in demonic delight. And then as she entered the room, his words brought agonizing, heart-wrenching fear to her mind. Her heart raced. The room suddenly seemed unwelcoming and strangely quiet. She looked around the room with curious eyes, wondering where the feelings were coming from. Whether illusion or reality, she accepted them as they surged at her.

Joe glanced at her as she entered the kitchen and smiled sweetly. "Hope you are feeling better today."

She wouldn't have been annoyed by the question itself, not in the least. But he grinned while he asked. Funny, she thought, how many times that expression would have made her happy, but somehow today, it only irritated her. She felt he was smirking, laughing at her juvenile behavior.

"Thanks for the coffee," she said smugly.

He stayed quiet, waiting and realizing she was still angry.

"It's not my job to make you happy and cover up all your mistakes." She snapped at him. "'Why did I marry him? Was it really a contract I can't break, one that has trapped me with no way out? Honestly, I've already paid enough.'"

Joe tried to reason with her but it was useless. "Grace, don't you think I understand?" he cried. "When we first fell in love, the skies opened. Everything seemed possible. But out of nowhere, it seems that evil forces are at work in our world, and all I'm trying to do is protect you from them."

She listened to him. But when he finished she appeared restive.

"Do you think that matters now after all that has happened? You should have protected my babies. Then they would still be here. Why did you allow them to stay at their brothers? He is just a young man and couldn't protect them." She blinked back tears. The sadness echoed in her voice, "Do you think I care whether it's fair, or whether it is your dream to have us back the way we used to be? If this hurts, maybe it's because you deserve it, maybe this is all your fault."

Her voice was getting louder, more panic-stricken.

He tried to wrap his arms around her.

"No, you don't. Don't touch me, not now, maybe not ever again." She stepped back, glaring at him, yearning to flee. A new sob broke from her chest. Joe was hurting her again. Was there anything he touched now that didn't get spoiled?

"Damn it, stop!" he shouted "I'm trying to make you feel better, Grace, I really mean it." His eyes ailing with their sadness began to fill with tears.

"I don't care what you want. It will never happen until you can make me forget the horrors," she screamed. "'I'm so lonely. My heart is locked in fear. I refuse to let you in and let you hurt me again. I dread every new day. My life is such a burden. I'm so confused. Every way I turn seems blocked. I don't know which way to turn. You can't solve my problems, so why don't you leave me alone? I've made so many mistakes, and I can see no way of undoing them. I don't even trust myself to pray anymore. I thought I had prayed for my kids to be protected. So what is the use of praying now? Clearly God forgot about that or he just isn't listening. Why is it every time we start talking, somehow the conversation always ends up getting around to our children; and it's too painful, and right now I'm too angry and too sad and too nervous. So if I don't talk about it with anyone, maybe I can pretend that's really not what happened, or that it's not really so bad; or that if I wish hard enough, the whole thing will just go away, and I can go back to things being normal, whatever that means. Maybe I will awake and find I've only been dreaming.'"

Joe's life felt so overwhelming. His future loomed large and unknown. The agitation and stress engulfed him. It wasn't like he had known all this would happen. But Grace had reacted so strongly, showing him the intensity of her pain. The sound of her agony still cut at him somewhere deep in his heart. Right beside it were all the other pain. Pain for the death of his children. Pain for his world falling apart. He felt selfish and hurtful. Why did he torture the ones he loved?

He sensed that she would slip away, so he waited until he heard the water begin to run in the tub. He did not hear her silent escape, but he could feel it. The absence he had assumed would come had left an empty space in his heart. Then he grabbed his mug of coffee and headed out to the deck. Joe wondered how much of whatever poisons she'd bottled up inside her would be waiting for him when he went inside. If she started spewing at him again, he was going to... "'Nothing,'" he thought. It wasn't Grace he was pissed at, he realized. He was pissed at the world. He should've expected her to blow at some point. She'd been handling things pretty well, rising up from each blow. But she'd been swallowing down the fear, the rage, and the pain. Sooner or later they had to spill out.

"'I can be noble, Grace. I'm not going to make you choose. I'll be happy, and you can have whatever part of me you want, or none at all, if that's better. I just want you to be happy again the way you used to be.'"

The nasty psychological warfare being waged against her was unfathomable. Joe just wanted an answer: why? The atmosphere in their home was tense. Joe was not sure how long he and Grace could continue to live this way. There seemed to be no solution to the problem.

"'I know I only have to handle one day at a time. Yet even this simplistic thought is overwhelming. Everything is too complex for me to understand. I need help, but who can I trust? Who has the answers? My heart feels restless. I'm addicted to anxiety. Everywhere I turn, even in the quiet times, I fear trouble is around the next corner. I anticipate danger, dreading the worst. My imagination dwells on negative things, frightening my heart. I need a new perspective, a more optimistic path. Lord, where are you?'"

When she came down from her bath, her hair was damp, and she smelled of lavender. Joe could tell she'd done her best to camouflage the fact that she'd been crying, and knowing she'd been up there, sitting in a bubble bath weeping, was another blow to his heart. More than anything, he was beginning to fear that he might lose her too.

The next evening, rain came just after two in the morning and woke her up. She'd fallen asleep in the guest room with the lights on and *Desperation* by Stephen King in her hand. Possibly it was not the best book, considering her mental state. Why had she told her book club she could handle it? What was she thinking?

There was a muffled roll of thunder under the slap of rain on the roof against the windows. She jumped at the sound of it, the windy power of it that made her uneasy. Her heart took one quick lurch. Trying to calm herself, Grace snuggled down, rubbing the kink in her neck. Tugging up her quilt, she gave a habitual scan of the room before closing her eyes to sleep. She froze!

The door was open just a crack. Shuddering, she tried to get up, but her legs wouldn't work. Her shallow breaths quickened as she trembled her way out of bed, then ran to the door and slammed it. She turned the handle several times to be sure it was locked. Grace tried to tell herself that she had forgotten to lock the door because she had accidently fallen asleep reading. She logically knew that no one was out there, but she could still feel an evil presence. She got back in bed and sat with her back against the wall. Grace woke up just before dawn, when light was just beginning to make an appearance in the room.

She lay amid the tangled sheets, knowing she needed to get up but unable to put the thought into action. Her body was heavy and limp, her eyelids dragged downward from fatigue. Disjointed thoughts formed and disappeared. Certainly her time with Joe should be over, and she needed to think about that—about what she should do. She knew what she wanted to do, and the idea was so new, so foreign to her that she could scarcely believe it. She wanted a divorce.

Grace didn't know what to say to Joe, only that pain was swelling in her chest again, a pain that threatened to suffocate her. She couldn't stay with Joe any longer. Silence closed around her—profound and terrifying. There were things she needed to do, she realized; but actually doing them seemed beyond her abilities. All she could do was sit there, barely breathing, considering the shambles her life had suddenly become.

She had just been screwed over by Joe, and she wanted revenge. He had been impossible to live with. Even her children had been tired of his harassment.

They would all be alive if it weren't for Joe!

Joe had to pay. She didn't know how, but she had to make him pay. She couldn't live if she let him get away with grinding her into oblivion. No matter how life had treated her before, she'd always managed to reassure herself. Rage bubbled in her like a thick tar, coating her brain in icy blackness.

"'How could I've been so damned stupid? Stupid, stupid, stupid! I'm disgusted with myself. I knew better than to believe in that happily-ever-after fairy-tale bullshit. Life is so shallow. None of my dreams have come true. Anger, tears, and sadness are my only friends. I give up.'"

Anger gnawed at her like a hungry animal. She would not cry over this. Crying hadn't helped anything. It did not bring her children back. She was choking on her bitterness.

Choked sobs tore free, born from despair so deep, she couldn't comprehend it. After dressing quickly, she went into the living room to watch the ocean as the sun rose. Grace was upset. She couldn't get a handle on her dreams. All she could remember was the darkness and the fear.

Joe saw her standing at the center window, staring out at the ocean. "'Slimmer than usual,'" he thought. With windswept hair and deep dark hypnotic eyes, she looked more like a portrait in a frame than a human being.

"'Where has Grace left the wife I love? Why did this happen to us? How can I make a difference? I wonder. How can I fix this?'"

Even before Joe had googled the side effects of the prescription bottles in the medicine cabinet, he had known what they did. What they did was take Grace away from him. The way they made her eyes glassy was bad enough. But when she took them, it was like he could see part of her—the part that was fun and loved life being swept away. And what was left was just a beautiful hollow shell full of fear and hatred.

The next morning dawned pearl gray and calm. While she sat looking at Joe, she realized she felt as if she were floating listlessly through life with nothing to look forward to. At her wit's end, she said to Joe, "Are you still maintaining your integrity? How can you say none of it's your fault? You played a part in all of this.

Do you get that? Our children were alive, now they're dead. If you hadn't been so demanding, they would still be alive. I would have had the party at our house, and they would still be alive. I should've said something. Instead, I just stood there and watched you badger them over your stupid rules. Would it really matter if they arrived home a few minutes late? Would the world end? Instead of feeling guilty, you have been short and snippy and dismissive. I wish you would just curse God and go to hell!"

A small spirit, Strife, floated next to Grace. He had nervous, restless wings that never stopped quivering and a blaring mouth that more than made up for his size. "'He lied to you all along!'" he shouted to her. "You don't know half of the illegal and scandalous things Joe has done. He thinks you are to blame for what happened to the children. You weren't a good mother."

Floating on the other side of Grace was Chaos, who shouted taunts to fill in all of Strife's pauses. "'Sexual! He has problems with sex. You'd better ask around and see if anyone knows about the affair. Talk to your friend, Kathy. She might know the juicy details.'"

The more she accepted the thoughts flooding her mind, the more enraged she grew.

Joe sat silently thinking, "'Wow I haven't done anything! Why does Grace treat me like this? What's wrong with her? How many other people think it's my fault?'"

Joe's life came to a halt right there next to his oatmeal and coffee. Grace used to be so supportive. No more. Everything had changed. Joe tried to think of a good reason all this was happening, but he couldn't.

He snapped, "Crying out loud! You are talking like a foolish woman. Do you think God only gives good and never sends trouble? How about a little peace and quiet for a change? Crazy stuff comes out of your mouth all the time. It's just insane."

In the shadow of fear and suspicion, life had lost its joy and simplicity, and Joe was unable to find anyone who could explain to him how or why this had occurred.

Her eyes might have been glassy, but they still had punch when they aimed at him. Grace fumed as she formulated her answer, "You're selfish, self-absorbed, and rude. The only thing you'll miss about me when I'm gone is having a hot meal put in front of you. So, screw you Joe. I'll just vent elsewhere. Maybe we should just not be together anymore. Maybe it would be better if I just moved out."

Joe shuffled his feet a couple of times, looking uncomfortable. He was careful to speak in a low quiet voice. His comeback was quick. "Grace that is not the answer, maybe you should try the counselor your friend recommended. Grace, if you don't find help somewhere, I'm afraid you will have a nervous breakdown. I'll call and see if they can squeeze you in today. I will even go with you if you think that would help. I am hurting too, but I am not to blame for all this. Maybe talking to someone other than me could help you deal with your anger and sorrow." Calculating in his mind, Joe figured he had only a few weeks before everything went to hell. He had to be ready. As soon as he could, Joe headed to his study. He would have liked to linger and clear some things up, but he could see that was a lost cause.

Not until he was seated at his desk did he recognize the symptoms. He realized what Grace had really said. Allowing his emotions to surface it felt like an arrow was piercing his heart, his breathing was labored, his body felt numb and stressed. Damn it all, he was frustrated beyond belief. The only woman he had ever cared about might leave him. Joe had no idea how he would keep her for doing it.

12

Life is, in fact, a battle. Evil is insolent and strong; beauty
enchanting but rare; goodness very apt to be weak;
folly very apt to be defiant; wickedness to carry the day;
imbeciles to be in great places, people of sense in small
and mankind generally unhappy. But the world as it
stands is no narrow illusion, no phantasm, no evil dream
of the night; we wake up to it again forever and ever; and
we can neither forget it nor deny it nor dispense with it.

—Henry James

The voice mail light was flashing when Grace got home from exercising. A feeling of relief came as she listened to the woman state that she had an appointment with the psychologist Dr. Gwen Abrams tomorrow morning at ten.

Driving down the boulevard, Grace saw that the business of the day was in full swing; people, grocery carts, and vehicles were circulating through Safeway's parking lot. Driving past it all, she stopped at the fourth light. Grace turned left and headed down Sepulveda toward the airport. Thankfully, she arrived at the office on time.

Doctor Abrams had a new office, now on the sixth floor. It was in a new structure of steel, marble, and glass and joined the other high rises in the area. "'Gwen's practice must be doing amazingly well.'" Room 615 was more than just a room; it was the whole west end of the floor. Her secretary was busy working, but when she looked up, she saw through the glass wall from where she sat that Grace was just arriving for her appointment.

Grace pushed through the doors and tried to address the secretary from a distance. "Grace Moretti, to see Gwen Abrams."

The lady smiled and nodded, "Yes, I see you have a ten o'clock appointment." She picked up her phone and pressed a button.

"Grace Moretti is here for her appointment." She looked at Grace. "She'll be right with you. Go ahead and have a seat."

Grace stood near the couch in the waiting area, but did not sit in it. She was too nervous to sit and apt to leave if the doctor didn't come out soon. Besides that, a man was already sitting there, and she caught him looking at her once, even though he was supposedly reading. Maybe he was reading, but maybe he wasn't. What was he doing there? With the way she felt right then, every person in the place might be a potential killer.

Her heart was pounding in her ears. If she shook much more, the doctor would notice. She tried to take some deep breaths to calm herself.

"Ms. Moretti."

That voice—after ten years, she still remembered it. She turned. There stood Doctor Gwen Abrams. She was very slim, with light-blond hair and beautiful grayish blue eyes. She had a sort of luminosity—that rare quality of self-assurance. She had a good figure and was wearing a tailored suit that accented her narrow waistline.

Grace's trembling was so great, it was hard for her to keep it from showing. She stiffened her body to remain steady, forced a smile, and extended her hand. "Hello."

Gwen shook her hand. "A pleasure to see you again. Come this way."

She turned, and Grace followed her back toward her office. Gwen hadn't changed. She was still the same, distinguished, stylish woman, the same articulate scholar Grace admired. She would recognize her anywhere.

She led Grace into her office and offered her a comfortable padded couch. Grace lay down and found herself looking up at just about everything. Rorschach inkblot paintings lined the walls of the office and seemed to tower so high overhead that she felt like she was sitting in the bottom of a deep well. The room was dead silent like a morgue.

Gwen took a seat in a high-backed, hand-tufted executive chair and relaxed for a moment; studying Grace's face, her hands clasped in front of her chest.

Grace looked back and tried to smile. She was beginning to feel the silence. It felt wrong. Someone should be saying something by now.

"So you're here to discuss the events of the last few months?" Dr. Abrams asked, still relaxed, leaning back in her chair. She knew how to listen with a particular animation, sensing what to ask, when to laugh, when to turn away with the tilt of her head and look as if she was concentrating in deep thought.

Demons dropped through the roof of the office to join the meeting. Black bulb-eyed things with dark wings whirring, spewing scandalous comments. The smallest one with spidery arms, hollered desperate chants filled with panic and confusion. The others joined in with a hideous chorus of profanity as vapors of red smoke rose to the ceiling.

The early morning briefing at headquarters had left them apprehensive. There was concern that Grace's visit to Gwen Abrams might actually be harmful. Was it enough that the sleepless nights had offered moments of anguish and bewilderment? Was Grace unbalanced enough or would intellectual rhetoric be helpful? It was a bit disappointing to see their work devalued. An ultimatum was ordered that they must secure their victim once and for all.

"Do not let a temporary excitement distract you from the real business of undermining Joe's faith." Satan wanted a full account of the doctor's visit and Graces reaction to it. "Let each of you think how to use this doctor's visit to our advantage. Be alert, for it has certain things inherent in it which may, in themselves, be dangerous to our cause. If we aren't careful, we may lose our grip on Grace." Those last words sent fear trembling through their ranks.

Lying on a couch next to Gwen made Grace apprehensive. "Yes, I think," Grace began, "I think I'm just very overwrought and lonely, and that's why I keep hearing voices." Immediately, Grace examined the counselor's face for her reaction. There was none. Her expression was stoic.

Gwen asked, "What kind of voices? What kind of things do they say?"

Grace thought for a moment, blankly staring with her baby-blue eyes. One minute she knew what she had wanted to say, and the next minute she felt that part of her brain was dead.

And Gwen was just sitting there, not saying a word. Silence filled the room; the air felt stuffy even though the room was air-conditioned.

"'Did Gwen's eyebrows just go up? Her look isn't exactly disapproving, but is that because she's suppose to remain neutral, but it feels definitely disapproving to me.'"

"Uh…What I'm experiencing is legitimate," she whispered. "I'm not crazy."

"Yes, I understand," Gwen said. "Don't be nervous. I won't bite. But do you think you can be a little more precise on what they say? Tell me about these voices."

Grace laughed. "I'm still a bit new at this, but I'll try to remember. When I'm alone, especially. Like late at night, when I'm laying in bed and can't seem to fall asleep…it's like a script to a horror movie, and I'm the star. The voices warn me of the impending doom that my friends will soon experience. I feel suffocated with anxiety." Idly, Grace toyed with the ends of her hair as she studied Gwen's face.

Insanity, his lips moving incessantly, shipped words right into Grace's brain. "'Your hope is lost, you're a worthless creature. It's only a matter of time; very little time until it happens.'"

"'You're insane,'" said another voice in her head.

Even though her mind was a little scrambled, she had to say something. But Terror was indignant and determined to have his way with her. He hung on her back like a vicious leach, sucking out her will, whispering confusion into her soul. The other three spirits that were also there circled Grace, taunting her with unkind words.

"'What was I thinking? Why did I agree to come? Why didn't Joe just leave me alone?'"

Grace stared blankly at the ceiling. Nothing intelligible would come to her mind. What was that thought? She just had it, she was going to say more, and now it was gone.

Gwen smiled a little but had no idea what to say. She had known Grace for over twenty years, and she always seemed sane. Yet with all the events of the last year, Gwen remained open to the possibility that Grace was encountering some type of neurotic psychosis. "Would you excuse me for a minute?"

"Certainly."

Gwen rose from her chair and hurried from the room, leaving Grace alone in the dark, oppressive room.

The silence closed in again, heavier than ever. She had trouble breathing, as if her chest were collapsing, as if the air were too thick to breathe. It had to be her imagination, the stress, the nervousness.

Grace closed her eyes and opened them again. The room still seemed dark, maybe darker.

High above her, the walls holding the paintings, felt like they were leaning in upon her. At the same time, the ceiling, close as it was, seemed to be escalating even further, making the pit deeper.

Like most art-forms, a Rorschach abstract allowed the viewer to determine his or her own interpretation of what was seen and what the painting meant. All Grace saw was a room full of evil, menacing, demonic beasts. Looking at the painting closest to her, Grace noticed that the shadows had a shape, an animated creature-like shape. Its leering bulbous eyes reflected the stark evil it held. Its gnarled head protruded from hunched shoulders. And rows of jagged teeth lined its mischievous smile.

Grace closed her eyes. She did not want to believe that her tormentors were lurking about.

"'Why are they at the doctor's office? What have I done to deserve this? I'm not an evil person. Maybe it's something Joe's done to curse our family.'"

She felt helpless, as though her path of escape was sealed off. Try as she would, she could not shake the evil presence. Her palms were wet. Her skin was crawling. This room was alive with evil and about to crush her. Had she made a mistake and walked into a death trap?

When Gwen returned to her office, she found Grace looking quite wilted and noticeably white.

"Are you feeling all right?" she asked.

Grace smiled weakly, "Oh, to be honest, I didn't sleep too well last night. Nerves, I guess."

"Oh, I'm very sorry. Let's try to proceed with the few minutes we have left. Grace" she asked, "do these voices ever say who they are?"

She could hear voices in the room taunting her, and it felt like sharp claws were rubbing against her skin. They remained invisible, hiding from her teasing, tormenting, and making her feel like a fool.

Grace didn't feel like proceeding, but she did. She thought for a moment. "I think one of them is from the Bronx and the other sounds Chinese. They always sounded so confident as if they were warning me of events that were coming. They keep telling me that Joe is the problem. I should divorce him, or even worse, kill him. Can you help me?" she asked with pleading eyes.

Fear saw his opportunity to finish her off. Grace was overcome with numbing, paralyzing trepidation. She willed herself to listen to Gwen, to think. He whipped her consciousness into a myriad of senseless thoughts. She would continue to answer Gwen's questions, but the session would be of no help to her.

"When did you first start hearing them?"

"It was a few days after the children's funeral. I asked Joe if we could move to get a new start, but he just laughed and said,

'Are you kidding?' I get so lonely and spend hours crying. I feel trapped like a caged animal with no way out."

"What was it they said at first? How did they introduce themselves?"

"I was alone, and it was almost like I heard them on the radio. Strangely, they asked a question, and I answered them. They said they were there to protect me so that nothing bad would happen, and that I should be careful when I was with Joe." Grace began to shed some tears. "I'm so afraid most of the time."

Gwen didn't know what to make of this. "Interesting," was all she could say.

"'I always thought that Joe and Grace had a perfect marriage.'"

Grace looked at Gwen with pleading eyes again and said through her tears, "I know what I heard was real. Not a dream, not a hallucination. Not figments of my fractured mind and hyperimagination. Whatever you think, whatever anybody thinks, I know what I heard. I hope you'll believe me. I've heard about you, and they say you are the best counselor in town."

"Is there anything else you want to talk about before you leave?" Gwen asked sympathetically. "You must be more than a little traumatized by all this."

"Will I ever be normal again?" she asked, her voice subdued.

"Time does seem to help in these matters," Gwen promised.

"How soon?"

Gwen shrugged. "A few years, maybe less. It might be different for you. I've never treated anyone who has gone through what you have. It should be interesting to see how all this affects you."

"Interesting," Grace repeated.

"I'll keep you out of trouble."

"I know that. I trust you." Grace's voice was monotone, dead.

Like most health professionals, Gwen had treated a few patients who heard voices. She preferred the wealthy, less problematic patients who really just wanted to have a friend to talk with. The world was often judgmental of their worldly eccentric behavior. Most of them were easy to handle with antipsychotic medications—the kind that could be treated with the one-size-fits-all solution. For Gwen, the content of any psychic distress—and certainly the meaning of it—matters less than the fact that it could be fixed with drugs. When more difficult clients came to her, she just referred them to her associates.

Gwen took a deep breath to steady herself. "'Time to take a recess,'" she thought. She knew she needed to process this, and she might even have to consult her colleagues. It felt as though she had entered the twilight zone. After stretching out her legs, she crossed the ankles of feet trying to get comfortable. "Uh," she said, trying to be comforting and nonjudgmental, "listen, I think it's been a fruitful hour…"

"Oh, it has. I feel so much better now that I've told someone."

Gwen had been sitting in her chair, turned slightly away from Grace, looking at the paintings on the wall and speaking in fluid sentences. Her fingers spread and her hands bouncing against one another, fingertip to fingertip. She turned her chair so that she was facing Grace directly. Her eyes narrowed and a smirk—it looked malevolent, no it looked like Joe's—slowly spread across her face. Now with hardly any pause at all, but with a strange, ominous change in her tone, she turned her chair toward Grace and continued her comments.

"Would you like to come again next week at this time?"

"Yes, that will be perfect."

Gwen stood up to give Grace the hint that the session was over. They really hadn't covered much ground, but that was enough as far as she was concerned.

"Now, let's both take some time to ponder these things. After a week, they may be a little clearer to us. They might make more sense. I also would like you to sign up for some classes on stress management and dealing with anxiety. These are classes offered at the local hospital and I think they might give you some insight on how to deal with what might be going on with your thoughts.

I will have my secretary give you a list of time and locations on your way out. Please contact my office once you know which classes might work best for you. Often times we can get through things better if we see other people's prospective and meet others going through similar loss. I hope that helps until we see each other next week. We will get you through this Grace."

Gwen's voice sounded dubious, and Grace could hear that. Her eyes appeared dark and critical of what she had just heard.

"That would be wonderful," Grace affirmed.

Getting Grace out of the door was such a relief and easier than Gwen had expected. Gwen closed the door and leaned against it. "Oh my God!" was all she could say.

Above and all around, demons were following Grace. At least ten taunting, torturing spirits were following her, buzzing about her head like angry bees. They followed her home. Her mind began to race again. She could hear the voices calling, mocking, cursing. Were there spirits in the car? She didn't see any, but she still could hear the slimy creature that was yelling at her. She wanted to be home.

Their lips stretched open, and their jagged teeth clicked and gnashed as they hissed out horrid thoughts. The loudest spit out insults like bullets from an assault rifle. Grace turned on the radio to drown out the horde of noises playing in her head. Yet the thoughts still came with the bursting rhythm of popcorn. Memories of her childhood and the devastating thoughts of the murder scene raced through her consciousness faster than she could watch them. "Stop!" she screamed, and there was finally a moment of silence.

Overwhelmed by her experience, she let her tires find the curb and rolled slowly to a stop. She slumped over the steering wheel and allowed the hate and fear to crush in on her. It was worse than she could imagine; the force of it took her by surprise.

"'My life is broken. All is lost. I'm on rocky times. Nothing will restore the harmony and balance I long for. Why do I feel so weak and failing? I'm so tired! I've been pushed beyond the limits, further than anyone should have to bear. I'm the black sky without any light. I feel so panicked. I'm lost.'"

But as soon as she walked in from the garage, they grew even louder. Thoughts saying, "'I shouldn't blame anyone else but Joe. No one else is responsible for the trouble I have gotten into. It's all Joe's fault. I should hold Joe responsible. Tell him it's over. After all, there is only so much I can take.'"

Entering the kitchen, Grace turned to look at Joe, "Oh, Joe," Grace sobbed. She tried to smile, but instead bit her lip as she turned to look at him.

Joe's eyes bugged wide and he jumped to his feet. "What happened? Grace are you okay?" he quizzed.

She shook her head furiously, trying to find her voice. A fresh wave of panic shattered her brief sense of confidence. Brushing back her hair as tears dropped one by one to the ground, she tried to cry softly, which was hard to do when her emotions wanted to rush out and punish him. Trying hard as she could, she was still unable to think of even one redeeming quality in Joe's horribly egocentric personality.

"'I hate that I married you. You've become so insecure and dependent. Yet when we go out to dinner, you stare at other women and forget that it is me sitting right next to you. I used to think you were the handsomest man alive. Now you're smelly, have bad breath, unkempt fingernails, and you wear wrinkled clothing! You're such a pig.'"

She was infuriated that his carelessness had disturbed her so much that she'd spewed out a great deal of her anxiety and dread. "Oh, go to hell Joe. You're so irritating and mean."

"What's happened to you?"

She wore nervousness and disapproval on her face. "Nothing, just leave me alone! Why can't everyone just leave me be?"

"How did your appointment with the doctor go?"

She didn't answer. Joe looked at Grace's face for a minute and then nodded. It was answer enough.

Grace turned toward the fridge so that Joe couldn't see her face. She closed her eyes and sighed deeply.

His eyes were anxious. It was mind-boggling, but somehow, he still hoped he had some type of hold on Grace. Joe anticipated a different greeting. He found himself wondering if he should even go to her, comfort her, and put his arms around her. Would she believe he cared? And if it were at all possible that he would change everything back to the way it used to be? He did care. His heart was breaking. He went to her and gently put his hand on her shoulder.

"I won't give you any pat answers," he said quietly. "I know this has been as hard on you as it has been on me. But deep down inside of me, I know there is an answer that will make it better. I know I've said this many times, so I won't say it again. I'll keep looking, and when I've the answer, I will let you know. I won't ask anything of you until then."

"I love you Joe," she said as she wept.

"I love you too, Grace."

She walked over to him and embraced him, giving him a kiss he would remember for a long time—a kiss when she held him desperately tight, when her face was wet with tears, when her body shuddered with her sobbing. Joe held her as tightly as his weakened body could, as if he were hanging on to his very life.

Even in all that had happened and with the unbearable stress, Joe did not give up on life. Sure he grumbled and whined. Just the other day, he was saying everything comes in threes, "Our dishwasher is busted, our refrigerator and freezer are dead, and now there is a leak under the sink. Fun times just keep on coming!" Funny he would say fun time sarcastically, when it really is no fun at all.

With his back against the wall, one more time he made an attempt at praying. He had tried very hard indeed, sometimes through the entire night. He would toss and turn throwing out questions to God. And at the end of the time, he still felt troubled. At least he'd made a start, he thought. That was something. Yet he was still plagued with one question: why?

Joel was pacing back and forth, his voice echoing off the walls. "I can feel it coming! The enemy is luring Joe into a trap."

Michael nodded his head and remained deep in thought. "Exactly what I was expecting. Satan has spent eons practicing and perfecting his deceptive ways."

"And succeeding too often, I say!"

"Yes, but things are going to be different now. People's eyes are opening, and they can now see the truth. They know who the true troublemaker is."

"Michael," Joel said, "will Joe win?"

Michael leaned back against the wall and replied, "We will have to wait and see."

13

Rarely do we find men who willingly engage in hard,
solid thinking.
There is an almost universal quest for easy answers and
half-baked solutions.
Nothing pains some people more than having to think.

—Martin Luther King, Jr.

Grace put away the dinner dishes, put up the towel, and made her
way through the house to the back bedroom. Her mind was full
of thoughts, turning things over, trying to sort things out. She felt
that a change was needed, though she had no idea what it could
be or which direction it would take. As she sat there in the dark,
she knew that she was at her wit's end. Grace sat there frustrated.

"'I've got to do something. I'm tired of pretending I'm strong
and unshakable.'"

There he was, swooping over her like a small black bat. Smug
shrieked thoughts to her, "'Calling Joe's friends might help. Maybe
they could straighten him out. Maybe he would listen to them.
Maybe they could point out to him what a jerk he has become.'"

She took her cell phone from her pocket and looked through
her contacts to find Mason's number. He was the most logical
choice since he and Joe were close friends. Mason lived in
Hollywood and became famous for his worldly wisdom. Millions
were made from his best-selling advice books and the articles
that were published each month in *Hollywood Review Magazine*.
A dignified silver-haired Tinseltown-native, he was respected as
a shrewd businessman and universal religious adviser. Still Grace
wondered why with all Mason's so-called wisdom he was on his
fourth marriage.

At Mason's suggestion, she decided to also call Jack and Owen.
Jack, an old high school buddy of Joe's, lived in Manhattan Beach,

a stone's throw from Joe's childhood home. You would often see him, a muscular sandy-haired man with blue eyes that crinkled when he smiled, skating down the strand, watching the young babes in their bikinis or relaxing while downing a brew on his deck with his wife and kids. He had married his high school sweetheart on his twenty-first birthday. He figured that way he wouldn't forget his anniversary and was guaranteed a celebratory party every year.

His dark blond hair, with its sun-bleached tips, was worn too long for the nine-to-five set, and his lanky build held ripples of muscles under his taut, tanned skin. His broad, calloused hands were those of a hardworking contractor. Jack was a likeable guy, one who's always there for you, no matter what.

Owen, who also lived in Manhattan Beach, on the other hand, was a guy to watch out for. A career bachelor whose baby-face, stylish clothes, and a certain fondness for ladies sometimes caught people off guard. An Irishman with red stubble for a beard, who cursed like a longshoreman at the least provocation, walked like Larry the Cable Guy and was as volatile as David Caruso. When he laughed, he laughed all over; but when he got mad, you'd better get out of his way. Owen's spiked red hair should have been enough to give anybody a warning. His family trust gave him a lifestyle most only dreamed of.

The three friends decided to rally around Joe and help him salvage what remained of his marriage. Joe's tragedies had affected their lives, and the problem seemed to hover over them like an unscripted horror film that they no longer wished to have parts in. They set out from their homes and planned to meet at the Manhattan Beach pier.

"Where is Jack? He said he would meet us here," inquired Mason.

"Oh, there he is," Owen replied. "See him? He is over there. He is the man in the very back row in the Dodger's baseball cap, turning slightly away, glancing at the girls in bikinis playing volleyball."

It was no surprise to either of them. Mason's waving hand caught Jack's attention. He elbowed his way through the crowd to join them on the pier. Mason spoke to Jack and Owen in muffled tones. After a quick discussion of Joe's ordeal, the facts were obvious to them.

Joe must be keeping something from them. He had hidden crimes and was getting what he deserved. Joe hadn't wanted to admit it, but he deserved it. No one was really as good a person as Joe pretended to be. Sure he worked hard, had great children, and volunteered in the community, but there must have been a hidden wrongdoing somewhere.

Joe had always said his family came first, but it seemed like he was always off, working. Maybe he even had an affair none of them knew about. It had to be something pretty bad to cause such wrath to come upon him. That much was clear as day. How would they help him? Simple, he must apologize for his mistakes. He must beg for forgiveness with all his heart, though whether or not God would grant his request was another matter.

After picking up some lunch from Old Venice Restaurant they headed down Highland Avenue to Joe's house. When they reached the Strand, they saw him from a distance; they could hardly recognize him. He looked so ill. Joe sat on his deck watching the surf. He picked up a bottle, twisted the top off and gulped down clear cold spring water. He noticed the approaching footsteps and heard the low murmurs of his friends.

They came up the stairs to the deck and nodded at Joe with their eyes level and unreadable. Mason was flawlessly polite, though he was having second thoughts about his friend's integrity. "Joe, good to see you buddy. How's things?"

Joe chuckled wryly, "Hell, things are horrible! One step forward, two steps back. Sit down, we need to talk. Look what all this has done to me; it's making me dump all my feelings on my friends. "

Mason gently patted Joe on the back as he continued, "That's why we're here today. We want to openly discuss our feelings regarding what happened, to put an end to everyone's speculations. If you have something you want to say, please feel free to interrupt. We are here for you, buddy. I think it would be good for you to have the first say. We'll just eat lunch while you tell us your story."

Jack and Owen grunted, "What's up?" sat down at the table and doled out lunch. They started off with a pita platter with amazing hummus and taziki, toasted pita wedges, and a prosciutto brochetta with fresh Romano cheese. The main course was lasagna, Greek salad, and garlic bread. If the wives had been there, they would have accompanied the meal with wine, but being the men they were, they preferred a cold beer.

Birds soared at the seashore, and overhead, fat, white clouds drifted lazily across the pure-blue sky. Smells of seaweed and salt danced in the air. The warm sunlight touched their faces while a cool breeze refreshed them.

They sat for the longest time and watched the tide roll in and crash on the shore. Joe couldn't say a word and felt disconnected from them, as if none of it was real, not even the heat of the sun on his cheeks. He only looked into their eyes, staring at each of his friends. He suddenly realized how much he truly loved them. He could see disappointment and sympathy on their faces. Beginning slowly, while picking his fingernails for stray remnants of dinner, he struggled to relay the details without bogging it down, without skipping over anything relevant. In silence, they listened.

"I never ever thought this would actually happen to me, and I sure didn't think anything would happen to my kids either," Joe remorsefully remarked.

Taking a deep breath, he immediately, even desperately, tried to compose himself. He could see it all as if it were happening again, even as he searched for the words to recount what had happened. He didn't want his friends to see him like this, and he could only imagine what they could be thinking.

"'I need to pull myself together. I don't want them to get the wrong impression. I've got to sober up. Why am I crying? I need their help, not their sympathy.'"

They watched, saying nothing.

"I never thought I'd come to this point. I almost feel sick to say I'm Catholic. No one ever told me I would come to the point where the familiar trappings of Christianity would no longer seem to work for me. You know"—Joe said, looking up at them—"I've no problem with the Christian doctrine of love. It is wonderful." He shook his head. "The trouble with the Church is they say they believe something, and then they do things totally different, as if they never actually believe it to begin with. And now, I'm having trouble trying to figure out why this happened." Joe sneered just a bit. "Aw, everybody's saying anything that comes in their mind and nobody has any answers, denying that they have any part in this whole affair. They don't know why it happened, but they are sure it's not their fault."

Joe stopped as an uneasy feeling came over him. He felt released that he had gotten it off his chest, but also a little ashamed as men weren't expected to share their emotions. Joe didn't want to appear weak.

The imps and guards in and around Joe's house heard a thunderous sound and paused in their duties of sending harassing thoughts to the men. Smug grinned, "I believe its Forbodden coming with fresh forces from Satan."

The swarm appeared, still a mile away, approaching like a flock of vultures. There were at least a hundred, flying in a random formation. The red glow of their words appeared against the sinister ghostly shadow of their wings. They hovered over Joe's deck, casting a spiritual shadow upon its entire length. The mood became so ominous that all the men felt it. The dogs in the neighborhood began to bark and howl.

A battalion of Satan's handpicked best descended with their wings, producing a roar that blew the smaller imps into the sky. Forbodden landed on the deck with thirteen disgusting demons surrounding him. The remainder of the group took positions around the perimeter of the house. The wings settled down; the roar receded.

Forbodden took a moment to size up the situation. His muscular arms rippled, his expansive black wings rising behind him like a royal robe, his jewels luminous and splendid in the sun. He watched with narrow scorching eyes. "It seems we will soon have reason to celebrate. I've received word that Criticism's visit with Mason was very successful. We have all our players in their places and a strong network at our disposal."

He stopped to think for a moment, his black talons scratching like hooks at the unkempt hair on his head. Forbodden spit sulfur and let his anger blaze. He sniggered a sulfurous snigger, "I can't wait to see my little imps in action. They're all here— Criticism, Strife, Gossip, Jealousy, Pride, Offense, Religiosity, and my favorite, Self-righteousness! These humans are pathetic. We will make them vindictive, unjust judges over this whole affair. There will be so much strife that not even the simplest prayer will be spoken."

Joe's thoughts went around and around as he sat trying to collect them. He watched the clouds move in and hide the sunshine, leaving the sky a gloomy, hazy gray. "I feel a little disillusioned. Well, it's more like I'm confused about who God is. The more I long to know him, the more distant he feels. Where is he? Will I really find him in all the religious trappings of the Catholic Church? I feel like I've been living like I ought to, but now my security blanket has been ripped from my arms. I used to feel safe, but…" Joe looked toward the ocean, pausing to regroup his thoughts.

Tears came to his eyes, and they sat in silence for awhile. Feeling Joe's pain made them uncomfortable. Standing, Mason said he needed another beer and headed for the house. The other men followed, hoping to let Joe have a moment to compose himself. In a huddle in the kitchen, they discussed his problems one more time. "Traumatic? If it were me, I'd be in the psychologist's office every day. He's bound to need help getting over all of this."

Returning to the deck, Mason offered Joe a beer. "Let's give this another try," Mason said.

Even though Mason was having some trouble in his own marriage—actually he was more concerned about it than Joe's problem—he still saw a great opportunity to share his worldly wisdom. His suffering had been a great teacher he thought, and a tremendous opportunity was available to point Joe down the right path. What Mason did not realize was that the mystery of the last few months had been asking all of them to look inward, further than felt comfortable and to look outward to a place just beyond the limits of their knowledge.

Joe began to grumble in discontent, he wished he had never been born. He began to speak almost incoherently and irrationally to his friends. "I shouldn't have been born! All my life has brought is sorrow. Everyone would be better off without me. I've contributed nothing to life! The world seems so dark. I hope everyone forgets the day I was born, and it passes forever from history." He paused. "It would have been better if I were aborted. My mother should have killed me, and I would now be buried with my family. I'd be in heaven."

Forbodden had waited to hear those words. He sucked in his breath through his fangs and began to spew profanity. It was the highest kind of ecstasy, a demonic exhilaration he felt only rarely, a precious and very ripe reward to be enjoyed only after much labor and preparation.

Joe took a deep breath and then sighed out. "All the killing in this world doesn't make sense, Lord. My children, Lord. Raw evil is everywhere. Nothing would make me happier than if I were now dead. Then I wouldn't have a life full of troubles. My life is so difficult. Why am I made to suffer? Why do I've to go on living? I would gladly remain poor if only I had some peace. My body is throbbing. I can't sleep, eat, or rest with all the troubles I have. Sometimes I even wonder why I remain in such a difficult position, such an uphill effort. But for me, I just need the answer to why all this has happened."

Mason nodded thoughtfully. He could tell that Joe was quite agitated. "Do you have anything to add to that?" Mason looked from Owen to Jack and back again at Joe.

Joe made no attempt to hide the anguish on his face, "I know I will win this battle if I can just find the answer. So much has transpired that I can't imagine what kind of an experience could reveal God to me. If God is love why didn't he stop this evil from happening?"

As Joe finished, Jack patted his arm and said, "You did fine. I think we all get the picture."

Joe was not sure. They both knew it was a lie, but Jack felt he had to say it.

Mason had always seemed like a likable guy, but now Joe was getting an uneasy feeling about him. He looked into Mason's eyes—strong eyes, steely. Eyes without pity. To Joe, it felt like Mason was trying to find some deep dark secret in Joe's soul. He wagged his fork at Joe before stabbing the last piece of lasagna on his paper plate. Mason was hard to ignore, and he liked it that way. After a big swig of beer, he belched loudly and leaned back against his chair studying Joe's face.

Joe was puzzled. He stretched out his legs and groaned. What was with Mason's surly attitude? Joe ate a bite of garlic bread, guessing that he would get around to giving his opinion about whatever was on his mind in his own time.

It seemed clear that there was the typical number of words on Mason's mind. "I've known you most of my life, and I hope you won't be upset when I tell you what I think. But I just feel I have your answer. In the past, you have helped so many of us with advice. Well, now it is our chance to return the favor. Your words have supported us, and now that you are discouraged, we will try to help you. If you were entirely blameless in all that has happened, shouldn't you be slightly more hopeful? God never destroys the innocent; you've said so yourself. It seems to me that those who do wrong or evil things eventually find themselves in trouble. God in his righteous anger has no choice but to destroy evil people. Just last night, I believe that God was trying to speak to me when I was having trouble sleeping. I awoke from a nightmare and was seized with fear. A spirit guided past my face, and the hair on my body stood on end. It stopped, but I couldn't tell what it was. A form stood before me, and I heard its hushed voice. It gave me a message for you." He stopped talking abruptly, as if he might have said something he hadn't meant to say.

Actually, if Mason had any genuine wisdom, he would have recognized his midnight visitor was in fact a demon. Criticism sat on the ceiling, a powerful conundrum of back-biting filth, shrieking profanities. Criticism straightforwardly shared his thoughts with Mason. His critical spirit was designed to cause division and trouble with no end. In a matter of minutes, he had convinced Mason to criticize Joe to such a degree that it would disrupt any type of harmony that remained in his life. His power came fresh from the pit of hell, and Mason ignorantly followed his dirty foul suggestions.

Joe considered what Mason had just said, his forehead creased in concentration. He tried to make sense of it. Everyone was silent, and it felt a little awkward. Joe's intuition told him Mason did not want to hear what he was thinking. He could feel his eyes on his face, waiting for Joe to give some kind of sign about what he thought.

"Hmm," he finally said, "your experience is thought-provoking."

A strange gleam came into Joe's eyes, as though something had just occurred to him. Mason saw a dim glimmer of possibility in Joe's smile and proceeded as if he were talking for God himself. "Can a man be more blameless than God? Can even a strong man be more pure than his Maker? If God charges his angels with misconduct, how much more will he accuse those who live here on earth? You can consult your priest, but will he have a better answer. Your resentment is already killing you. You are just skin and bones. It is like your family has been cursed. Your hardships did not spring from the ground, yet it appears your family is doomed to tragedy."

Mason smiled, as if he could read Joe's thoughts; perhaps he thought he saw an obvious sign on his face that indicated that he was on the right track. "The only answer I have for you is to plead for mercy. You have seen in the past that God performs miracles. Just yesterday he sent the rain to water the earth."

Mason would not hesitate to point out to Joe his many flaws and imperfections. As much as he was willing to impose his views on Joe, he had once told him that he would love to kill anyone who tried to impose their values on him. In truth, he loved giving people a hard time. "I've seen many people face tragedies in their lives. It seems that those who mourn and are remorseful eventually find peace. However, criminals are caught and punished for their craftiness. They will pay for the suffering they have caused others. Look what happened to Bernie Madoff. God saves the poor from scoundrels and powerful men who are unjust. What is it you've done?"

Suddenly, Mason leaned forward with a strange smile on his face, his hands folded tightly, and his gray eyes giving Joe a numbing, penetrating, strangely ominous gaze.

That didn't sound right to Joe. "How about trying another angle? I don't think you're going down the right track. I haven't done anything."

Mason stopped, considered, and then continued, as if he was trying to sell Joe something. He could see that he wasn't getting through to Joe, who was looking around impatiently and scratching his sores. "Just one more thing," he soberly stated trying to hold Joe's attention.

"You should feel blessed that God cares enough about you to correct the wrong you have committed. Do not become high-minded and scorn his discipline. I know you feel wounded, but he will restore you if you just repent."

Joe flinched back from Mason's highly criticizing remarks. His mouth hung open, and he quickly shut it. He was visibly upset. Joe deflated a little. The conversation was turning sour. Joe just couldn't accept what Mason said. It was just so difficult to hear the things he knew weren't true. Joe stared at Mason, attempting to mask his emotions.

He didn't like having this conversation under the present conditions, yet he knew to find the answers he was searching for, a smart person, would look at all sides before he came to any conclusion. But what he just heard in the conversation wasn't relevant to what had happened to him and Grace.

Mason figured he'd better retreat while he could. He leaned forward and began to speak in a low voice filled with intense passion, "Once things are back to normal you can stop fearing, and your life will return to what it once was. I've thought about this a lot. Please take my advice. I'm only telling you this because I care so much for you and Grace."

Joe's throat suddenly felt dry and tight, and his stomach startlingly queasy. He got up and sat in a lounge chair next to the table. He took a sip of water before he could answer. "Can't you see how depressed I am? Do you know of anyone who has been through what I've been through and not gone insane? The trouble God has sent to my family is a poison. I miss my children, I miss them so much."

Joe combed his hair with his fingers, a nervous gesture, then asked, "I've one desire and that is that God would tell me why. How can I have any hope when I'm suffering? Please, God take me out of my misery. How can I help myself when all my success is gone? I'm feeling lousy, and I don't know what to do. I feel empty, useless, and worthless."

Joe said his last statement with a rather growling tone. "You don't seem to understand this at all. I'm sure you wish I would just cheer up and get over things. You think I can just 'snap' out of this, but it's not that simple—I wish it was. I'm feeling lousy, and I don't really know what to do. Rather than acting like a friend, you turn an accusing shoulder. I thought we were bros. Bros have each other's backs. You are useless. I don't want you to BS me, and so far I haven't gotten any answers." He spoke quickly before the pain developed into something too great to bear. It was obvious that Joe had been so consumed by his anger, he'd become uncertain about what to say next. He became conscious of the thunderous pounding of his heart. His breathing was quick, his muscles were tense, his heart racing, and adrenaline was coursing through his bloodstream, his fight-or-flight response was fully activated.

A big spirit who was standing next to Owen shrieked out an order, and seven imps converged on him like starving predators, the words flashing and the tongues wagging. Laughing, taunting, and teasing, they stayed there to make complete confusion. The imps were in a blind rage.

His denial only seemed to fuel Owen's offensiveness. "It's not like that; you just don't understand. Mason is trying to understand and help you," Owen defended his friend, suddenly vehemently. "What's gotten into you Joe?"

Suddenly, Joe clamed up, but his face showed he had more to tell. Uneasy, he continued his discourse, "Did I ask you to bail me out? No! You've known me for years. Have you ever seen me do evil things? I'm in deep trouble. I thought I could count on you for help. If you guys could just show me what I've done that is so wrong that I deserve, this I will shut up. Truthfully, do you think I deserve this? Why are good people punished, and the bad people get off scot-free?"

He paused for the effect, "Have I ever lied to you? Maybe you would like to reconsider your advice."

Joe didn't say another word, but his face showed his resounding anger. Sighing in pain, he tried to think things over.

"'I don't like Owen's tone of voice. What's up with him? It's like he has a bee up his butt! What impulsive, imprudent, or overassuming mistakes have I made? Why isn't Mason extending me a little grace just this once? It's not like any of them are angels. All of them have done worse things than me and nothing this evil has happened to them. Where is the justice in this?'"

In the past, Joe had understood that bad things happened to corrupt people. Over the years he had watched as his friends and family dealt with unfortunate circumstances when their choices were to blame. His brother had gotten his girlfriend pregnant at homecoming, big mistake. Then to compound the sin, he had paid for the abortion.

William had thought it would be no big deal. When he went to bed that night, he realized that he had paid to have his own child murdered. He was confused when his girlfriend was okay with having an abortion, but he found himself depressed, feeling guilty, grieving and shame-filled. He felt isolated and weird, and his only relief came from drinking and drugs. After several years of counseling, he was better, but it was as though a little demon sat on his back, reminding him of his past. At his son's first birthday, he realized that the child he aborted would have been eight. One more shadow passed by, it was a reminder— don't make decisions that you know are wrong.

His sister, Mary, was another story. She was an angel. Everyone said so. Everyone one loved Mary, including that deadbeat she meant in college. He was a smart talker, the true woman's man. His bad boy attitude was like a magnate. Although the priest who gave them counseling before the marriage warned Mary to reconsider, she gave no credence to his wisdom, ignoring the fact that marrying an ungodly man was unwise.

"I love him! And you always taught us we should love everyone. I know I can help him be a different man. If not, I will take it as my cross to bear and live with it the rest of my life."

Well, Paul didn't feel the same way. After three children and six years of marriage, he left her for a twenty-two-year-old and moved to New York. Joe's sister was an angel, but a very naive one to say the least. Check point number two: don't make foolish decisions when you haven't done your homework on that topic.

Trying to find some new revelations of truth was lonely at times. Joe just felt so tired of everything. Maybe Mason thought his words were prophecy, but to Joe it was a lot of hogwash. How would he know if God really spoke to Mason? He hadn't heard anything. Everyone seemed to have a cure for what ailed him: "You know that what you sow is what you reap. You need to repent of your evil deeds and come back to God. Read your Bible and pray more."

"My God, Joe," Mason finally replied. "How long will you continue to whine? Can you truly say that God has punished you unjustly? Are you that twisted? Come on Joe, you must realize that when your children were out partying, they must have done a few bad things. Don't you think they might have brought this upon themselves. Maybe their hidden sins or indiscretions opened the door to their on distruction." He waved one hand in the air as if he were giving a sermon.

Joe was a little stunned to hear the words coming from Mason. Joe listened attentively to Mason's homily, recognizing there was something strange in the tone of his voice. The guy was being slanderous, he thought, but selling it all very well. Joe figured he was due a large heavenly reward for his patience, he couldn't imagine anyone else would have listened to such bullshit.

"'I just wish these attacks would stop. I've tried to logically understand, but I can't. It's just so miserably unpleasant, and I want it all to go away. It's as interesting as the way a gall bladder or heart attack are interesting: a pain you want to end. Why do feelings of doom and terror have to keep bubbling up? Why don't they just pick up stones and throw them at me? I don't think that would hurt as much.'"

Mason was still waiting for his answer, giving Joe that numbing gaze. "But if you will actually tell God how sorry you are for all the things you did wrong, I'm sure he will forgive you and set things right. Things might seem bad now, but your future will be brighter. You're smart, and I'm sure you can make millions again. Ask your dad. I'm sure he can point out where you went wrong. You know that bad things happen to people who forget God."

Joe was ready to talk, but not to be stared at. Joe ground his teeth in an effort to control his frustration. Despite everything he had promised himself, Joe saw red. He jumped up and dragged Mason out of his chair, grabbing him by the front of his shirt.

Mason held up both hands and smiled. "Hey, don't get so riled up. I'm only trying to help. What's wrong with you, Joe?"

The air was filled with deafening cries of the hideous spirits, and demon after demon tried to outdo one another. The demons were foaming and frothing, wailing and hissing. The intensity of their onslaught was shocking, surprisingly strong. They were bold, brash, and reckless, attacking with screams and shrieks, even grinning mockingly. Without angelic intervention, they were invincible. And while the order for angelic forces to stand down was in effect, the demonic warlord tried out some new tactics.

Giving up on his current method of preaching, he uncrossed his arms and leaned forward, examining Joe intently. He opened his mouth to speak, closed it again, and rubbed his hand over his jaw. Joe watched him with faint bewilderment. He acted as if he was perturbed by something, yet Joe saw nothing unusual.

"Surely, God has not found you blameless. He only does this to evil people. If you just get up and turn yourself around, he will once again bring laughter into your home. He'll clear your path for victory, and your business rivals will be put to shame."

With that, Mason could tell he overstepped his boundaries. Joe looked irritated and amazed at the same time. Joe forced a toothy smile, "But how will I ever prove to God my innocence? His wisdom is profound and his power is beyond anything I can comprehend. Who has ever challenged God and won? God speaks, and the sun stops in the sky. He alone created the heavens and causes the tides to turn. He set our universe on the hinge of Pleiades. He performs wonders and miracles I do not understand. The problem is that we never see him. Why is he so mad at me?"

Joe began his comeback carefully, trying very hard to sound like a sensible individual as he related his major points. He struggled with the words. He was trying to avoid making Mason become defensive. "When he let my children be taken, I could not stop him. I can't seem to find the words to argue with him. Though I haven't done anything wrong, I fear he will crush me with a storm and multiply my suffering for no reason. He is most surely stronger than me, and who am I to challenge his justice? It appears to me that he destroys both the innocent and the guilty. Look at all the scandals in the newspaper. Although America has fallen into the hands of criminals, he seems to have blinded the judges to condemn them. A murderer is sentenced to two years in prison while the drug user is sentenced to fifteen years. Where is the justice? If it's not the Sovereign Lord, then who is it?"

Joe was impressed by how easily Mason was becoming flustered, but he tried not to press his challenge any further. Not yet anyway. Instead, he picked up where he left off and brought it to a finish.

"Even if I could muster up the courage to put a smile on my face, I would still dread the suffering. Since I've already been found guilty and punished, I can't understand why I still want to fight on and prove my innocence. Tall as I am, I look like a matchstick. My hair is very dry and unmanageable, and my eyes, which were once piercing, are now listless and dull. I constantly feel fatigued, and my unbearable tiredness does not go away even when I rest. If only there was someone who could talk to God and get him to show me a little mercy, then I would be able to talk to him without fear. But as it stands with me, I cannot."

Joe was disturbed when he thought that Mason was going to try to top what he'd already said.

Jack saw that Mason was getting nowhere. He flinched, and finally took a deep breath asking, "Have you ever thought that these murderers could ever be God's appointed messengers?"

Jack's message caused Joe to shake his head in disagreement a number of times, and he grumbled some evasive reply. Joe, in his wildest dreams, would never believe that they were the chosen ones whom God appointed, or that God gave assignments to brutally murder good people.

"'No, no, no. How could these men ever have been selected to carry out the work of God?'"

His deep discomfort showed on his face as he continued to think. How could Joe explain how he felt without sounding self-pitying? He was once again frustrated and close to tears. He hadn't come to hear a sermon. He wanted answers.

"'Instead of one unlucky event, this would mean that God was predetermining the killer's every move and the death of his children.'"

It made him even more furious when Jack suggested that maybe it was an "accident"—being in the wrong place at the wrong time. He wanted to scream out loud as he grasped the absurdity of it all. Was he crazy? This was no accident; it was premeditated murder. His heart, which had gone sluggish with discouragement, sped up, and Joe could feel his pulse hammering in his neck. There were no accidents; there was a reason for the home invasion, just as there was a reason for Joe being who he was.

What made Jack's comments infinitely more ludicrous to Joe was that he was so full of doubt; he expressed doubt in the most eloquent and sympathetic ways. In his completely logical and convincing view, the Bible was a book with a troubling plot, but a plot that could be understood: God created us out of love, but we don't want God, or we don't believe in Him, or we pay very poor attention to Him. Nevertheless, God continues to love us, at least, He continues to try to get our attention. And the real trick was having faith, he said, even if things weren't remotely going the way we thought they should. Intellectually said, "You must do something. You just need to work and strive and seek. Maybe a little meditation and yoga would help."

Jack knew all the best stories in the Bible and assured them that doubt was the essence of faith and not faith's opposite. He hemmed and hawed, but Jack didn't manage to say anything coherent or helpful. "Well, maybe God has some purpose in this. If God wants you well, why doesn't he heal you?"

Joe was bewildered. He stood up and paced around waiting and wondering what to say next. It was like some kind of disease. Everyone was infected, and no one could recognize the injustice.

"'Why are my friends indicting me? I know they hear what I've been saying. Friends are supposed to listen to what you say, but best friends even listen to what you don't say. It would be better if they sat silently rather than say things that make no sense. Have they lost their minds? I used to think they were intelligent guys! I thought I could count on them. My life feels so empty. I'm being swallowed whole by vicious sharks—ripping, shredding—leaving me in pieces.'"

Joe slapped the side of his head, pretending there was something wrong with his hearing, "Did I hear you right? You're unbelievable. But this is one thing I do know, God wants everyone saved, but not everyone is." He growled. "Somehow I must have to play a part in this. I know I've seen God initiate healings on His own some time, but I don't think that is the way he usually does it. If I just sit around waiting for a miracle, I might just die. I just have to find the answer to why all of this has happened."

Joe recoiled back and bit his lip. Jack could see that his words had bothered him, but he couldn't figure out why. After all, Joe had invited them there to give their opinion.

Owen leaned toward Joe so that their faces were only an inch apart. "There's no reason for you to be so upset with Jack. He is only trying to help you find answers." Owen rolled his eyes signaling that he was not amused with Joe's attitude.

Joe started to say something—something angry from his expression, but he stopped himself, took a breath. His face looked as if it were carved in stone. He contemplated not responding to Owen but instead blurted out. "You don't seem to get it! I didn't choose this. I don't know why it happened." His voice turned bitter, "I lay in bed longing for sleep so that these months of misery will be hidden with sweet dreams. Yet the night drags on, and I toss and turn until the sun rises. My body is racked with pain, and my breaths are labored. I can't image that I will ever be happy again." He let his thought trail off, and they restarted in a swell of quiet sadness. "As a sun vanishes across the sky and is never seen again, so I hope to die and never return. I despise my life. Why are you testing me, God? Even at night you give me terrifying dreams so that now I desire death more than life. Please, God, in your sovereignty, have mercy on me. I've suffered more than one can endure. Shouldn't you pardon my sins and forgive me?" Joe laughed once in disbelief.

They all heard the edge in his voice, "My wholesale business is so harassed and so sabotaged by an unseen monster. I guess I would call it that. I became too great an insurance risk. I can't fill my orders, clients are seeking other suppliers, and I just can't seem to stay above water anymore. The business is stretched to the breaking point. Why do they say you can't keep a good man down?"

Joe's furious glower made it hard to answer.

"You know, Joe, you're awfully self-righteous, considering all that has happened to your family," snapped Owen.

Joe waited a moment before he answered, and he knew Owen was experiencing the same frustration as he was. The tension was making them both lightheaded. A dozen emotions were sailing around before he settled on being pissed off. Joe actually grabbed Owen's shirt in his fist. His eyes were wild, and he hissed the words silently through his clenched lips, "Idiots!" He hated to say this about his friends, but all of them were morons. "Stop right there! Not another word!"

Owen said nothing, but he didn't back down either. Joe didn't like that at all. His eyes flashed back to Owen, and they exchanged a loaded gaze. He pursed his lips for a second, deciding what to say. And then, he glanced abruptly at Owen, as if he might grab him again.

"You don't understand. You just don't seem to be able to hear what I've been saying," Joe repeated, scowling at Owen. "You could be a bit more understanding. You have no idea how truly difficult this ordeal has been."

Owen stared at him disbelievingly. He looked into his face at his defensive eyes. He noticed how his eyes had deep, dark circles; that he was extremely uptight. He frowned at what he saw. It was a while before Joe noticed. Everything was dead-silent for an endless minute. Joe tried to be strong, but he didn't think he could hold back the tears. Hysteria was edging in on him. He could feel it pushing him closer to the brink. Shaking almost uncontrollably, he steadied himself by grabbing Mason's shoulder.

"You'll get through this," Owen promised. He sounded convincing and persuasive, and Joe clung to the promise of his words.

"It's going to be all right, understand?"

Joe nodded, desperately wanting to believe him.

To ease the tension that was so apparent, a serene voice with a heavy Southern accent asked, "Are you all gonna eat the rest of the garlic bread?" Matt had his eyes locked on the only remains of the huge meal the men had consumed.

"No," Joe sighed with sadness, "I seemed to have lost my appetite."

Owen smiled a smile of pity. He put his hand on Joe's shoulder and spoke condescendingly, "Joe, come on. If you really think that we're that hopeless and unhelpful, maybe you should ask your gardener for help. He seems to be able to take care of your garden maybe he can fix you too!"

So Mason, Jack, and Owen decided to stop questioning Joe. Clearly there was no convincing him that he done something wrong; he continually swore he was innocent and was not to blame for what had happened.

Matt Scott, Joe's gardener, had been eavesdropping on the conversation while eyeing the remains of lunch no one seemed to want. He thought Joe was acting a little self-righteous. Why was he defending himself and blaming everything on God? If something or someone was to blame, surely it wasn't God.

Matt had his own theory, but so far had said nothing. Matt Scott had been Christopher's best friend. He was a young, attractive man in his late-twenties, with unkempt brown hair and large tiger-like eyes. Matt was just about to complete his MBA from UCLA. He felt a bit intimidated talking in front of Owen.

Something seemed to draw their attention to him, a small, mischievous troublemaker imp. He was lackluster-black with bight ruby eyes. He had pointed ears, slanted thin eyes, thin, elegant hands, and the most malicious grin with slightly yellow, very sharp teeth. He prompted Mason to ask Matt for his opinion. Matt's anger was aroused because no one had found a way to refute Joe, and yet they continued to condemn him.

Taking several deep breaths to calm himself, he began, "I'm young and clearly you maybe wiser than I, but I think you are speaking foolishly. I had to bite my tongue when I heard your absurd reasoning. Not one of you has proved Joe wrong. Why do you refuse to answer his questions?"

He was right. Every man at the table hated to admit it, but Matt was right. There was a long, fidgety silence. They all looked at the view of the skaters passing by the ocean, and only occasionally at each other.

This longest of days seemed to stretch on and on and on. Joe wondered if it would ever end.

A smile flickered across Matt's tense face. He decided to break the silence. His voice was soft and accented by a slow southern drawl that allowed him to pause to make his speech more affective. "I will now have my say, and I'll admit that I feel like a volcano ready to erupt. I will tell the truth without trying to flatter any of you. Joe, please listen carefully."

You have said, "I'm squeaky-clean, I've done no wrong; I've not sinned. Why has God chosen me to be his enemy? Why has he allowed this to happen?"

As he talked, his eyes scrutinized Joe. Matt responded to the questions saying, "Aren't you misrepresenting God and discrediting his loving character? God is mighty, yet just and quick to warn and forgive. Joe you have always been a kind and honorable man, but you aren't perfect. Perhaps your biggest mistake is that you have said God does not speak. I say he does. He tells us where and when to go and keeps us from falling into harm's way. Do you have anything to say to this?"

Matt ended his statement and brought it to an orderly finish.

But Joe wasn't sure he liked what Matt said either. He wasn't even sure he heard it all. He suddenly felt very weak and angry, and he couldn't figure the source of either. And what about his suspicion? He knew he didn't buy anything this guy said. Or did he? Or had he just misinterpreted him? Joe couldn't think straight or feel straight. He just felt so tired.

"Sorry, guys, but I just don't buy anything you've said."

Matt pointed his finger at Joe and looked down that finger with cold brown eyes. "Now right there is a problem in itself! You've lost your objectivity in this whole thing, totally and completely. If we had given you the answer, even half an answer, I don't think you'd admit it!"

Matt's face went blank and suddenly red. His hands started to shake. "You have your own ideas, and that is all you are willing to believe. We don't know the kind of person you are when we aren't around. None of us does. And if you are unwilling to listen to reason, I don't think any of us will be able to trust you anymore."

The nausea began coming in mild waves, crashing over Joe and then receding. He felt like he might vomit, but instead, he let a loud belch escape through his lips. His sense of time got blurry. He began to perspire profusely, and when the nausea passed, he was dripping in sweat. Joe felt faint, and he worried that he might pass out, aspirate, and die. When he mentioned it to them, they responded that he looked a little pale. This increased his anxiety because if they were worried, then he should be really scared, he thought. On the other hand, at that moment, at some level Joe wanted to pass out, even if that meant dying.

Joe took a moment to be quiet and break the momentum of this building confrontation. He spoke softly. "Guys, you need to give me a little slack here."

"Listen, we mean no offense; please understand. I mean, we all appreciate your position. You must realize God's ways are mysterious." Mason pushed his chair back and stood to stretch his legs.

"Joe, I'm sure you realize that we have some strong and some weak arguments on our side, and maybe even a few of our points are arguable. But please, do not be so headstrong. You aren't perfect. In fact, sometimes you are very wrong in your opinions," Mason hit him one last time.

Joe challenged Mason, "Can't you at least pray that I will be healed of this debilitating disease?"

Mason took a moment, then replied, "You are much too excited, Joe. It's best to say God's will be done."

Joe became angry. He had heard enough. He glared out at the horizon, fuming. In frustration he stood and told his friends, "Well, don't worry about me, I'll make it through. I know I will see things more clearly when I find the answers on the other side. This is my journey, and my faith will get me through. I'm sure I'll find the path to God." He turned and walked toward the house. "I'm a little tired, so I think I will have to go inside for a nap. Thanks for coming, and I will consider all you said."

Forbodden basked silently in the moment, letting his thoughts run free. Success was just around the corner. He pointed his crooked finger at no demon in particular, and then at one overly anxious fighter.

"'Do your worst tonight while Joe mulls over the day. Joe isn't angered by mere misfortune, but by misfortune conceived as injury. And, thankfully, Joe's sense of injury is based on his legitimate claim that he has done no wrong and has been denied his answer. We must, therefore, zealously guard his mind from finding the true answer. He must never be permitted to doubt that his deductions were wrong. Our next attack has a better chance of success because Joe's whole world is cold and empty and miserable.'" Forbodden's thoughts echoed in the minds of his underhanded squad.

Joe examined their faces for just a moment, and then went inside his house letting the door slam behind him. Joe was fuming. He hesitated. Then he snapped. His voice grew hushed and grave. "What a bunch of dumb shits. What business do they have snooping into my daily affairs? It's not like their lives are perfect." Joe observed that medication—Xanax, Klonopin, Celexa, and alcohol—were more effective at soothing him than his friends ever could be. Now his legs were weak and numb, and his breath so labored. As he stood, taking a pee, he noticed it was a light shade of pink. Things weren't shaping up like he had hoped. Feeling hopeless and trapped, he wondered if he should be driving himself to the emergency room.

Joe sat on the couch, his head on his arms, sobbing his heart out to God. "'Oh, God, surely I don't have to die! Why did you make me sick? Are you the author of the sufferings that are in this world today? What is happening to the world? Where did all this malice and cruelty come from? I guess I've lost everyone. If only one true friend would walk in, I would gladly let the others go. My questions demand an answer, but none of them really gave me an answer; they just gave me some theological concepts that do not amount to anything.'"

Joe only made a disgusted face because he knew no one was there to see it. He was clearly unhappy. So the consensus was that Joe was just supposed to forget about the deranged killings, his almost bankrupt business, and his crumbling marriage and just go to confession to ask God for forgiveness.

His calm had completely worn off, that is, if it had ever even been there. He certainly did not want their pity—there were so many things he wanted to know! Were his friends all nuts? Joe knew it wasn't even worth a minute of his time to consider their suggestions.

Joe wanted to be sure his friends were gone, so he leaned over to peak out through the slider door. The coast was clear. His emotions had covered a full range in a single afternoon. He was energized when he saw his friends arrive with lunch. There was no other word for it. After lunch, he had felt like a kid caught with his hand in the cookie jar: guilty, depressed, accused of wrongdoing. Now just minutes after they left, he was thrown into despair, convinced beyond a doubt that he'd never have the answer to his question, "Why?" He sat down on his bed and thought for a moment. Exhausted from the ordeal, he lay back against the pillows just to rest, and before he knew it, he was loudly snoring.

14

You can get a thousand no's from people,
and only one "yes" from God.

—Tyler Perry

His friends were good at what they did. Joe had to admit it. Their words were forceful, well-choreographed, and persuasive. They expressed all the points good religious people always said. The disturbing part was, before all this had happened, Joe might have thought the same things too.

"So they're just rambling on and on, and no one bothered to pray?" Manuel said.

Nigel nodded. "That's about it."

Gabriel thought about that and nodded. "Sounds like a smart move on Satan's part. If he can divide them so that they are at each other's throats , it will make his job a picnic."

"It looks as though it's spreading." said Nigel. "First with Grace and now with his friends. They're at each other's throats."

Gabriel paused to evaluate their situation. "If things don't change, we may lose Joe."

"And we won't have the prayer backup to succeed in anything."

"But what about those pesky imps?" demanded Nigel. "Surely they would be easy to root out."

"No," said Gabriel; he was quite angry and frustrated. "They have the right to be there. Joe hasn't denied them access. He has given himself over to them, and until he learns the truth, this cancer will never slow its spread."

"So what now?" asked Nigel.

"Joel and Lionel are working to find a breach in the enemy's ranks, some weak spot in Satan's plan that we can use to help Joe. In the meantime, all we can do is watch."

No, it was no demonic army, not even an alarming spirit, only a small, horrid messenger, audacious enough to fly right over to them.

"Are you Gabriel?" it cried out.

"I am," said Gabriel.

"Satan has a message for you!" The little imp hovered below them, calling out its message with a high, raspy voice. "He says, 'I've cut Joe down, and he will soon be mine. Be sure you do not interfere in any way. You do not have the right! That goes for Michael too. Archangels may be fierce. You may be heaven's most terrifying weapon but to Joe you are useless."

The imp darted away like a little fly.

Gabriel grimaced as he said, "We can only hope that Joe's parents have more wisdom than his friends."

Joe's mom hesitated at the door to his bedroom, not sure whether to knock. She decided to peek first, hoping that he wasn't asleep. Seeing that he was snoring, she decided to head out to the deck to let him rest.

When Joe woke from his nap, he was pleasantly surprised to find his parents sitting out on the deck. The sun slowly drifted behind some clouds, creating a beautiful sunset. "You've been so very distant and quiet for the past few months, we thought we would stop by and see how things are going," his father remarked with one raised eyebrow. "Is everything okay between you and Grace? Your mother is a little concerned."

Joe looked at his parents, his face calm and ruddy. He appeared haggard, gaunt with only a careful blankness on his face. There was no animation in his dark eyes. He noted his parent's question as seriously as they meant it, thinking carefully before he answered.

It was hard for his parents to look at his face. They discerned that the last few months had been continually hard for him.

Joe looked at his parents for a long time. Then, with some effort, he rearranged his expression into a slightly respectful smile.

Joe's mother was always more insightful than his father. Perhaps it was because she spent more time praying and reading her Bible. With her hectic schedule, sometimes she only spent a few minutes, but at least she tried. Juggling her responsibilities with family, work, and church sometimes made it difficult. She seldom had time for herself.

His father was always busy with work. He attempted to fit in time for his grandchildren's sports events, but little else. As soon as their traditional hugs and kisses were out of the way, they sat for a few moments in silence.

"Joe," his mother asked, looking out toward the pier and the crashing waves as she spoke.

"What is it Mom?"

She sighed, not looking at Joe, "I'm worried about you and Grace."

"Why? What's wrong? Do you know something that Grace hasn't told me?" Joe asked, feeling fearful at once.

"Ah," she mumbled, fixing her eyes on a scantily dressed jogger.

"You two just don't seem like the happy couple we once knew. I know you have been through more than almost anyone can bear, but I hope your marriage will survive it." She paused to hold back tears. "There is something…strange about the way you two look at each other…a hidden darkness."

Joe frowned; he could see the waterworks coming. He bit his lip. Nothing bothered Joe more than tears. He was never going to get through this.

"'Why today of all days? It's true, Grace and I barely touch each other anymore. But is it really any of my parents business? I know it is difficult for Mom to ask this type of question, but I wish she hadn't. Why is she so overprotective? She is treating me like I'm a small child again.'"

He laughed, though he did not meet her gaze. He struggled to find the right words. "We're fine. The road has just been a little bumpy. Things are different without the kids. We just need some more time to rebuild and find our way. I think you are imagining the worst, Mom," he said quickly, struggling to keep his voice happy.

Right then, he could not resist the urge to comfort her. He crossed the deck and leaned over patting her hand.

"I'm sorry, Joe. I know you hate to see me cry."

"It's not your fault, Mom."

A smile flashed across his face briefly, and then he sat down to watch the ocean.

"I know." She took a deep ragged breath, trying to control herself. She wondered how she ended up being the one who was crying when she had come to comfort Joe.

There was a knot brewing in his stomach. He'd forgotten how well his mother used to read him. Her prayers had cut right through all his disguises, and she saw the naked truth all too well.

He looked up at the sky, his stare intent, as if he were reading something written in the newly appearing stars. He clenched his teeth together, glad he wasn't looking at his mother's face, fighting against the sobs that threatened to overtake her again. He wanted to be truthful, but he had no idea how. Until now, he had never hidden secrets from her. He didn't have the courage to tell her everything.

His parents let the subject drop. They were all quiet for a moment. They seemed to be waiting for Joe to say something. He was trying to think of something to say.

"Can I tell you what the worst part is?" he asked hesitantly when his parents said nothing.

"Will it help you?" his mother whispered.

"It might. It couldn't hurt."

"What's the worst part then?"

"The worst part is knowing what could have been. Knowing that I'll never see my children married or have any grandchildren. It seemed so effortless, comfortable, and easy. We were on the normal path everyone takes." Joe stared into space and waited for a moment. "If the world was the way it was supposed to be, if there was no sinister evil hiding behind each corner..."

His parents could see what he saw, and they knew that he was right. If the world was the sane place it was supposed to be, Joe and Grace would still have their children. And they would still be happy.

If it was still out there for them, Joe did not know. He had to believe it was. "I used to think Grace was my only sunshine, but now it appears clouds have settled in," he sighed. "The clouds I could handle, it's the tsunami that is overpowering me."

His mother touched his shoulder, laying her head upon it. He exhaled at her touch and closed his eyes. It was very quiet. For a minute, Joe could hear the beating of his heart, slow and even.

His father elbowed him playfully. His voice was very calm and practical. "How about dinner at El Sombrero? I'm sure Grace would like a break from cooking. You two always seemed to like that place. Me, I'm an old meat and potato man myself. It would be a nice walk, and we can watch the sunset."

Returning home, Joe was greeted with a sharp jolt of unease. It felt like sharp claws were tugging at him. They remained invisible, hiding from him, tormenting and inflicting pain. Piercing his stomach, he realized how short his time might really be. Nothing the doctors had prescribed seemed to make even the slightest improvement in his physical condition. Fear—one of Satan's best—was now his ever-present companion. Joe was overcome with numbing, paralyzing dread. He willed himself to think clearly. Many spirits gathered around Joe's head, stripping his consciousness into a heap of senseless fragments.

A drastic change in something would be necessary, and the key to what he wanted more than anything else in the world was getting his life back. He wanted it more than everything else in the world put together. Through clenched teeth he whispered, "Please, Lord, help me. I want to be normal again and feel your presence. I trust that you will help me."

A laser thread flashed, delivering the request to the throne of God. The demons who were frolicking in their successful day gave it no notice.

Satan's eyes narrowed with cunning. "We will wait. Have patience. We will watch, we will follow until the moment for our final victory arrives. We will confound Joe, strip him of his power. We will have victory!" Satan hacked a hideous chuckle. "Such a marvelous thing, betrayal delivered by friends."

"'If Joe decides to pray, I must make sure that his only way to gauge its success is how he feels. A successful prayer must produce the desired feeling, which is very difficult to accomplish when one is ill. If Joe ever figures this out, our situation is, for the moment, desperate. I must decide how to use this present state to our advantage rather than enjoy our most recent triumph.'"

At Joe's home, the demons abruptly called it a day. A few of them swooped down, spit out some evil thoughts, and then the majority of them soared off like a crazed flock into the night, leaving only Smug and Gloom on watch. The sudden silence was jarring.

Gloom was nothing significant, nothing to revere or dread. He was small, thin like a salamander and repulsive. He knew his lowly station, but his blows still had impact. He was part of the master plan. His lips stretched open, and his ragged teeth clicked as he mumbled his evil words. Gloom barked out another sulfurous laugh and rolled like a playful pup. But even with only the two small demons, Joe found little peace.

Alone in his study, frustrated by the day's events, Joe began to throw things around, smashing everything he could get his hands on. He screamed so hard that drool frothed from his mouth, he yelled that he was so scared, that he couldn't take it anymore. He wanted to die. Joe was desperate for some relief. He grabbed the decanter of whiskey and glugged it down. Stunned by his exertion, he collapsed on the floor sobbing. Even after he was considerably drunk, his anxiety persisted. He was unsure how he would survive the next few days.

15

Be wise with speed;
a fool at forty is a fool indeed.

—Edward Young

Tomorrow would be Sunday, and perhaps a walk along the beach with a trip to his favorite spot to think would help. Joe could only hope. He was so tired.

Returning from his walk and whale sighting, Joe pondered the idea of going to Mass. He placed the binoculars on the fireplace mantel, hoping that he would see Joshua walking down the Strand. His spirits were high and maybe he could invite the new priest, Father Timothy, to dinner. Perhaps an outsider would have a better perspective of things.

Joe had heard Father Timothy say "I became a priest because God touched my heart with grace, and I want to help him touch the hearts of others. That's why I gave my life to Jesus Christ." Father Timothy felt it was important for Catholics to know the Scriptures and be able to coherently explain their faith.

Father Timothy looked for opportunities to help people every day. He found them when he actively pursued them. The inquiry may come from a colleague in his office, from the clerk in the grocery store, or from the fellow sitting next to him on the plane. It might come in one of a million forms—"Gosh, I've always wanted to ask why you Catholics have a pope."

When he was growing up, his parents hadn't really belonged to any church. His father was in the Air Force, and they would just attend the service offered on the base. Since they were stationed overseas in Guam, there were two chaplains, a Pentecostal minister and a Catholic priest.

The services were very different, but both offered paths to the truth. After a long period of seeking and questioning, his parents decided to become Catholics, having found meaning and joy through becoming members of the Catholic Church.

While he had been attending a private Catholic high school in Hampton, Virginia, a priest, Father Ronan O'Maney, led a retreat day at the school. He spoke of the priesthood's mission to share the gospel and the Catholic faith beyond the church's door. When Father Timothy heard Father O'Maney's story, he knew he wanted to explore becoming a priest.

The big problem was that he had been interested in a career in journalism, and he had difficulty figuring how being a writer and a priest would mesh together. After spending time in prayer, he suddenly saw that he could use his interest in writing to help explain the Catholic faith to persons who were not Catholic. Like his parents, others were searching to find the truth and the message the gospel could bring them. Once he made his decision, he wondered how he would tell his parents. Surprisingly, it seemed that people were more intrigued than anything in how he had come to the decision to be celibate the rest of his life. The reaction was one of curiosity. He was so young and had an entire life ahead of him.

But in his heart, he knew that nonbelievers, fellow Christians, and especially, fallen-away Catholics needed to see his good examples of prayer, faith, and an upright moral life. They needed to hear him mention God in his conversations. Mostly, they needed to know that he was a happy and committed Catholic. He tried to live these virtues everyday as a priest and encourage the people of his parish to do so as well.

The few little demons lurking about Father Timothy's church service could only cringe and scoff. Some did manage to stop the ears of the people they owned, but the onslaught of his sermon was particularly severe and painful. To them, Father Timothy's preaching had all the soothing effect of having your teeth drilled.

Michael had agreed to let Gabriel watch the church while he was looking after Grace. On the top of the church, Gabriel and his warriors refused to back down. Satan dropped by with a sizable flock of demons just in time to see Joe enter the church, but Gabriel would not step aside.

"You know better than to tamper with me!" Satan warned.

Gabriel was firmly polite. "We cannot allow any more demons into the church this morning. Father Timothy spent the better part of the night praying for the protection of his parish and unfortunately for you, Joe is one of them. You must realize that even you can be held at bay for a time by the prayers of an intercessor."

Satan did know, but that had never stopped him. He defiantly attempted to maneuver around the truth. Frustrated, he gave up trying to sneak into the service. Frozen in thought, he reasoned to himself, "'After all, what could one church service do to change things? Joe's destruction is so close, I can almost feel it.'"

After delivering a few choice insults, the whole bunch roared off into the air, bound to see what mischief they could inflict upon Grace.

Joe, even after all the suffering and pain, still loved Grace. Even her abusive nature could not cause him to give up, because he knew that, underneath all the anger and the sarcasm, Grace was in pain. Right now it was crystal clear to him. He had to try to find a solution. It was more than that; he owed her. It was because her pain hurt him too. Grace was a part of him, and he never wanted it to change. "'I can't believe I'm sitting in front of this stupid computer again. What does it care if my life is in shambles? I pretend I'm not in social isolation. I can put my words into order, so everyone thinks my life is glistening. Although I really don't know if anyone is listening. I know that if I read a book, paint, or go running or biking I'm doing something productive and present, not reserved and recluse. But I feel so much safer hidden behind this screen. What I need to do is get out to see people and push away from the computer. I need to stop staring at my contact list and just contact someone. Meeting up at Peet's would be a good start. It might even generate a little business.'"

Slowly typing at his computer, Joe almost unconsciously continues posting irrelevant comments. Reading his feeds, he is annoyed by being interrupted by advertisers who flock to try to sell him things he does not want and can no longer afford. Why can't the world leave him in his own private peace?

"'I'm becoming unsocial. It is no longer satisfying to engage with my friends and look into the sadness in their eyes. The house is so quiet, it gives me a chill. I need to shut off this stupid computer and make the most of this day. If I could just make one real connection, life would feel real. What a difference it would make. I'm caught in the net—is there no escape? I spend hours posting pointless comments to people I've never meant! I need to go out in the world and leave distractions behind.'"

It was an act of faith when Joe set two places at the dinner table. It was an act of faith, trusting that somehow this new young priest would have the answer he longed for. Joe sat at the table, staring at Grace's empty chair.

Just then the doorbell rang. Joe jumped a little. He sprang to his feet and almost skipped as he went to answer the door. There stood a young man, blond and neat, glowing like a saint, yet appearing somewhat timid. Shaking Joe's hand, he politely declared, "Good to see you, Joe. I've been looking forward to meeting with you all day."

Joe nodded graciously, stepping aside, "Yes, please do come in." Joe took him into the dining room and let him have a seat. "Thank you very much for coming. Somehow, I know you have the answers that I need."

For the first half of their meal, they indulged in small talk and a general review of Joe's experiences.

Father Timothy was visibly moved, "I will do my best. But first let me say a quick prayer before we start. Father, we thank you that you give us the Spirit of wisdom and revelation in the knowledge of you, that the eyes of our hearts find the truth so that we will know the hope to which you have called us. In Jesus's name, amen. I find quoting this scripture from Ephesians sets the right atmosphere when I'm searching for truth. I don't believe God's purposes are ever thwarted for long. He has His own special way to get people through their difficulties. Remember, you don't have to carry this whole thing by yourself."

Joe relaxed a bit, leaning back in his chair. "I don't want to bother you."

The priest glanced in Joe's direction, and he started to chuckle. The laughter came deep from inside him and a wrinkly smile creased his face. "I'm honored that you have invited me to be a part of your life. You're not bothering me. Listen, as soon as you're ready, we can go over everything, recheck everything. There have to be some answers somewhere."

"Father Timothy," Joe said at last, "can I tell you what's on my mind? I'm not very sophisticated in my knowledge of the Bible, not as wise as I thought I was. I only read it occasionally, except for those passages that I hear read aloud to me when I go to church. I read my prayer book often and my Bible at Christmas and Easter. I've always been a pretty regular churchgoer. With all my fears coming true, I just don't know what to do! Lately, I've started skipping Sunday services. I can no longer make any claims that I'm pious. What little faith I still have seems to be fading. I just don't understand why God is doing this to me."

"Do you really think God has done these things?"

"Why else would they happen? Isn't God the ultimate power of the universe?"

"Have you ever read the book of Job?"

"I'm sure I have. Do you mean that you've uncovered something new I might not know?"

"Joe, I think you should take a day or two to study this book. Go off to the mountains, and let God show you some things. Well, anyway," Father Timothy said, bringing in the punch line, "I think you will find your answers, and your life will follow a new path."

"Well, it can't hurt," said Joe, stirring his coffee absent-mindedly with his spoon as he contemplated what he had just heard.

"I'll even go so far as call a friend of mine who has a cabin in Big Bear. I'm sure he'd let you borrow it for the weekend. But before I leave, I would like very much to say a prayer for you."

Joe dragged in a deep breath, preparing to answer, shaking his head yes; his words seemed stuck in his throat. Finally, he whispered, "That's what I was hoping you would do." He was surprised to hear himself say it. With his head bowed and eyes closed, he held tightly to every prayerful word.

"Father, build a hedge around Joe and Grace, and let them hide in your secret place of protection until Joe finds the answers his heart desires. In Jesus's name, amen."

"I think I would rather stay here at the beach. This has been the place where I've always found my answers. I feel God's presence when I sit watching the waves crash upon the shore."

By the time Joe and Father Timothy went on their separate ways, Joe seemed to see the church in a new light. Perhaps it was more than coincidence that the wayward beach comber named Joshua had recently come across Joe's path.

Michael and his troops gathered once again in the second heaven, and the mood was better this time. They reviewed the words of the first battle; a victory, even though a small one, had been won that night at the dinner table. More of them were allowed to intervene on Joe and Grace's behalf. The original one hundred had grown to a thousand as more mighty warriors had gathered, called by the prayers of the priest.

"On your feet, all of you!" Satan shrieked with an intense glare.

They complied instantly.

"Who is this nobody priest that attempts to stop me?" With that profanity spewed from Satan's mouth. "This priest is a subtle warrior who knows more than I had anticipated. We need to find his limitations." Satan trembled in his rage, adding extra force to his words. "I should have realized something was up when I was barred from Mass."

Those words brought a chill to the group. His eyes darted madly around the chamber, casting a contagious uneasiness on the crowd. The littlest imps gazed down to avoid eye contact, hoping to avoid the escalating tension. Nervous and indecisive as to what his next action should be, Satan paused for a moment of thought, "'Michael and Gabriel are too wise to have sent anyone less knowledgeable to pit against me. Now Joe seems a little revived and that is very dangerous. The priest's strength comes from his daily prayers and Bible readings. I'm discovering more and more about Michael. He is quite a strategist, a master of subtleness. Thus far, the forces of heaven have been ineffective and largely invisible. Michael is waiting, maneuvering. He is a layer of traps, a setter of snares. We will not make that mistake again!'"

Satan's eyes shot toward the sound that had interrupted his communication. His eyes focused on them, and his irises were a shocking brilliant red. They were almost glowing. Two small demons were playing around and softly screeching, distracted by a new powerful force. Feeling Satan's gaze, they suddenly bowed, apologized, and begged for mercy.

"There will be hell to pay!" The two demons, startled and terrified, backed away.

"Please, pardon us. We did not mean to interrupt you, my prince!" said the one.

"Please, pardon me. We just couldn't help ourselves. The force of those prayers are disturbing us," he said with eyes wide and mouth gaping.

"Words are so powerful," alleged the other.

"Silence, you two!" Satan bellowed. His eyebrows squeezed together to form a crease across his forehead. His eyelids were tight and straight. It was unmistakably clear how angry he was, and all of them felt the strain.

Satan fought the force of the words. "Why is this happening? The probability that this might occur was infinitesimal. I thought we had the advantage."

Smug and Envy couldn't process what Satan was saying. Their concentration was ripped to shreds by their fear. They were breathing faster, but they couldn't help themselves. They started to gasp, "We're going to be punished!"

The two demons braced themselves for a horrifying chastisement; their terrified red eyes peered out from behind their black wings. But Satan did not strike out at them. He seemed more concerned about the words he had just heard uttered from Father Timothy. He staggered slowly around, strangely troubled in a way the demons had never seen before.

"'Bedamned.'"

A low gurgling wail came from deep in his mind as his nostrils belched forth red vapor. His gnarled face registered a burning hatred that slowly rose from deep within.

Then, like a slowly swelling tsunami, his roar shook the room and terrified all the demons of hell. His initial explosion released, and he began to storm about the cave, growling indiscernible phrases of profanity. Distraught, the demons gave him time to vent before daring to ask any questions.

Timidly, Forbodden, the once-powerful demon asked, "Can you tell us what happened?"

Satan spun around in fury, his wings unfurling like a clap of thunder, and his eyes like hot coals. "Can I tell you what happened?" he shrieked, and every demon fell on his face. "The man of God has repaired the hedge around Joe and Grace. It is only temporary, but it may be the final blow that defeats us."

Satan kept pacing and deliberating and snarling. "There isn't much time. We must lay a trap to make them stumble. Be sure to be subtle. Remember, no frontal assault will work."

Strife stepped forward. "We are working overtime on Grace. Joe derives a great amount of his strength from her. With one last attack, we hope to sever their relationship forever."

"Do it any way you can."

"Leave it to me, my prince."

Grace's second appointment with Gwen did not go as well as the first. Even though nothing wrong was happening Grace's nerves made her feel tense. She was worried she might say something wrong or embarrassing. Her hands were clammy and her heart raced. She hated that she felt this way and she wasn't even sure why. It was just the way she had become. She had so many worried thoughts race through her mind and she accepted all of them. Her anxiety had changed her thought pattern. Her thoughts made her worry, even when she should not have been. Her continual whining was negating Father Timothy's prayers. You would hear her say, "I'm just lost and I don't know what to do anymore. I feel so down and I realize that there is no shoulder for me to cry on. I feel alone, unloved, unwanted and forgotten. It is one of the worst feelings in the world."

Before Grace arrived at her appointment, a black bug-eyed imp, its dark wings whirring, its breath pouring out red vapors, arrived and took its place in the corner of the office. Its spiny arms flapped slowly as it disgorged evil contorted words. The demon's tricks and maneuvers set the atmosphere in the room while his fiery words cut an arc through the air.

Grace was finding it more difficult to talk about the barren times—the lonely hours in the empty house. She didn't want to talk about the pain she had suffered. Her voice distorted around her words, "I need to try to help Joe. I can't just give up on him, he needs me. Just because he's not human all the time doesn't mean he's not there for me. Sometimes I don't even feel human myself. You don't know what it's like—the voices, nightmares, hallucinations. Actually, I feel nervous to the point of nausea whenever I think about them. I shouldn't really be talking to you. They will punish me tonight, I just know it. I try not to even think about it. There is no escape from their omnipresence." Grace hesitated. "If Joe hadn't helped me, I'm not sure what I might have done."

She looked guardedly over at Gwen. Her eyes were wide, and her jaw taunt.

Gwen rolled her eyes in frustration, "You do understand that good and evil are necessary counterparts, in the same way as any quality and its logical opposite: blackness can occur, it is implied, only if nonblack also occurs. But unless evil is merely the privation of good, they aren't logical opposites, and some further argument would be needed to show that they are counterparts in the same way as genuine."

Shrieking, cursing, blow after blow, Confusion consumed Grace's thoughts. His friend Madness, a loud-mouthed imp, cursed and taunted Grace, filling the air with blasphemies. He was quick and confident and knew he would prevail.

Grace lay on the couch, clutching her head and gasping for air, taking long deliberate breaths, trying to clear her head, trying to make even the tiniest bit of sense out of what Gwen had just said.

Slightly late for his assignment, Despair floated in through the roof. A pitiful slug of melancholy filth, he whimpered and watched. Several other dark spirits followed him there, staying low, muttering, hissing, and slobbering in agitation. They were a motley band of destroyers, deceivers, and harassers. Their words were having an abominable victory.

Grace's imagination was miserably out of control. Suddenly out of nowhere, she heard a distinct whooshing sound come into the room. She looked up and saw a room filled with hideous bulging red eyes. She screamed out, "Oh my God, look! Do you see the demons?"

No sooner had she spoken than they had disappeared.

Gwen's day had been normal up until then.

"'Wow, Grace's imagination has her sadly out of control. She has taken a perfectly normal afternoon and twisted it into a nightmare requiring an exorcist.'"

Grace needed more therapy than Gwen could offer. Gwen wanted out. There was no way she would any longer consider counseling her. Grace's mind had become too warped.

In a velvety voice, Gwen replied, "I don't know how to phrase this properly," her tone a little bleak. "It might sound a bit cruel, I suppose. There is something very wrong with you."

Her statement was blunt, without much in the way of sugarcoating. Gwen didn't specify what was wrong, but it was clear she felt Grace was mentally deranged. Her morbid mental and physical state contributed to her abnormal behavior.

Gwen got up from her chair and walked over to the door. "I've come to the conclusion this is beyond my expertise. I need to refer you to Dr. Lieberstein. He has numerous years of experience in these conditions." Opening the door to her office, "I hope you can find the help you desperately need."

Grace nervously ground her teeth. Not only were the words coming out of Gwen's mouth demeaning, but it infuriated her the way she drew out her statement in a sarcastic drawl.

"Fine, I'm sure Dr. Lieberstein can help me," she stated between clenched teeth.

Suspicion returned. Grace's eyes were fixed on Gwen as she spoke. Anger pulsed through her automatically: an instinctive reaction to the tone in Gwen's voice. Her expression was agitated; there was only the slightest wildness in her cerulean eyes as she spoke, measuring Gwen's reaction. "They have gotten to you too! I knew they would find out and you would abandon me. How can you call yourself a doctor? You're a witch!"

Grace had to get out of there. Right now. She rose to her feet but wobbled there, feeling faint, light-headed with terror. Words wouldn't come. There weren't any more left. She hurried to the door, running past Gwen. Grace dashed for the hallway, and then rode the elevator to the first floor, pushing her way outside as if she were running for her life. Suspicion stroked her hair and rested on her shoulder.

Grace sat in her car, her elbows on the steering wheel, and her head in her hands. She had to hold still for a minute. She had to try and think, be rational. How could she sort out her feelings when her counselor had just quit. She didn't move for five minutes. The only sound in the car was her heavy breathing. It occurred to her how still everything was and how alone she felt. She *was* alone, covered in darkness, and no one cared.

"'No one loves me. How divine. I feel so lonely. Suicide—am I really that desperate? Maybe I should send Joe a letter, and just move to another state. That's it. Start over where no one knows me. Oh, but how will I stop the nightmares? I just feel so angry and humiliated.'"

Grace drew a long, tired breath and leaned back in her seat. No, she finally decided. She was better than that. She wanted her old life back, the one she had with Joe. She reached in her pocket, pulled out her keys, and started the engine.

Next to the car in the shadows of the trees, two red eyes were watching her, two taloned hands curled in hate. The imp let out a little snicker. In the tree another spirit, squatted like a monkey, its black wings hanging at its side. Its red eyes were also following her.

As she pulled away from the curb, two black shapes hovered over her car. They flew in back and forth patterns with their shadowy wings flapping. They sailed over her, slobbering and cursing, spawning fear from their lips. Her old friends were back. Grace's heart was beating fast, and her body was getting weak. "No, please, not again. No, I can't take it."

"'I need a vacation from my life. I feel so broken. Why can't I enjoy what I still have? I think I need a trip to Santa Barbara. Maybe with a little time alone, I'll find the peace I crave. I'll call Joe and leave him a message. I'll tell him I've gone to see an old college friend. All we seem to do is fight. He probably could use some breathing room too.'"

Tears welled up in Grace's eyes. Switching lanes, she headed north fleeing the doom that encased her.

When Grace arrived in Santa Barbara, she took off her watch and planned to never put it on until she was ready to return to Joe. In the morning, she would wake up, have a light breakfast, and dash out to wander the ocean trails. In the afternoon, she walked to the nearest Starbucks to have her favorite drink, a skinny mocha with extra whipped cream.

This was the first time in a while she didn't feel panicked. She loved wandering around in a city where nobody knew her. Nobody looked at her, nobody talked to her, and she spent her days in delicious silence. Nobody wanted anything from her. She had nothing to explain or justify. She was nobody. She was lost, but at least the vicious voices in her head were temporally quiet.

There was one advantage to staying away for a few days. The new conversations in her head were more palatable.

"'Who is responsible for all this suffering? Why us? I suppose this whole thing was an act of God. He must have needed some more little angels in heaven. I guess his ways are higher than mine. He knows what's best. His grace is sufficient. He will help me carry my burdens. God giveth and God taketh away. Job sure got that right. All things work for the good of God.'"

Smug and his cousin, Distorted sunk down through the ceiling of the Starbucks, chuckling half truths about God as they descended. They might be small unattractive creatures, but they still had a powerful evil influence. Wild and uncontrolled, they spit red vapors that crept across the room and filled the air with an eerie glow. Like a whirlwind, their onslaught attacked any sense of sensibility that remained in Grace's mind. Their hushed, gargling conversations penetrated the room. Grace was putty in their hands.

"This is easier than I thought it would be. Grace must have listened to every falsehood she was ever told, and then stored them away without questioning their validity." The belligerent egotists patted one another on the back.

That day Grace realized that she had the answer Joe was searching for. It was clear that they should divorce and go their separate ways. Then God could work it all out for good. Sitting in a leather chair, she writes from a desk pushed up against the window, looking on the ocean. It is a list of things she must do when she returns to Manhattan Beach.

Joe intended to be patient with Grace. Her sudden departure to visit an unknown friend in Santa Barbara had left him rattled. It wasn't that unreasonable of a request; it was just that he didn't understand how women thought. He had no idea how he would help Grace, but he knew that first he must help himself. He didn't know how much he owed her, but he figured it was his life many times over and possibly his health as well. Grace's suffering had always triggered Joe's protective side. It was not entirely rational. Grace was hardly in any physical danger. He hated when she grimaced, trying to cover the pain in her heart—a poor attempt at bravery. He still saw the suffering in her eyes, pale and blank.

One shadow in Joe's house did not stand still. It crawled, quivered, moved along the hallway toward the kitchen. Any light it crossed seemed to sink into its blackness, as if it were a fissure torn in the atmosphere. This shadow had a shape, an animated, demonic shape. As it neared Joe, its sounds could be heard; the scratching of claws along the kitchen floor, the faint rustling of membranous wings, drumming just above the creature's shoulders, and vile comments.

Its leering, bulbous eyes reflected the stark fluorescent light in the kitchen with their own red glow. The gnarled head protruded from hunched shoulders, and wisps of rancid red breath gurgle in labored hisses through rows of pointy fangs. Strife either laughed or coughed, as wheezes puffed out from deep within his throat. From its crawling posture, it reared up on its legs and looked at Joe. The black leathery jowls pulled back revealing a fiendish smile. Its black hand passed into Joe's mind like a bayonet. With an eerie cry of rage and indignation, the membranes on its back began to billow.

There was a heavy weight on Joe's heart and emptiness inside. At times, he could barely breathe under the pressure, and even his heartbeat seemed labored, heavy, and slow from his misery. He'd never felt such pain as if he would never be free. The ache from so much tragedy was ever present. It throbbed, ebbed, and flowed throughout his body. Sometimes it felt like a parasite was imbedded in his mind, behind his eyeballs. It took all his willpower not to scream from his agony. It wasn't fair; he didn't understand.

Hoping to find some relief, Joe decided he would attempt to do something to comfort Grace. The only thing stopping him was his uncertainty that she would welcome him. His pride and ego had taken such a beating, and he didn't want to risk being rejected one more time. There was an aching sensation in his chest that made things too difficult. He shut his eyes, and then swallowed painfully.

"'Did I do this to her, hurt her so deeply that I've destroyed all the joy in her life? I've got to make it up to her, somehow, someway. Why hadn't I appreciated things more? Now it seems as if Grace is broken. Broken. She has been so kind and devoted to me. Why have I been such a jerk? I don't understand why God just doesn't tell me why this happened. It would be so much easier if he would just leave a note under my pillow—you know like the tooth fairy does. It would be nice to have some clear and specific directions as to what to do or what He's wanting from me. '"

Joe was having difficulty getting his head around it. He was afraid that Grace might be making plans to leave him. Suspicion was now becoming second nature to him. He felt a little betrayed because this wasn't what he had expected from Grace, what he had become accustomed to having. She hadn't married him because of convenience and money and protection, or any of the other reasons a woman might hook up with a man. She had married him because she loved him.

He was confused and furious and scared. Joe didn't want this. He wanted everything to be exactly the way it had always been, and the thought of losing Grace made him sick and panicky. Even if he could replace her with another woman, he did not want that. He didn't want to lose her. He didn't want another woman. He wanted Grace. He had to stop this line of thought and shut it down now.

Just a few months ago, Grace would have been asking if there was anything he wanted, catering to him, fussing around him to make certain everything was just the way he liked it. Now she would spend hours in bed, making no effort at all to even have a conversation, and the chasm that separated them felt as if it were a thousand miles wide. Now she was listless, moody, depressed, angry, fuming.

Slowly, sitting there in the brightly lit kitchen, he began to hope that his new journey might lead him down a path that included Grace. This new weird mixture of euphoria and fear made his heart race and his stomach jump. He could understand the power of love, and he felt as if he had taken a mysterious drug, so instantly addictive that he craved more.

Father Timothy had told him the book of Job would have his answers. He wanted to read it from beginning to end without interruptions. Joe got up early and walked into the kitchen. He took his cup of coffee and laptop to the table. "Lord, please help me understand the wisdom I'm about to read."

Until he found his way through his troubles, it would pay to find out more about how God worked. He booted up just as the timer began to buzz. Turning off the timer, he took the pizza out of the oven. Grabbing the cutting wheel in the drawer next to the oven, he cut four slices. As he put them on his plate, he grabbed a couple of paper towels and two chocolate chip cookies Grace had baked the day before. That should last him for a few hours.

"Well, Lord," Joe spoke out, opening his Bible randomly. "What have you got for me today?" Joe liked to open his Bible randomly and let his eyes fall on whatever verse they came too, and he believed God had something specific to say to him that day.

He began to read out loud verse 42 Then Job answered the LORD, and said,

² I know that thou canst do every thing, and that no thought can be withholden from thee.

³ Who is he that hideth counsel without knowledge? therefore have I uttered that I understood not; things too wonderful for me, which I knew not.

Joe could feel a knot in his stomach, he had found something— something new that he had not heard before or just glanced over in the past. It was like those times when he was studying in school and would turn the page in a book to find he was reading without fully understanding. He had to go back and start again, and the words seem even more disturbing yet maybe a little comforting. The words seemed unfamiliar and sounded strangely in his head, yet they sent a piercing arrow into his heart. He grabbed Grace's Every Day Life Bible from Joyce Meyer's that was lying on the nightstand. Maybe reading it another way, he could glean some more understanding. Job 42:1, "THEN JOB said to the Lord, I know that you can do all things, and that no thought or purpose of Yours can be restrained or thwarted [You said to me] Who is this that darkens and obscures counsel [by words] without knowledge?"

Joe paused, taking a deep breath to evaluate things. He had just tasted the sweet love of God and was overwhelmed. As he grew nearer to God, he saw more clearly the purity of His Word. Feeling giddy, his body was tense and his heart was pounding. Then just as quickly, he felt light and calm, laughing at his discovery; he sat there with an off-centered smile. He took another deep breath, hoping that as he continued to read he would learn more. "Therefore [I now see] I've [rashly] uttered what I did not understand, things too wonderful for me, which I did not know" (Job 38:2).

"'Why was Job repenting? What had he done wrong? How did he stop God's plans? What knowledge did Job lack? What didn't he understand? What are the wonderful things I need to know? God, I need to know you. Help me. Lead me. I will follow you forever.'"

Joe stared amazed at what he was reading; he flipped to the reference page of Job 38:2 and read, "Who is this that darkens counsel by words without knowledge? (Job 35:16).

Another reference. Joe needed to know more where was God leading Joe for an answer to all his current problems. He flipped to Job 35:16 and read aloud, "[U]selessly opens his mouth and multiples words without knowledge [drawing the worthless conclusion that the righteous have no more advantage than the wicked]."

Frozen, breathing like a statue, he could not believe what he had just read. Joe couldn't hold back his excitement. Was his own mouth condemning him, just like Job? Was he stopping God's plans for his life by what he said? Like Job, what did he not understand?

"'Was it true that I played a part in my own destruction? What wonderful things do I need to know? God I need to know you. Help me. Lead me. If you give me the answer, I will be as Job and change my ways. I will follow you forever.'"

Joe ran to his desk, grabbed several markers, two notebooks, and a Bible concordance. Spreading them across the table, he flipped his Bible to Job chapter one and began his journey to a new life.

On Friday morning, Joe couldn't get the upcoming meeting off his mind, which was probably to his advantage, considering the condition his body was in. He felt it was now or never. Time appeared to be running out. The answer had to be close at hand. Questions were swirling in his mind. Question he felt sure that Father Timothy had the answers to.

Joe loved and admired his father, Joseph Senior. His father had taught him all the tricks of business, how to behave, how to dress properly. His trust for his father brought him a sense of peace and comfort. But sometimes, when it came to ethical matters, in ways that he could not clearly formulate, he sensed that his father had some shortcomings. It was as if, at times, his father did not believe in a concrete right and wrong. He like to dabble in what Joe thought were gray areas.

And Joe needed certainty. It was part of his innate character, the part that needed to believe—to find what was right or wrong, good or bad. Joe experienced a secret sense of disappointment in his father. Though he was basically a good man, at times he had allowed himself to be involved in somewhat shady dealings. It was the reason, he thought, that his father, though kind and generous to a fault, was shallow and lacked the wisdom he needed.

Joe preferred Father Timothy's advice. He believed he was wise beyond his age, and even though Joe was sometimes unable to follow the many turnings of his shrewd mind, he realized he would have the answer. There was an absolute certainty to what he believed in his heart. The rules he lived by were fixed and eternal. Father Timothy would pray over his decision, meditate on what the scriptures said, and by the end of the day, he knew exactly where he was going and why he was going there. Everything considered, Father Timothy gained revelation from the truth.

And then it seemed to Joe that he understood. Father Timothy was a gift from God. He had sent the priest to save Joe from his dilemma, help in the time of need. Freedom was so close, it was touchable, believable—attainable. Signs of it seemed to appear from everywhere. Things started falling in place.

"Uh," Father Timothy looked for an empty chair, and finally moved a pile of reference books. "Have a seat. Pardon the mess."

Joe sat down on a chair.

"What can I do for you?" Father Timothy smiled broadly, leaned back in his desk's swivel chair, and rested his hands behind his neck. It seemed this was going to be an enjoyable day.

"Wow," Joe gleefully declared. "So we dare to infringe on sacred ground!"

Joe looked around the room in mock suspicion, searching for eavesdroppers, then leaned forward and said in a lowered voice, "Listen, there are so many things I did not know. I had heard Christian clichés about God, but now I know Him. Yes, now I know some of his promises."

Joe's countenance brightened up even more as he said, "God isn't responsible for the evil. It was all done by Satan. I had the power to stop it, but I lacked the knowledge to know how to do it. I was as stupid as Job. Just like it says in Micah, 'My people perish for the lack of knowledge.' I thought it was against the rules for normal people—people like me and you—to know about the clandestine world full of demons and imps that secretly existed around us. Now that I know about that world, it will be easier to stay out of trouble.

"I thought it was God who was taking my children. I mean, I was always taught he allowed it, so it must be his will, what he wanted. God gives and takes away, I had been taught. But what he gives is good and what he takes away is evil. Why are people so blind? Why hasn't anyone ever talked about this before? The Bible offers an open book test. I will never, never ever be fooled again! I now know that the word of God can stop Satan's actions."

With a mischievous glint in his eye, Father Timothy observed, "I can see that your eyes have been opened, and at last you see the truth. In the future, it will be important for you to be willing to lay aside any theory that you have been taught if it is contrary to the plain Word of God. Try to accept things at face value and refuse to question God or make His Word a lie about anything it says."

When Father Timothy put it like that, Joe knew he was right . He sat up in his chair, his sudden hope kindled. Beside him, Father Timothy sat like a tightly wound clock.

"Are you trying to tell me that God means what he says and says what he means?"

Father Timothy focused his gaze on Joe as he answered. His voice was vibrant, faintly softer than a roar. "If God says anything, He means it. You have all the right in the world to believe that He is an intelligent being, and that He can and does use the human language as well as any man."

He eyed Joe for a moment. "There isn't a thing to be gained by doubting, questioning, and arguing about everything that He says. Joe, you stand to lose everything both now and hereafter if you pursue such a life. We also play a part if we continue to listen accept, believe and speak the lies over God's truth. In fact, fear is the opposite of faith and can actually be considered sin in God's eyes. God teaches us in James 4:17 'Any person who knows what is right to do, but does not do it, to him it is sin. Now you know that stress, fear and anxiety are not characteristics of someone who is Godly. So instead choose to live in what God calls the fruit of the Spirit – love, joy, peace, patience, kindness, goodness, gentleness and self control. If it is not from God know it is not truth. Refuse to accept it any longer."

"Why is it so hard for me to understand this?" Joe hesitated.

Father Timothy fixed his eyes more intensely on Joe. "It is the purpose of the devil to get men to live in doubts and unbelief concerning what God has promised, so as to rob them of the benefits of faith in God's word. If God did not mean what He said, then He should not have said it in the first place. But if He did say it, who are you to make Him a liar? Wouldn't you rather blame the one that deserves this title—Satan? He is your worst enemy, and all your unbelief and doubts are his work. He wants to ruin your life."

Joe didn't answer. Father Timothy looked at Joe, then evaluating his reaction.

"Job 28:7 taught me that when I pray in faith, God puts a hedge around me where no demon can penetrate. The fowls and vultures of life are kept at bay."

Several dark shadows kept a wary eye on everything from their perch atop the church roof. Dishonesty, more nervous than ever, paced and spewed a rampage of curses. What worried Dishonesty the most were the angels that were hanging around. As Joe's fear began to diminish, it became almost impossible to keep his enemies at bay. The hosts of heaven were back in the game and seemed to have the advantage. So far, Michael's presence, as well as the presence of so many other warriors, had a taming effect on the demonic hosts. There had been no incidents, and for now, Michael was pleased.

Father Timothy continued, "Most people no longer want to acknowledge that we have an enemy—the devil—arrayed against us. They fear that people will see them as unintellectual, uneducated. That makes it so easy for him to rob and cheat us out of the best things in life."

"Can you tell me why there are so many Christians who are are still sick?" Joe earnestly asked.

"Well, healing doesn't just fall on people. It seems to me that either people haven't heard about God's healing power or they *did* hear it and rejected it. I'll give you an example. Many years ago, I prayed for two men I knew who were facing death. I shared with both of them the truth I'm sharing with you. One of them rejected the truth and died. The other said, 'Yes, I see it. It's in the Word and I accept it,' and he was healed and raised up from his deathbed. The number one reason people fail to receive healing is that they do not believe that it is God's will for them to be healed. You need to settle the question about this before anything else. Every promise of God is a simple declaration of obligation to men that God will give them certain benefits when they meet certain conditions. All the promises of God are conditional, as can be seen from my example. If one wants the benefits promised, he must believe the promise for what it says and meet the mandatory conditions."

"But how can I settle this? I'm not sure I know what God's will is."

"It is God's will to heal not only you, but also everyone else who are sick. You can see it clearly written in his word. Please settle this in your mind and heart. I'll get a Bible and prove it to you. Read 1 Peter 2:24 aloud to me."

And Joe did.

Then Father Timothy said, "Notice the last clause of that verse. What does it say?"

Joe said, "By whose stripes, ye were healed."

"Now is *were* past tense, future tense, or present tense?"

Joe looked at Father Timothy in amazement, and yelled, "Why, it's past tense! If we were healed, then I was healed."

"That's exactly it!" Now just thank God for it. You're not going to be healed, you *were* healed."

Joe bowed his head and began to thank God. "Lord, I'm so glad that you healed me." As he opened his eyes, he noticed that his body ached less and the rash on his arms were gone. "This is it. I know I'm healed." Even though he had some of the symptoms, he continued to praise God.

And Father Timothy had one last thought before Joe ran off for the day, "Don't forget about the process of training. This is a lot of new stuff for you to digest. There is a process to all of this. Just because it gets hard doesn't mean it's wrong—it means its difficult! Don't expect to nail something that you are new at. Yes, that's what I said! Give yourself some realistic expectations. You are training you soul and body right now. Your spirit became new when you were born again. Your success will be dependent on how you react when you slip up (because you will at first!). But if you embrace this, you will get back on the path; failure and quitting will not be an option. So, just as it takes time for medicine to take effect, it will take time for God's medicine to take effect on your body."

Joe made sure he had his daily dose of God's medicine: His word. He dug up old articles on faith, prayer, and healings. There were so many things he had never learned at church. He should have listened better and not daydreamed so much.

So Joe decided to spend as much time as he could examining the Scriptures on the subject of healing. Letting go of old traditions was a challenge. It was something the Morretti family didn't have much experience in. They were used to holding on to things, like a dog with a bone.

Taking out his notebook and Bible, he would sit in the sunshine under a tree, out in the fresh sea breeze. He would lean back in his chair and read, pause, and contemplate the scripture's meaning. After three days, he became convinced that divine healing belonged to him. So without being any better, with symptoms still screaming at him, he wrote the following: "Having studied the Bible, I've come to see that healing is mine today, just as much as the forgiveness of my sins are." When he wrote this, he still felt weak. He knew everything was not quite right.

Joe's mind struggled, "I'm a fool. Who am I trying to kid! It can't happen—I can't be healed.'"

As long as Satan could hold Joe in the arena of reason, he could defeat him. He could defeat him in every battle. He began to feel his grip loosen. The arena was changing. Why? Slowly, deep from within, came a cry.

"'Wait a second, those thoughts are wrong. I need to remember what Father Timothy told me. Faith says with God all things are possible. I can do this. My worry says God isn't able to help. I must not listen to this worry. For I'm not moved by what I see or how I feel. I'm moved only by what I believe, and I believe your Word and that you have healed me. Even if I can't see it, he has healed me.'"

Suddenly strength came to his body, and for the first time in months, he started to feel good.

At church the next Sunday, Joe understood the Eucharist, Holy Communion in a new way. The broken bread represented Jesus's broken body, broken for him. He had always taken part in the routine ceremony, but it hadn't meant a thing in the world to him; it was just a ritual. But today, he was receiving the wafer as a sign, as evidence that he was partaking of Christ's broken body, and therefore healed by his stripes.

Joe was learning to not let his thoughts get the best of him. He had been religiously brainwashed that God had some purpose in his sickness. Sickness and disease aren't from heaven; they are from Satan, the deceiver. When he got this settled once and for all, he had won at least fifty percent of the battle. Now that he knew where sickness came from, he would not be so quick to accept it.

Joe had been asking anyone who would answer a long list of questions. He read several books and talked to Grace and his closest friends. Father Timothy and Joe spent many days out on the deck, talking and looking out across the blue green ocean. Through these conversations, and especially the meetings with Father Timothy, his understanding of God and his purposes were profoundly changed.

Joe came to understand the common thread of disappointment and failures of faith that many of his friends had experienced. They had not received from God the perfect spiritual equation that would solve their problems and make them whole, and that led them to believe that the promises had not been made for them.

Healing began in Joe's spirit. Even his physical healing for his body began in his soul. God didn't start work from the outside to the inside. So Joe no longer looked on the outside for physical healing. He knew to look on the inside, the place miracles came from. When he stopped paying attention to his outward symptoms, he found that they were gone.

It was funny that Joe knew things on the inside that he didn't see on the outside. They were things that his mind could not comprehend. But because he knew it in his spirit and believed it, he began to say it. And because he said it, it came to pass.

Joe gave the Word the same opportunity that he had given the doctor's medicine. God had promised him a happy and prosperous life. There would be attacks, but Joe would come out victoriously. And by the end of the week, every single one of his symptoms had disappeared.

Joe was so glad that he had not reasoned, "Well, if I'm healed, why am I still in pain?" He could have reasoned himself out of his healing. But instead he praised God. He stopped by the church to tell Father Timothy the good news. He packed up a bag of chocolate chip cookies as a treat they would share over a cup of coffee.

As the sun was setting, Father Timothy remarked that, at the end of each day, he went to the chapel to pray, and suggested that perhaps, Joe would like to accompany him.

"I hoped you would ask me," said Joe zealously.

The chapel was silent; they were alone. "Each time I pray," Father Timothy observed, "I like to remember that I'm in the presence of God, thanking him for the promises he has given to my parish." He smiled. "It lets me know that there is an answer to everyone's troubles."

Father Timothy went to a small altar, sank to his knees, and loudly began to pray.

Joe knelt beside him and did his best to do the same. Father Timothy's presence was encouraging. Joe felt a sense of peace. Surely, he thought, in this quiet sanctuary, he would be led to his answer.

A soft muffled sob came from deep inside Joe. There, kneeling in earnest prayer, his head resting in his hands, he looked very vulnerable and much older than his age. His lips moved without sound as he poured forth his prayers with passion and tears. At last his prayer crumbled, as all his thoughts and feelings came to rest on her name, "Grace," and he cried and cried.

Two angels watched, looking down on the remorseful man in prayer.

16

The best way out is always through.

—Robert Frost

"Victory!" came the sudden ear-piercing war cry from Gabriel's powerful lungs, and the entire room instantly burst into a blinding flash of bright light as Gabriel shot up out of the ground, blazing and sparkling, making dazzling arcs in the air. The demons covered their ears, flinching and whimpering. The room echoed with triumphant words, which sent forth piercing darts that danced like comets for minutes upon the walls.

Gabriel's body was shifting unconsciously as he watched, tensing for the words he would say. His hands were clenched at his side. He stood tall and strong, and he bellowed out a laugh that shook the ground. "Now, you foul demons, God rebukes you."

Forbodden's eyes were black with hate. He did not smile, his lips were pressed into a tight line. There was a striking reptilian quality to the way he coiled his body, a serpent waiting for an opening to strike. His restless gaze flickered between Gabriel and the other demons. Tension rolled off him, nearly visible in the air. You could feel his passion, the all-consuming desire to destroy Joe. His plan was obvious as it was practical. They easily outnumbered Gabriel, and the advantage appeared to be theirs. It would be quick, he had no time for games. It would be thorough. Something that not even God could repair. He shrieked out an order, and all twenty demons converged on Gabriel like starving predators, barring their fangs and screaming obscenities. However, an arch angel equip by the power of prayer was not something to be messed with.

Gabriel shot straight up out of their midst, and with one final commanding word said, "Be gone in the name of Yahshua!" The demons unfurled their wings and shot into the sky like loose balloons fleeing in blind rage.

Smug rolled his eyes toward the sky and wailed in his fear and frustration. "Satan will have all our hides for this. Those who did not fall in battle will surely be punished by him."

Smug counted the demons around him and came up shorter than he hoped. "What happened to Fear?"

"Gone," they all screamed. "One of the first to fall."

"And Terror?"

"Vanquished to the Abyss, I imagine,' said Worry.

"Anxiety, Despair, Trepidation, and Poverty?"

Smug only got desperate glares. He looked around, and his body twitched. He could not fathom what had gone wrong. "It should have been an easy task. We accomplished so many times in others."

Smug moaned, "Wait until Satan finds out."

Smug flapped frantically into the air. His wings had seen better days. One wing was twisted and jagged. He hurried away, complaining and sniveling as he went.

Insanity yelled, "And when you are through with telling Satan, come back and help us with Grace!"

On top of all the fantastic things that were happening, Joe still wondered when Grace would be coming back from Santa Barbara, "'Did Grace's friend really need her that much? Maybe I should ask Grace if she wants me to send her some healing scriptures. How will Grace hold up while trying to help someone else? She barely seems to be functioning. I'm going to patch things up with Grace. Man, I just have to get through this; much more of it, and we wouldn't have much of a marriage to come home to.'"

Part of Joe and Grace's difficulty came from the fact that they were approaching their problems from two different agendas that didn't seem to coincide. Joe, with his intellectual, emotionally tainted agenda, wanted answers; whereas Grace, with her standoffish bipolar insanity, was looking for relief. The approach of one did not work for the other.

When Grace finally came home in the midst of so much suffering, it was not the time for Joe to offer answers. It was a time for him to listen and empathize and say things that could comfort her. She did not want him to give answers; everything was so emotionally wrenching. Rather, she hoped he would show compassion and empathy and just be there with her, not judging because his continual intellectual answers did not offer her any relief.

The weeks came and went. And in those dark days of that year, Grace seemed to be wrapped in a mantle of sadness. Joe had been able to convince her to give him a year before she would leave. They tried to pretend everything was back to normal. Joe did his best to be cheerful in her presence. If he read funny story online, he told it to her, and she seemed to enjoy it.

But as gray December began, with Christmas approaching, he could see little joy in her face.

Joe's fear of emotional outburst kept him from checking on Grace in the guest room. Though she was quiet, he found it difficult to sleep without her in their room, so nights would drag on relentlessly.

Unable to fall asleep, Grace would often end up in the guest room. Seated beside her on the bed, a mischievous, waiflike spirit, Torment moved his finger about in her brain as if he were stirring a bowl of stew, chanting softly to himself, chuckling a little between his singsong irritating evil verses, as he painted pictures in her mind.

There were three other spirits in the room, one hanging from the wall like a spider, one flat on his back on the hardwood floor with his clawed feet in the air, and one lying on the end of the bed. They were little hoodlums merrily committing sin in secret.

"Oh, don't give her that thought again. Use some imagination," said the spirit at the end of the bed.

"Why not?" said Torment. "She always believes it."

"I can do better."

"When she falls asleep, it will be your turn."

Torment's red eyes flashed with delight at his own cleverness, "Ooooh, remember her screams as he raped her? Remember all the blood?"

Grace sat on the bed and rocked with her arms clasp around her knees. What was that? Grace heard it. Drip. Drip. Drip. She couldn't believe it! Joe had left the faucet dripping again. The faucet seemed to mark off segments of time, announcing the passing of each horrible event in her life. One moment, and another moment, and another moment; like a clock, never stopping, never slowing just one steady drip, moments passing.

People were walking, laughing, and riding bikes along the Strand, but Grace did not hear it. A siren wailed once; she cringed, visualizing her children's deaths. She had no strength, no will to rise from the bed, her hands limp by her side. She lay there in her pain and misery.

She just lay there, staring vacantly at the ceiling, listening to the drops. Drip. Drip. Drip. "'It's all Joe's fault.'"

Drip. Drip. Drip.

"'He's the one that has caused this disaster!'"

Drip. Drip. Drip.

"'He's so manipulating and condescending. I should just divorce him and get over this ordeal.'"

Drip. Drip. Drip.

"'He's lost all our money! He's going to make us bankrupt with all his manipulating.'"

Grace had no tears. She was too devastated to cry; there was no soul within her. She continued to gasp for breaths, wishing it would end.

The demons imposed on her—Torment, Strife, Dishonesty, and now Suicide. They stabbed at her, whispering to her, scratching away at her soul one layer at a time.

"'It's a lonely world. How will I survive?'"

Pain was upon her, an aching deep in her soul, and with gritted teeth and a stifled whimper, she cried, "Oh God, help me!"

Returning home from his office, he saw her sitting on the deck, watching the ocean. Grace was alone. She must have heard him come out, but she did not turn, as though silently letting him know that she wanted him to leave her alone. He was about to go into his study but then, thinking better of it, he quietly sat on the bench beside her. He did not say anything but observed the sadness in her eyes and the stiffness in her back. And after a time, he reached over and took her hand and said, "I'm so sorry."

She said nothing. But at least she did not draw away.

Joe assured Grace, purposely making his voice light. "I know you are unhappy," he continued quietly. "I'm sorry for all your pain, I do understand. Please don't shut me out."

He put his arm around her shoulder. "Don't worry. Things will get better," he urged, and then he kissed her on the forehead.

After a pause, she responded.

"The truth is, Joe, I don't know if I can live in this world without my children. I just don't see the point anymore. Life without them just isn't life. I have no purpose anymore."

He removed his hand from hers. He put them in his lap, and stared at the ocean.

Then he felt Grace put her arm around his neck, and as he turned toward her, she rested her head on his shoulder.

"I understand," was all he could say.

Grace seemed to be in a decent mood when Joe got home. She didn't even go out of her way to be vulgar. Grace being Grace, however, insisted on cleaning up the dinner dishes before they did anything else. Joe expected that, as in keeping, everything in its place made her more peaceful. What had happened to them heightened her organizational bent. At this point in life, she not only wanted things to be in their place, but she needed things to be in their place. It gave her a sense of security.

For himself, most days, he felt he was doing pretty well if he could get dressed in a somewhat cohesive attire. Because he could see how she wouldn't be satisfied otherwise, hoping to placate her, he dried off dishes and put them away. But largely, he knew to stay out of her way while she boxed up the leftovers and wiped clean the stove.

Grace's moodiness left her feeling joyful one moment and irritable the next. She was on an emotional seesaw, and there was no apparent cause for her frequent mood changes. Her hostility was wearing on Joe, chaffing him raw. It hurt that she was frequently angry at him, and that they weren't really even friends anymore. He struggled for the right words when they talked. He took deep breaths in an attempt to remain calm. Joe took a moment, keeping his eyes on hers. He didn't see fear or discomfort in them, only a spitting fury that made him nervous. Why was she so defensive? It did them no good for her to be that way.

Her nerves could spring from anywhere, and for now, she had been strangely quiet with them. Time had not yet made her immune to Joe. There was still a glimmer of hope that she would not take him for granted. Joe's eyes traced over her soft features: the soft curve of her lips, her radiant eyes, and the straight line of her nose.

Walking over to Grace, he held out his hand to her and waited until her gaze shifted to him, "I'm looking at a very brave woman who has survived. Not only were all of your children taken in a heinous crime, but we are almost bankrupt. Everything you knew and cherished has been taken for no rhyme or reason. I understand why you have a shattered sense of security and an endangered sense of what some would call sanity. We are standing here because you have chosen to fight back step-by-step, in your own time, in your own way. I think you are one of the strongest people I've ever meant."

Tears ran down her cheeks, and she wiped them with the back of her hand. She muttered something unintelligible. Within a few seconds she was smiling at Joe.

Joe kissed her cheek, "I love you."

Feeling courageous, he softly prayed, "Lord, I thank you that you will give Grace the wisdom and knowledge to know you better. That your grace will shine upon her and give her peace."

Fiery words cut an arc through the air. The surrounding demons met it with their own curses, and the blow sent them spinning. Mayhem's jaw tightened, and he squared his shoulders. His eyes emptied, he was filled with confusion and suspicion. He had overwhelming fear. He tensed himself for the attack. He did not spare one glance for the demons he had promised to protect. His eyes were on Joel, filled with a hate so ferocious that he looked deranged.

"No," he said again, through his teeth, as the angel started to move toward him.

He looked gnarled and haggard, but he was able to fling vicious words toward Joel. Not quite circling because Joel would not let him, he slithered back, moving side to side and trying to find a hole in his defense.

Joel faced his assailant, shouting, assaulting blow after blow; he recognized his holy power, and one by one, they withered away. He turned and soared higher, his words emanating a circle of light. He blazed with the fervor of battle, the passion of righteousness. Spewing fiery words, he stalked Mayhem with perfect precision. Joel roared in fury, and the demons skipped back, amazing light flowing from his mouth as he took a swipe at the mangled demon. Joel's words struck Mayhem from the side, and something tore with a hideous, grating shriek.

Mayhem roared in fury, and Joel put up his word-shield—he was amazingly light on his feet. Mayhem yelled one last word with terror pouring from his eyes. He showed his teeth and hissed at Joel, but with that, he became mute. You could see the burning desire to kill warring in him.

He shook his head fast and jerky, fighting to find the words. His face contorted in frustration, and then he shifted lower as though he were a snake about to strike. He slithered deliberately forward, trying to appear lethal. His eyes were anxious for help from his fellow demons.

Joel bellowed and launched one last massive backhanded verbal strike, which caught Mayhem in the middle of his broad chest. Mayhem's huge body soared into the air, and an anguished wail escaped from his lips. The battle was over.

Joel's squad fought honorably, commanding demons from the sky like foul vultures, vanquishing them with strong words, relentlessly pursuing them and honoring no pleas.

After taking a deep breath, Grace was finding it hard to say what else needed to be said, "Underneath all my strange and bizarre actions, I know I'm a sensible, contemporary woman. Joe, you aren't to blame for my feelings. I just need to figure out why I have them and where they are coming from. But when you go through what we have gone through, you learn not to take things for granted. Children, love, time, blessings. My therapist was the one who had me start to keep a journal and helped me to get to my feelings, my emotions—ones I haven't been able to talk about, ones I'm only able to write down."

Grace seemed to smile more from her eyes than from her mouth as she paused for thought.

"But I see that you are healing quicker than I am. All the meds I'm taking only mask my feelings. My emotions are hidden but resurface when I least expect them. It's almost like someone, or better yet, some invisible monster is controlling my thoughts. My thoughts are so alien, extraterrestrial. I think I would like to meet with Father Timothy. He may have the answer I'm looking for. Maybe I've been a little foolish to sit around, stressed and weak, waiting for the next disaster. Life seems so dangerous to me am I just asking for trouble?"

Grace walked to the desk in the kitchen, ripped a blank page out of her journal, and started writing down questions for Father Timothy; her handwriting more illegible than normal, thanks to her excitement.

The Holy Spirit had silently erased all the panic and tension from Grace's soul. With his remarkable power, He controlled the emotional atmosphere. Grace felt calm and peaceful. He reassured her that she was taking the true path. The calm would continue until she had her first meeting with Father Timothy.

Raphael and Nigel shot out of the trees, along with about fifty other warriors at the end of the walkstreet where Joe's house was located, taking the demons by surprise. Another cluster of demons was just coming home in an automobile full of Joe's arguing neighbors. The heavenly warriors flooded over them before they knew what was happening and removed that complication immediately.

In reply to Raphael's cry, the remaining one hundred warriors swept in a fiery sheet around the home and rushed through its interior like a flood. Demons spun about, and then shot forward from the trees and buildings with piercing cries and vicious wails. Words clashed, wings gyrated, sparks flew. The angels were engaging the demons' full attention, fiercely battling two, three, six demons at once, but they were prevailing.

Strife was distracted by the violent battle, his eyes anxious for his partner's help. He bellowed and launched a massive burst of malicious words. His red eyes were brilliant with fury. The evil spirits were losing their ground.

Nigel shot and zigzagged through the trees, this way and that, in, out, up feinting fiery word-darts. Crash! The demon came at him, and the words met again. The demon was visibly shaken!

Nigel's backhanded wordy blows sent Strife's body soaring ten feet, and it crashed into the rocky wall at the edge of the yard. You could hear the breath whoosh from his lungs. He rebounded off the stone wall and fled to safer ground. A low sigh of defeat escaped though Strife's teeth.

The expansive cloud of spirits beyond the home heard the cries and saw the battle. Out front, his fangs protruding past his chin and his head bristling with spikes, Mayhem roared a command. With an echoing, ringing, flourishing of red glowing blasts, the returning warriors attempted one last assault.

Michael had heard enough! "Be gone, you vile spirits, as God commands!"

The angelic guard came in like a meteor flash. In a long streak of light, the battle was won.

With a quick prayer, Father Timothy and Joe began their weekly meeting. Joe asked if Father Timothy might have time to meet with Grace. "She sees how much my meetings with you have helped, and she is hoping you can give her some answers too."

Joe had been bothered, almost taunted, by his conversation with his friends. They had suggested things he used to think were true, but now he wasn't so sure. He needed Father Timothy to clarify some things. "Isn't it just the will of God to take one and spare another?"

"No," Father Timothy answered his confusion, "it doesn't work that way. The same truth is presented to everyone. One of them rejected it and the other accepted it. I think you should go through the four Gospels carefully and underline with a red pencil all the individual cases of healing. Or better yet, write them all down on a sheet of paper. After writing them down, I believe you will find that the faith of the individual plays a large role in his/her life. Mostly, you will learn to fear not—only believe. Only believe."

Joe nodded thoughtfully. He was beginning to understand how the spirit world operated.

Father Timothy paused, his face pensive. "But instead of accepting what the Bible says, most people say, 'Yes, but you don't know my circumstances. It's different in my case.' Let me just tell you a thing or two. Well, I can't find a 'yes, but' in there anywhere. God wants us to take him at his word. Why not just try accepting what it says?"

"But that wasn't how I was taught to interpret that verse."

"Exactly," he paused, thinking for a moment. "I'm not interpreting it. It plainly says, 'He took our infirmities and bares our sickness.' I'm not interpreting it; I'm quoting it.".

"Yes, but I don't think it really means that."

"Why not?" Father Timothy challenged.

Joe's innate calm was visibly shaken. He stood and began to pace toward the window. He stared out into the foggy morning with a pained and ambivalent expression. Then something changed in Joe's voice, and he asked Father Timothy to explain.

"I didn't say it means anything. What if I said to you I had a hamburger for lunch yesterday? How would you interpret that? Would you think I ate a hotdog? Or would you just understand I ate a hamburger. Wouldn't you just take my word? Why not take God's Word for what it says?"

Pausing for a moment, Father Timothy gave Joe a change to digest what he had just heard. "Every man should literally accept the promises given by God, as if a man promises the same things to them. Begin to act upon these promises and believe them just as they are, without question. They do not need to be interpreted. Please Joe, do not attach conditions to them that aren't stated in the Bible. Meet the conditions stated, and you will receive the benefits. You must not, even for one moment, question what they say. Just like when you were a small child when your father said 'no,' you knew he meant it. The very moment you start to question what he said is the moment you are in trouble. The same is true with God. The very moment you begin to question the promises is when you are being attacked by the devil, and demonic powers get you to doubt God's Word. This is what caused the Fall in the beginning, and this is the very first thing you must get victory over. Joe you must do this to get the benefits of God's promises.

"Learn here and now that you cannot doubt God's Word and make Him a liar and still get the benefits you desire. God will not make a special pet out of you or anyone else. He demands your faith in his word before He obligates Himself to meet your needs. This is the first lesson I hope to teach you. You must learn it well. It is absolutely imperative! In time, you will learn that it is God's will for you to have everything in life that you want. God loves you and wants you to be happy, healthy, wealthy, and successful in life beyond anything you have ever dreamed. Believe God! Change your attitude, Joe, and believe that He means what He says. Begin once again to cooperate with Him in asking and receiving these blessings of life. God will not force you to accept these things. It has to be that you are willing. He will not give you these things alone, regardless of how much He desires to do so. He made the plans of the universe eons ago in his Word concerning what you must do, and also what He promises to do if you do your part. He cannot break His own laws, and He will not fail to meet his own obligations—the ones he has promised."

"Leave!" Michael ducked and held up his word shield as the blazing laser-like words slashed over his head. Red eyes! Gasping jaws!

Michael's wings exploded into a brilliant blur. He shot across the church parking lot, the demon's words like a shrieking chainsaw at his heels.

"You can't be here!" The other demon appeared in front of him like a bomb blast, fangs bared.

Michael spoke, and his words formed a fiery arc.

Michael and the demon went sailing into the church's foyer. Michael let out a powerful shout that echoed over the church.

The demon, a hideous monster, yelled one more obscenity.

Michael shot upward with a burst of power. Another demon from above swooped in like a hawk, shrieking as he passed. Increasingly frequent righteous words were flung at the demons, and shocked hissing made it clear the strikes had met their marks.

Something powerful and white whistled through the air and collided with Poverty. The impact sounded like an explosion, and it threw Poverty against the wall. He landed on his feet again, crouched and ready for attack. Words flew in Michael's direction.

Michael blocked them, their words met in an explosion of fiery sparks, and Michael tumbled onto the floor. A second kick of adrenaline hit like an electric shock, and Michael's next words were crystal clear. With one last powerful cry, he sent the demons spinning crazily away. "This is God's property. Joe's faith has allowed God to rebuild the hedge of protection, and you do not belong here," he commanded.

Even though Grace had grown up as a Catholic, she was still nervous about her first meeting with Father Timothy. She didn't know what to expect. She told herself to relax; he knew his sacramental calling and would find some way to help her find peace. It might even be easier than she thought.

"Hello," she said in a dull voice.

"Grace. I'm so glad we are able to meet today and get to know each other better." Father Timothy tripped over his words as he hurried to get them out. "I trust I will be able to help you as much as I've helped Joe."

"Hopefully you can get me unstuck on my faith journey," she breathed anxiously. Apprehensively she continued, "I've a tendency to mull things over in isolation, sometimes endlessly; I struggle with living without my children, I've problems praying to God, and I even hear voices."

Father Timothy smiled, and then a sly look came into his eyes. He pulled up a chair and offered Grace a seat. "Well, I suppose we should get to work." Gently he encouraged Grace to talk with God about these thing—to make them part of being in God's presence.

Father Timothy put Grace on a path of peace. They discussed her prayer life. She wanted to know when and for how long she should pray. "Will God really respond to my prayers?" They also discussed her relationship with Joe.

"You're confused," he said to her, his deep voice very quiet.

There was no question in his assumption. Father Timothy knew what Grace was feeling, what anyone in her circumstance would feel. "Perhaps the most essential area you need to understand is spiritual discernment. Once you get that, you will know why all of this has happened and how to stop it from happening in the future." Father Timothy gestured theatrically and sat up straight in his chair. "I understand how frustrated you must be, and why you are questioning God about these events. It is easy to be angry, but there isn't a thing to gain from that. He isn't your problem."

His expression was tender, like Grace had been missing something immensely important.

Grace just stared at him, trying to understand. She yearned to flee, to escape the pain welling up from inside. She refused to be swayed by her emotions. Of course, that was exactly what the demons wanted. But what she needed was to put an end to all the pain, the fear of death, and the hours of loneliness. That was all that mattered.

Father Timothy's expression was casual, he was determined to help Grace. "For most people, I've found that it is a lack of knowledge that has caused most of their problems. I was wondering, do you feel God had a part in all this evil?"

Grace sat totally motionless, gripped by the question. "Of course. He is omniscient so he must have chosen to have it all happen."

Grace thought she saw a flash of something in his eyes that she wasn't supposed to see.

"But he did not. The fact is that the devil has been working to cause your problems. At times you may have even questioned your own actions, but I can say that after getting to know Joe, I'm sure you were not the problem. Lately, you've been right in your heart but wrong in your head." He imagined how horrible it was for her these past few months.

Father Timothy took a deep breath before he continued. "In my study of the scripture I've discovered that Satan gets his power through deception. Many are deceived into believing that everything that happens to them in life is God's will for them. Just stop and think: What won't be in Heaven? Sickness, disease, death, poverty, and all that is evil. Why would God bring it here? Remember the Lord's prayer, 'As in Heaven so on Earth.'? That's the way God wants it for you. He wants you to experience now what he has promised will be in heaven."

Grace nodded with a slight smile on her face. "'If only this was possible. I have said the Lord's prayer probably 10,000 times in my life and never really knew what it was saying or maybe I never really believed it. It was more of a routine, what you are suppose to do and say. Guess it is just like when I bake a cake. If you leave out an important incredient you have a mess. I guess saying it without adding any faith just gives you a mess.'" "But how?" she asked.

He stared into her eyes as he answered, "Here are some steps you can use to resist the wrong influence of the spirit-world and join with the forces of the angelic kingdom. First and foremost, study your Bible. It is quick! When you speak the words written in it, you release unseen power to change your circumstances and conform to God's will." He knew Grace might find what he was saying hard to believe, but he pressed on.

"Second, use your faith. Faith is the unseen spiritual force with an energy that can move physical things like mountains in your life. It is the substance of things hoped for, the evidence of things you haven't yet seen." He waited, watching and listening, for her reaction.

"I'm not following you," Grace sighed, resting her head in her hands.

He spoke the words slowly, "What do you believe? Who do you believe? I challenge you to choose to believe the Bible as it works mightily in and through you! You see, for your faith to work, you will have to use your imagination to create images and feelings you desire. In the past, you have let your thoughts meditate on fear and failure. Choose the thoughts you will have from now on. Create an image of victory in your life."

There was a brief pause to let her digest what he had just said. He tilted his head back and smiled at her, love pouring out to her. "Finally, if you find you are up against hard situations, find someone who is strong in faith and ask them to agree with you in prayer. Be certain they have the faith to truly believe you will receive the answer you prayed for. Ask God for his best. Speak God's words in faith, for when you do, you are giving angels an assignment to help you. That's all."

Grace sighed and bit her fingernails. She knew herself well enough to know it would be a difficult path to follow. A shiver raced down her spine. Swallowing her pride, she mused, "'My imagination is a funny thing. Could be dangerous too, but I'm willing to learn. Now's my chance to get better. I hope you can teach me what I need to know.'"

Father Timothy continued, "I understand this might be a little hard for you to grasp, but God is able to go forward and backward in time. After all, he created it. God sets up our tomorrows because of our prayers and how we seek him today. He orders our tomorrows, but He orders them because of what you pray or don't pray. As you pray, God will give you checks and balances in your spirit. He will confirm the plans he has for you and give you direction by telling you, 'yes,' 'no,' or 'not now.'

"Invariably, when you pray, God desires to send a blessing your way, and Satan wants to steal it away or trip you up. When you fervently pray, it releases the Angels to go into your tomorrow and lay a trap for the devil and make sure your blessings are there, right on time."

And then, although she hadn't anticipated it, a gentle peace flowed over her. And for a second, she saw that life could once again be happy and peaceful. Standing to leave, Grace asked, "Can we meet again next week? I know I will need your help to understand this. And perhaps you could suggest where I should start reading in the Bible."

"Oh, just one more thing," he insisted, gesturing for her to remain seated. "I'll e-mail you my suggestion on topics you might want to study before our next meeting. Would next Thursday at ten work for you?" he asked.

She was on the edge of her seat ready to stand and walk out. "That would be perfect. I think I will head over to the chapel for a little prayer time. It is always so peaceful there," Grace replied.

He brightened as he noted her desire for prayer. "Yes, that is exactly what I was hoping you would do."

As Grace sat alone in the little chapel and prayed the rosary, you could see in her very face the trouble pass and the weight of the world lift from her shoulders. She looked at her wedding ring. She pulled it off and looked at it again. It shined brightly, reflecting the light from above. Softly she muttered, "For better or worse, for richer or poorer."

Her wedding vows were foremost in her mind. She wondered what strange power had brought her to this place, but she understood right then where her solace lay. She knew she had to surrender to God. If she did so, she could withstand the powerful forces aligned, fairly or not, against her. She knew, as long as she had Joe, her family, and her faith in God, she was going to be okay. She immediately felt renewed. It was out of her hands and into his.

That night flew by dreamily and then it was morning, and life was once again staring her in the face. Her last dream stayed with her—a silent encouragement. She had seen the most beautiful angels carrying golden censers filled with her prayers. Her prayers were their precious cargo, and they were carrying them with care. No prayer went unanswered, even wrong prayers. Each prayer was brought to God, and instantly, the angels left to go back for more.

Reaching for her iPhone, she read Father Timothy's e-mail. Then she grabed her Kindle and opened it, so she could read along with the audible version of her Bible. Grace began the long journey back toward peace.

When she came down for breakfast, Joe was already gone. He'd left the newspaper on the table, and that reminded her that she had some shopping to do. Scanning the ads, she noticed a play being held at the Chandler Pavilion. If she's lucky, she would be able to purchase two tickets and surprise Joe with an evening out on the town, which was probably just what the doctor ordered, or should she say, *priest?*

Joel and Gabriel were there beside her, wings unfurled, words waiting on their lips. For now, the demons were hiding.

After his last meeting with Father Timothy, Joe at last felt vindicated. He could turn to Grace and say, "This is why all this happened. It was all about the fears I held in my heart."

But what would be the price of his guilt? He hoped for God's forgiveness, the relief it would bring.

"Please, Lord forgive me for my sins and cleanse me from my unrighteousness, amen," Joe prayed.

Feeling a great weight of fear fall from his shoulders, at last, he murmured the words he had missed for so long, "I love you, Lord."

It was impossible to explain, even to him, how much easier those words made it to go on and say what he thought. In hindsight, it seemed unbearably clear that every mistake he'd made, every bit of harm he'd done—the small things and the big things—had originated from fear. Each pain he'd caused Grace, each wound stacked up into a neat pile of fear. He would no longer ignore or deny it.

It took longer than he thought it would for the peace to come. It happened though, and he was overjoyed. Unconsciously, the full relief came like a medicine. The healing power brought with it a brighter outlook. Instinctively, Joe had known that the tear in his heart would mend. Time would make it easier. But more than that, he longed for Grace to get better too. That she could be happy again. Joe had to believe that Grace would be happy. But that required trusting God—a trust he was willing to give.

He was staring at her with cautious respect. "I care about what happens to you."

"I know you do."

For the first time in months, Grace had a bizarre feeling that things were different. It felt more like the way she and Joe used to be: the easy, effortless friends. Odd that she should find it here again when she had thought it had been lost forever.

Her hand felt soft and friendly. "Good. Want to take a walk? Down by the seashore, maybe?" Joe asked.

And for the first time in a long while, he saw the combination of surprise and delight on her face, her eyes grew big, and a smile snuck upon her face. Right at that moment, with his hand warm in hers, she believed him. She smiled at Joe, swallowing against the lump in her throat and holding back tears. "That would be nice. We haven't done that for a long while."

"The sun won't be setting for an hour, so there's plenty of light, but you'll need your jacket as it's breezy."

"Right." She stepped into the closet to grab it.

He moved in behind her, deliberately reaching over her for his. Grace stiffened at the light brush of his body, sidestepped, and reached for the front door.

Her nerves pumped once like a pulse, then seemed to evaporate into the cool air. "It's gorgeous tonight." She breathed it in, the fresh sea breeze. "I haven't been able to go out alone at night. I've thought about it though"—Grace pulled her jacket on as she walked—"But it is either too quiet, or I see too many strangers, and I come up with a dozen reasons why I should stay home." She glanced at Joe while shrugging, "One night last week, I was restless and wanted a walk. I actually thought about taking my gun with me, in case I had to defend myself against a homicidal maniac."

"A gun!" exclaimed Joe.

"Yeah. A gun seemed like it could do some damage if I was attacked. But I decided against it and watched an old movie instead. It's ridiculous. But now, I'm here with you, and I feel safe."

After stopping for a moment to digest what Grace had just said, Joe started walking again. Without seeming to think about it, he reached over and took her hand. They silently walked across the sand to the edge of the water. They looked like a couple who was deeply in love.

The clouds moved slowly across the sky, dimming and brightening the setting sun, filling the horizon with a beautiful array of colors.

When they returned home, she took a chance; a big step for her, like jumping off a cliff into the ocean. She lifted her hands to lay them on his face, rose up to her toes. And then she touched her lips to his.

"I'm afraid I'm going to screw this up. I'd like to go to bed with you."

"An excellent idea."

"I get them occasionally. Maybe you should kiss me again before I lose my nerve."

"He kissed her and then led her to the family room."

Jerking her up toward him, he kissed her with heat, with passion. All she could do was hold on while fears and needs warred inside her.

Part of her was falling in love again. And part of her was pulling away.

Grace headed up the stairs, and Joe followed. He lounged on their bed and gazed lovingly at her, seeming oblivious to the battle that was raging. His expression was carefully bright and optimistic, there was no trace of any anxiety.

Right behind them, so close, so dangerously close, the demons followed. The first demon began his maneuvers, he could feel the power of his words as distrust and fear covered the room. His fiery words cut an arc in the air. Shrieking, he turned to face his assailant. Cursing, parlaying word for word, looking into the fiery eyes of more power, more glory, more holiness than he'd ever feared before. And he could see in the angelic eyes that the warrior would never turn away. Never.

The demon withered even before the words struck its final blow. It slipped from the bedroom into the outer darkness, gone in a tumbling puff of red vapor.

The warrior turned and soared higher, spinning and reciting God's words. He shone with the heat of victory, emitting a circle of light. The fervor of righteousness began to spread around the room.

On his right, a long slithering spirit yelled one more curse at his heavenly assailant. On the left, a loud-mouthed imp boasting curses filled the air with blasphemies. He was quick and confident and hoped to win.

His head went spinning with one command from Michael.

"Let us go," the others pleaded.

And then it was over. The demons were gone. And once more, peace filled the room.

For a moment, Grace felt frightened, wanting to flee. Gasping, she said, "I think I—"

"Need to trust me," Joe finished and kissed her again.

She felt his hand running up and down her body. Lovely little touches. He unbuttoned her shirt as he kissed down her neck until she trembled. He let his hands run up her shoulders, sliding the shirt away as he traveled down her arms. Then his fingers opened the hook of her bra, and her eyes closed.

She cried out as she slid over the first peak, a shock to her system, a sudden surge of sheer delight. She moaned, "I love you."

"God, thank you, God," she sobbed.

They lay there arm in arm, blissful, and grateful and without a clue of what to say or do next. Joe opened his eyes lazily, "How are you doing, Grace?"

"Truth? I'd stop believing I would ever feel this way again. Just something else I had lost. Thank you for sticking it out with me. You're my only love." Grace toyed with her hair for a minute, then nuzzled up to Joe and fell asleep.

The sun was already up when Grace awoke. She smelled bacon and knew that breakfast was awaiting her in the kitchen. Joe had already headed to work, but he had left a note that he hoped she would join him for dinner that evening at El Sombrero, their favorite Mexican restaurant.

Feeling calmer than she had in over six months, she rationalized that there must be some solution to the dangers she felt lurking about, some way, if she were truly repentant, that God would grant her protection from the demons that harassed her. Perhaps if she confessed everything to Father Timothy, he would offer her some advice.

"I know you want to see our children again, Grace. You've been talking about them in your sleep. Worrying actually."

"I have?"

Joe nodded. "But clearly, you are still unable to deal with this, so I interceded on your behalf."

"Interceded? You threw me to the enemy! Now that he knows all my fears he is sure to get me."

Joe rolled his eyes, "You aren't in danger. You haven't been hurt, you are just imagining and taking your thoughts and dreams as if they are real."

"I told you I wasn't ready for a spiritual battle—not yet. I can't take any more."

"Nobody said you had to. Trust God to protect you. Remember to thank him when this is over."

"How do I trust God when he let this all happen to us?"

"We don't have all the answers Grace, but I have learned one thing recently. We need to have faith that God has the answer. He has your answer. If you just ask him I know that we will make it through this."

His face was serene as he gazed at her. The cogs were turning.

Getting up early every day changed Joe's perspective. He saw more sunrises and had time to read his Bible. He got more work done, which was going to help their financial standing. It gave him more time to study and consider the possibility of change. Prayer was the place in which God abided and where the devil would not be able to find him. His prayers made a way where previously there had been no way.

Every night just before he was about to fall asleep he would say, "Grace and I love each other just as we did on our wedding night."

17

When a man is getting better he understands more and more clearly the evil that is still left in him. When a man is getting worse he understands his own badness less and less.

—C. S. Lewis

Joe took a break from his computer at noon, went to the kitchen to switch from coffee to a Diet Coke and a handful of peanuts. He was munching down on them when the phone rang. He scowled, as he always did, when the phone rang when he was overloaded with work projects. He lightened up when he saw the caller ID showing his attorney.

"Hi, Mike. What's up?"

Mike told Joe about the new plans for the business reorganization. Joe smiled when he asked if he had time to talk about the proposal.

"Yeah, I got a few minutes. What did you think?"

Mike Parnelli was a smaller man, barely five foot eight, with slightly thinning hair, a hooked nose, and sharp blue eyes. He wore very good suits, black with the slightest charcoal hue. His suits were specially tailored to project the image of power. He was well-traveled and played the piano at Nordstrom while he was in college.

Mike had spunk and sparkle, and Joe knew him as a priceless associate, a friend who could come through with almost any much-needed favor or advice. He was tough and decisive—his associates used the word brilliant and refined. He was ambitious, a real go-getter, and he drove a red Porsche. Mike was intimidating in court, and Joe was glad to have him on his side. He was good at his job.

Mike agreed to evaluate the proposal. "I will need to do a little research to build a case to support it. I will make recommendations, but any information relating to the job must come personally from you. I advise you to consider hiring a private investigator to help out. I'm sure that on this last project, there was a crook somewhere on your team."

Mike swallowed hard, came to a heartfelt decision and added, "I'll reduce my fee by half, and you can repay me later when you are back on your feet. One last thing. You can pray." Mike emphasized. "Specifically, pray for some friends in the right places. You've got a fight ahead of you."

Joe had a nice little home office with two small desks, a copy machine, a multiline phone, and a fax machine. The afternoon sun was shining in through the big windows, offering him a scenic view of the ocean. Under different circumstances, he had enjoyed working there.

When he hung up, he scratched around through his piles of notes for the copy he'd made for the upcoming meeting. Things were beginning to take shape. For another hour, he paced about his study, going over things this way and that, glancing from time to time at his computer. He was laying his cards on the table, holding nothing back.

His every waking moment would need to be devoted to this project. No one needed to tell him how tight the schedule was. He knew what he had to do to see that the project was brought in on time. At night, he would work until three and then tumble out of bed at sunrise, fuelled by coffee and ambition. It had become personal to him in a way he could never have explained. For him, it was a test of his faith. It was the project that would make or break him. Despite the fact that it appeared he was going to pull it off there were still many things stacked against him.

"'I can do this. I have a plan, and I will work my plan. God is on my side and will make me victorious.'"

Joe sat quietly, rested his chin on his knuckles, thought for a moment, and then nodded in agreement with his own thoughts.

He could have been bitter right then. He lost his children in a horrific crime, his businesses were in shambles, his salary was pitiful, and his wife was often annoyed at him. It just didn't seem fair. Even so, Joe remained true to himself. He would remain a righteous man, a man of principle and fortified by his newfound conviction.

Joe's office seemed to be an oasis of peace, a professional spot for reflections on upcoming business; in the spiritual realm, trouble was within its borders, hiding in the shadows. Only a few dark demons had accompanied Joe into his office. They were some of Satan's best. Ruin sat on his shoulders, dangling his skinny fingers into Joe's brain while Trouble sat on the desk and watched. They fussed and chattered all around him, itching to get in on Joe's downfall. A rustling went through the room as Misery's black wings began to quiver and red glowing words flowed from his mouth.

Joel and Michael and a few other warriors were staying out of sight, sitting on the rooftop bidding their time. They didn't want to be spotted by the evil powers that only spirits could see. It was nice to see them so cocky; demons in that state of mind, unaware of the upcoming battle, were easier to catch off guard.

Joe was far from cheery that afternoon, and his mind began to wander from his paperwork. He missed his old life, the way it used to be so easy, uncomplicated. Yet he was glad that he still had the memories. Out of nowhere came the fear—the fear of being wrong. He feared the ridicule that might follow being wrong. He ultimately feared for his career. He could envision his allies smearing his reputation. A single misstep, a single misstatement, a momentary misunderstanding was all it would take.

Joe was frozen in his chair for a moment. He stared down at the envelope, his stomach in a knot, his heart pounding so hard he could feel it. The envelope was starting to quiver in his hand.

It looked like a lawsuit had been filed against his last remaining assets. Joe leaned against his desk, all alone in the room. "Oh God," he prayed in a whisper. "Thank you that you direct my path."

Things had gone wrong for much too long. Joe was mired in debt, abandoned by his allies, estranged from his friends, unable to sleep, unwilling to eat, his career was in tatters, and the crushing wait of it all felt stacked upon his shoulders. Beyond Grace and his parents, he was not sure there was anyone he could count on. Desperate to steer his mind away from his problems, he knelt to his knees to pray to ask God for his help and, perhaps, a miracle or two.

Michael and Joel made a low sweep over Joe's house and saw how distraught Joe was becoming. Michael gave the signal, and the others, with an explosive surge of wings, shot forward, etching the even sky with streaks of light. They rushed into the office, they came to a halt and settled next to Joe. The moment their feet touched the ground, the glimmer around them faded and their wings folded and vanished.

A minute later, he remembered the article he had read in the doctor's office that showed that classical music can act as a cause to slow down your breathing and heart rate, which, he was sure, would be helpful. He found his iPhone and clicked on Pandora, selecting songs by Vivaldi. The playful tunes of *Spring* instantly lifted his spirit.

Suddenly, Joe's mind clicked on just a little, and again for the millionth time, he tackled the same vexing question: if his life was so senseless, so empty, so disturbing, why was he trying so hard to hang on to it? Why did he keep on going? Maybe it had something to do with what his heart told him—nothing poetic, just that mysterious desire—that life had a purpose. A purpose that he needed to find. He would keep things simple. He would only concentrate on the task at hand. He leaned forward and began to study his notes for the meeting one more time. The two propositions he would present would save his company from liquidation. Suddenly, and contrary to his instincts, he knew there was nothing to worry about.

Waking early, Joe stood in front of the bathroom mirror, double-checking his appearance. He straightened his tie, spiked his hair; his hands trembled, and his stomach was queasy from the anticipation. That morning, Joe was jumpy as he climbed into his truck. He was glad it was a Saturday, and the freeway had less traffic than usual. But the future of Moretti Enterprises hung by the narrowest of threads. Joe pulled to a careful stop in his usual parking space and got out in a calm businesslike fashion. He was being cautious, sensitive to his emotions, careful not to let his edginess show.

Moretti Enterprises was nestled within the grid of a major metropolis in the center of downtown Los Angeles. In every direction, it was just across the street from the noise, litter, gridlock traffic, and a few homeless people. All the offices had floor-to-ceiling windows with dazzling downtown views. Everything was at one's fingertips, from a haircut or a manicure to grabbing a bite for lunch at the delicatessen to dry cleaners and tailors. You'd find them located on floors four through six. Joe's office was on the tenth floor.

Joe went to the front with his Mac in his hand. The room had a high twelve-foot ceiling, dark-stained mahogany trim, and hardwood floors. It was deathly quiet, except for the noise from the air-conditioning. The fluorescent light fixtures were at full brightness, but the room still seemed gloomy. Perhaps it was because the massive drapes were still drawn over the windows.

He attempted to look like a hassle-free man with a bright expression and smooth voice. He was going over his defense in his mind, trying to come up with something persuasive. Surely, all the members of the board knew his character, his ethics.

Joe had mixed feelings about this meeting. He felt prepared in some ways and frightened in others. He only hoped that Edward Stadham, one of his very vocal opponents in the past, would remain mute today. But there he sat, dressed up in a black suit, flanked by his office assistant, ready for the meeting to progress.

He heard Mike complete his remarks, "And now, I think all of us are anxious to hear from Mr. Moretti."

Joe rose, buttoning his jacket as he gazed around the boardroom. He walked toward the podium and mentally rehearsed his arguments. Taking a deep breath, he addressed his audience, wandering back and forth, studying the pattern on the carpet, waving one hand in the air as if conducting a choir. "I have a few items to address before this group," he conveyed. "First of all, from the business side, things have begun to turn around. Our expenses have been cut ten percent, and our revenue has been increasing over the past several months. In other words, we're turning the corner and entering a profitable market. I personally have no doubts why. There were many issues we needed to resolve, and your support in these matters is greatly appreciated."

It was his voice, the intonation, that hit the fearfulness somewhere deep inside Joe—where his nervousness lay: a nonconscious, hard-to-govern nerve, probably in the pit of his stomach. It was the quality of his voice, soft and yet rough, anxious to the ear. "Secondly, I know that I've made some mistakes in the past, but I have faith in the group here, and I think we can turn the whole thing around and start doing things right in the future. I say let's do it."

For a moment, no one said anything. Even Mike's pen went silent. Joe was trying to keep his cool, but nothing seemed quite right. It wasn't. The demons played by different rules than the rest of the world. Something definitely went out of Joe that moment. His heart dropped. His eyes lost their luster. His mouth quivered. A thousand things raced through his mind as he tried to regain his composure and stay strong, if nothing else than for the thought of Grace. He stood there, staring at everyone, as though he were in shock.

Joe felt the darkness descending on the room like a cloud of smoke. Things were getting grim. It began to occur to Joe that people thought he had done something much worse than he actually did.

"'But what, Joe wondered, what crime do they think I've committed?'"

He stopped cold. This project was too big and the stakes were too high. It was more than he could handle.

"'Well, Joe you did it again. You thought you could handle this all on your own. Better do something.'"

Joe made a decision: he refused to get upset. It was not the first time he had felt their presence. He might not know the Bible as well as he wished he had, but deep from within it came; somehow he found himself quoting under his breath, "Thy rod and thy staff comfort me. I'm over my head again, but with your help, I will be more than a conqueror."

He stood there and slowly scratched his chin, looking at the table in front of him. He felt angry with himself, but he knew he couldn't let it show, he couldn't let it out, or he'd only make things worse. Life and death were in the power of his tongue.

Joel and Nigel came swooping into the office with blazing words and sweeping power, as the demons disintegrated on all sides. Other warriors shot flaming words into the sky like flares from a cannon, plucking fleeing demons out of the air and silencing them.

Joel could feel Joe's prayer, but he was also distracted by a bad presence in the room. Somewhere, somehow Satan had planted an invisible, insidious infection in the room, and he was attempting to make it grow. Satan had performed cunningly; no one had noticed and it would be difficult to expose the truth. The hearts of the people would have to remain pure to keep the germ out. Thankfully, Joe was growing and had ignited the power the angelic force needed to get the job done.

And so the morning went for the better part of an hour, as everyone took turns discussing the issues the company faced. Nerves flared, bottoms got numb, but eventually, laughter filled the room. Joe had taken his jacket off, loosened his tie, and rolled up his sleeves. They poured over the projected financials until they reached the bottom line. Joe took a deep breath, and then he began to give a final recap of his proposal. Joe looked over at Mike, hoping for his approval. Was his smile a good or bad sign? He couldn't help trying to guess what everyone was thinking.

"Okay, it's time for a vote," he said, handing out slips of paper to two employees who were to pass them out. "Let's keep it simple. If you think we are on the right track, write 'yes,' and if you want to shut the place down and recoup what we can, write 'no'."

This was his moment. He rolled down his sleeves and put his jacket back on because he was feeling nervous and needed something for his hands to do. He also took a moment to say a quick silent prayer.

Joel nudged Michael. "Will Joe have enough votes?"

Michael shook his head, "Yes, I think Joe's prayers have made a difference. Things appear to be turning around."

"Let us hope others are praying as well."

At Joe's request, Father Timothy at that very moment was in the chapel, praying for Joe's business.

Writing a simple yes or no didn't take long, so the votes were immediately collected. Michael stood on the left side of the room, looking fiercely at as many demons as would look at him. Some of the smaller harassing demons flitted about the office, trying to see what the employees were marking on their ballots. What they saw was very unsettling, and their scowling and cursing indicated that things were not going well. Someday soon, maybe even tonight, a directive for their retreat would be issued.

Then came the long, second-by-second wait. Joe scribbled a note to himself and then looked about the room trying to determine how the crowd was voting. A tense silence fell over the room.

A flock of panicking, hissing demons materialized in the room, wanting to see the outcome for themselves. Michael stepped out too. It was only fair, he thought.

Satan swooped down from the ceiling, looking somewhat anemic and hissed, "Get back in your corner."

"I wish to see the outcome, and your downfall." Michael said.

"Oh, I bet you do." Satan sneered. "And what if I decide to strike out at Joe's employees? A nice heart attack or stroke could spice things up!"

Something in the way that Michael answered, "Try it," may have caused Satan to reconsider.

Michael's answer also sent the little demons trembling away like a herd of monkeys. He bent over the two employees who were counting the vote. Cheating made one last attempt to sway the decision. Screeching, he said, "The vote is lost. No votes win. The business will be auctioned off."

The writing on the small bits of paper started to change.

Michael roared, "God's will be done." Immediately the slip retained the original vote. Downcasted, Satan slipped from the room.

Minutes later, the official tally of the votes was announced. The proposal was accepted, and bankruptcy had been averted.

18

Let no feeling of discouragement prey upon you,
And in the end you are sure to succeed.

—Abraham Lincoln

Grace did not want to admit to Joe how hard it was for her when he was gone to attend the stockholder's meeting. She had suffered from an abandonment nightmare. If she had told him that, it would make him feel horrible. One step forward, two steps backward. It had been like that in the beginning, but she thought she was through that obstacle course.

Joe must have realized how hard it would be for Grace to stay home alone. He saw through her. There was a note next to her favorite coffee mug.

> I'm powerless to control this overwhelming love I have for you. I'll be back soon.
>
> Until then, know that you carry me in your heart. Let the peace of God be with you.
>
> Love,
> Joe

The leaves on the impatiens were green—that fresh, new green they wear in late spring. The garden was filled with a myriad of reds, pinks, and oranges. From their small table on the deck, Joe and Grace could watch the ocean crash upon the shore, and the birds flit about the water's edge, diving for sand crabs. This spot on the deck was Grace's favorite. It was so peaceful here, almost a world away from the strifes, questions, and disputes of the past. They lay back on shay lounges looking for pictures in the clouds.

They watched the swells roll toward the shore. They heard them beat upon the sand. They gazed until it was late, long after dark, as the stars spread across the sky. Joe looked at Grace's face, searching it for a brief time.

"What?" she asked.

"It is just that you look so beautiful and peaceful today. I see something different in you."

Grace noticed that too: for the first time in many months, she felt peace inside. Her heart was at rest. It was an all-encompassing peace, and she didn't know if it would last, but she could feel it and knew she wanted more.

"I think, maybe I understand things better, at last I am understanding more how spiritual things work," she said.

Meanwhile, with very gentle, very subtle flitters of his wings, Joe stood behind Grace, stroking her blond hair and speaking sweet words of comfort to her mind.

Joe did some thinking the next day as he walked along the Strand. He thought about his conversations with Father Timothy and his friends. "I've made some mistakes, but at least, even if it is slower than I wish, things are turning around. I know how to handle them if they ever happen again. I'll make better choices. I know how faith operates. I'll gladly surrender my entire life to God. No more fear. Imagine how it ruled me, threatening my every move; I was no more than a slave to it.'"

His newest discovery seemed the most potent. Joe had never realized how the unseen had been at work in his life. Everything had always been so easy. He handled himself well, and blessing just seemed to rain down from everywhere. It seemed as if he were God's favorite. Nothing could go wrong.

He never considered that Satan was in the business of raining down destruction with a resume like no other. Oh, he hadn't singled Joe out in this area. Good or bad, all Satan desired was everyone's destruction; the sooner and more gruesome, the better. He swung the gauntlet over everyone.

That was when Joe first began to think about certain events or specific things being *important* and having a *special effect*. Until then, the notion that only one careless thought or word had a designated, much less, a special purpose, would have been cuckoo to him. He was captivated by the thought. Now Joe was a believer in the *special purpose* of certain events or specific things.

It was a red-letter day for Joe when he first understood the truth—that day he sat thinking of his children. He felt an intense stirring of emotion. It'd been little over a year since their deaths. He wanted to have lunch with them, hug them, to show them the man he had become. Although it was a simple desire, it was one that God could not grant him. Instead, he would have to live with their memories.

He watched the sun sink into the ocean until it went from blazing gold to fire-red. He could see the bright cluster of stars overhead and the Pleiades, the seven sisters, the hinge of the universe. Returning home, he let himself in the front door. Instead of going back to his office, he walked to the living room and began to read the book of Job one more time.

Grace was trying to return to her once-happy life. Every morning, just after she awoke, she would read her list of scriptures about being free from fear and how to live with love, joy, and peace. Grace felt humbled for a brief moment. Her temper was no longer a problem. It was easier now; something she just did, natural. The black haze didn't wash over her anymore. Her voice was calm when she answered Joe.

She was feeling a bit more relaxed and decided to head out to the market. Hoping to please Joe, the meal naturally should include red meat. Maybe a little pot-roast with a Guinness sauce. Cooking the roast slowly all day would fill the house with a wonderful fragrance. She would also need new potatoes and carrots. A manly meal complete with homemade peach pie for dessert.

As she returned from the store, she stopped, pressed her fingers to the center of her forehead where the headache was sneaking back. She felt safe when she was at home. She wanted a glass of wine, but even more than that, a nap in a quiet dark room with a soft blanket. Hopefully no dreams, just oblivion, peace. Should she just quit, take two Tylenol, and go to bed? Obviously, she was making herself crazy by trying to make the perfect meal. Wiser and stronger, she yelled, "No, you don't devil. I'm healed by the stripes of Jesus."

She switched on the light and went straight for some water. Standing with one hand braced on the refrigerator, she gulped it down straight from the bottle. When she lowered it, a faint tapping had her glance toward the window over the sink.

She saw the shape of him. Struggling for breath, she stumbled back as the bottle dropped out of her hand. The plastic bounced on the floor, and water spewed out over the tiles. She covered her mouth tightly with her hands, trying to keep a scream inside, trying to keep quiet. She couldn't get her balance. In a flash, he stood a few feet in front of her.

She didn't look at the demon, didn't move, didn't blink, she was thoroughly frozen. Her own pulse roared in her ears, her heartbeat like thunder. The hugeness of what Grace was seeing was so overwhelming, she couldn't process it. Her body and most of her brain had gone numb, but a part of her mind still functioned, still grasped the monster that was standing there. She had to get away.

The demon gave her a stab and a kick, cackling and shrieking with delight when he saw the fright on her face. Life flooded back into her body, and she fled. Her body acted on its own volition, driven by desperation, without thought or plan. She dashed toward the hallway. The dark spirit fluttered after her as she ran, chattering and spitting. He was sure that he got her this time. How could she escape?

Desperately, she looked around. There was no safe place, no haven where she could hide. Even knowing that admitting it, she couldn't just stand there; she had to get away from him. It was a wonderfully cruel attack.

She reached the bedroom and rested against the hard plaster wall, panting in fear, hurt and angry. "O Lord, help me!"

Mayhem slipped and fell. His words were losing their grip.

The silence in the house, the emptiness of the house when Joe was out was taunting. Right now, she should have been preparing dinner for her family. She missed them. But she was alone, frightened, and so tired. There was a scream in her, trapped by shock and terror and doubt, tearing wildly at her throat. Gasping she cried, "I will fear no evil!"

The angel had been watching, waiting for his turn. The small prayer started things buzzing. Joel stood still, watching his moves, sizing him up. It was nice to see the demon acting so arrogant, as it would be easier to catch him off guard. A cry! A scream, a shaking traveled through the house.

Fear's massive heinous body twisted and morphed as it sailed into the living room and then dropped to the floor, screeching loudly. His black body spewing sulfurous dither, hollering and shouting profanities, and thick red vapor pouring from his nostrils. The room was filling with a putrid haze that almost obscured his shadowy image.

At the end of the room, Joel was glaring at the pitiful demon, his huge powerful body taunt for battle. He took one huge step toward the center of the room praising God, bowing, and folding his wings. The room echoed with the sound of his voice. Then the order exploded from his mouth, "Peace, be still!"

The force of Joel's words was more than enough to get Fear started, along with his friend, Mayhem. The house came back to order, filled with peace and tranquility. Under Joel's protection, Grace was safe.

Satan could sense the change in the atmosphere. He paced back and forth and sank on to his throne with a deep scowl.

"'How could this happen?'" he bitterly mused. "'We sought to destroy her, or at least make her insane. How will I use her to defeat Joe if she is under their protection?'"

The demons stood like statues, silently waiting for his next word.

"'Dam them all!'" he continued to muse.

He fumed and drummed his talons, glaring at them all. "These humans! I hate them all! So now Fear has blundered, and Grace is slipping from our grasp. She is a worse threat to my mission than she ever was!"

A demon stepped forward and bowed, "Will my lord consider abandoning his plan?"

Satan straightened, and his fist thundered down on the sides of his throne, "No! Not this plan. Too much is at stake, too much has already been established. It is the only way I can win. There is too much to be gained. Joe has to be destroyed!"

Satan tried to relax, leaning his head back and letting his breath slowly escape through his pursed lips.

"'This offer was so perfect, and our power so strong, so numerous, so unbeatable! I worked so hard to establish this deal. We have to win'".

Satan continued his mental review, "'Joe was so self-assured, so intellectual, so far from really knowing anything about how the spiritual world worked. He was the perfect specimen for this project.'"

His beastly face grew tight and bitter.

"Until they started praying and reclaiming their rightful power…"

Satan sealed his thoughts.

Then the image was gone. Grace stood frozen in place, trying to get her breath, her sanity.

She didn't want people looking at her out of the corner of their eyes again thinking she was crazy, but she would rather fight back than crumble in fear. Besides, she was making progress. She was back cooking and doing the one thing that always brought her joy. Joe would have the dinner she had planned. Nothing would stop her now.

As Grace entered the den, she caught Joe snoring. She studied his dreaming face and liked what she saw. While he slept, every trace of the fear and torment had disappeared from his face. In these moments, he looked like the young man she had married twenty years earlier, the man who had been her very best friend in the world. He was always happy to see her and would sit for hours and listen to whatever she wanted to talk about. He looked like her beloved Joe.

Grace nestled into the couch next to him, hoping that he would sleep a little longer until the buzzer called them for dinner. She flipped through the channels, but there wasn't much on. She settled for a cooking show, knowing as she watched that she might try cooking the recipe for dinner some day.

Grace felt relaxed, almost sleepy too. Their house felt safer now, probably because she realized God's protection was there. It was hard to believe that, not so long ago, she'd found the world frightening and lost sleep to unimaginable nightmares.

She let her mind wander to happier times, memories of the children. She could look at things more objectively now—it was time for a new beginning. "I'm fine, now. I'm fine. I'm okay. I have Joe. I refuse to be scared. I guess the impossible is made possible by God.'"

It was hard for Grace to define, even to herself, how the miracle occurred. There was just something about putting everything into God's hands and accepting his promises. Her faith may have been childlike, but she liked the idea. She felt she belonged to God in a tangible, quantifiable way. In heaven as on earth, as God's prayer said.

She had done all that she could do. Grace tried to accept that, and put the things that were outside of her control out of her head, for tonight at least. The thought was very comforting.

Then, for just a second, she saw a vision of Joe and her on the deck, with four young children. It was like another world. There are so many wonderful memories: Saturday mornings when Joe would take out his guitar and sing Beach Boys songs with the children while she cooked waffles with sun streaming in the windows; Christmas morning with the smell of fresh-baked cinnamon muffins in the air, watching Christopher as screams and laughs trying to ride his new bicycle in the living room; building sand castles and digging for sand crabs as the waves crashed around them spinning rainbows on the shore; standing with tears in her eyes as she watched Jenifer and Heather walk hand-in-hand into their first day of kindergarten, and Joe wearing Mouseketeer Ears, slumped in a chair at Disneyland, holding Travis as he slept. A world where she was a mother. A simpler place where love was defined in simpler ways. The buzzing from the timer in the kitchen brought her back to the present.

"Honey, dinner is ready," she whispered.

"What?" Joe sleepily asked.

"Hey, sleepyhead. Sorry to wake you but dinner is ready."

"Wow, I was just sitting here praying, and I must have dozed off."

Grace kissed him, "Don't feel bad. I'm glad you got some rest."

He yawned and stretched. "I wanted to talk to you. I can't believe I fell asleep."

"You can talk to me while we eat," she encouraged.

He pulled Grace off the couch and then led the way to the kitchen.

Entering the dining room, there were scents, ones he was glad had not been lost forever. Something succulent was on the stove, something fresh from the pile of farmer's market vegetables. And a combination of both the succulent and the fresh, that was Grace. When she turned, he could see the love and joy in her eyes. They were deep, they were bright, and they were warm.

"For this one night, could we try to forget everything in the past besides just you and me?" she asked, unleashing the full force of her smile on Joe. "It seems like we haven't had any time like that in awhile. I need to be with you. Just you."

That was not a hard request for Joe to agree to, though he knew avoiding the past would be easier said than done. Other matters were on his mind now, so knowing that they had this night to be alone would help.

There were some things that had changed. He felt ready to hope that they might have a family once again. The fear and guilt he had felt had taught him much. He had a chance to concentrate on this new beginning as he gazed into Grace's liquid-blue eyes. He knew he would no longer panic. The next time something came at them, he would be ready. An asset, not a liability.

So they had something to work out that night. After everything he'd learned in the past few months, he didn't believe in the word *impossible* anymore. It was going to take more than that to stop him now.

Okay, well honestly, it was going to be much more complicated than that. But Joe had decided he was going to do it; not just try it, but do it.

As decided as he was, he wasn't surprised that he felt peaceful. He didn't know exactly how to do what he was trying to do, and that guaranteed that he would need to study hard and spend more time with Father Timothy. Joe began to feel cautiously optimistic. Perhaps getting what they wanted would not be as difficult as he used to expect.

"Great idea. Something smells delicious. Do you ever write any of your recipes down?" he said, his tone conversational.

Grace ordered herself to pick up her fork to eat, despite the fact that she wasn't feeling hungry. "Sure, I was organized and a little more carefree before all this happened. I've got recipes filed on my laptop with two thumb drives as backup. You never want to lose a secret family recipe. Why? Are you planning to take over my job as cook?"

"No, I was just wondering why you'd haven't created a family cookbook."

"I used to think I might, eventually when the kids were grown," she added with a smile.

"Eventually never gets done. You want to do something, you do it."

"I'm not sure I could handle it now."

"Maybe it is just what the doctor would order to help you turn things around. I know how much you love cooking."

"Maybe, I will try."

"If you put together a proposal, I will find you an agent." Joe ate the last bit of meat on his plate. "Amazing pot roast. Be sure to put it in the book."

Grace knew something had happened to Joe. She knew it was what he had been searching and waiting for, and honestly she wanted to know what he had found. She turned toward him and scanned his face.

"You know what I think? Joe asked Grace.

She laughed. "No."

Joe smiled.

"What do you think?

"I think I've found the answer, and I can now see how the spiritual and physical worlds are connected. I can't believe we have been through all this because we were so ignorant and arrogant.

Why didn't we realize that the greatest and most important work of Satan was to conceal the truth in order to destroy us?"

Her eyes narrowed as she thought about it.

"But how do they get their advantage?" Grace pondered.

"Foolishly we didn't know any better. I wasn't walking in faith, I lived in fear. For God's blessings to be in our life, we have to use our faith to activate it. Like all the promises, we have our part to play. Things are different now. I plan to wait and pray until it is clear beyond all doubt that God wants me to take action. I only want to do what God tells me to do. I finally understand that all acts of God will be primarily for my liberation from sin, for my deliverance from pain, sickness, and want. All of Satan's works are sent to blind us, causing sin, discouragement, lack of faith, and failure in life. Just as Satan requires lies in our minds to hold us in bondage, so God requires truth in our minds. 'For the truth will set us free'," he insisted.

Grace shook her head in agreement, "Anything is possible."

Suddenly Joe was serious. He took her hands in his, holding them firmly so that she couldn't look away from his intent gaze. "Wow," Joe said, and a strange, fierce half-smile spread across his face. "We are the victors now. We have the advantage. God's blessings are sufficient for us!"

Joe put his arm around Grace and pulled her tightly against his side. "It's going to be amazing, Grace. Trust me."

"'Sure,'" she thought to herself. "'Trust him.'"

After such a delicious dinner, Joe rose to clear the table. He pushed up the sleeves of his sweatshirt, then took the piled-up dishes to take to the kitchen. He washed them off and put them in the dishwasher, then poured some soap in, and shut the door. When the dishes were done, he got to work on the table. He considered blowing out the candles but instead asked, "What's for dessert?"

With that, he took her hand and pulled her to him. His mouth captured hers, firm and strong. All those feelings were there again. Being intimate again was monumental for them. The passion. They reminded each other there was sweetness in the world. And love and kindness. It was good to be part of it again, to feel that again. And it was then that Joe and Grace knew that God would bless their family with more children.

"It could be any time now. Are we ready?" he asked Raphael.

"Yes, the victory is ours!"

On that night, the angelic host waited while Joe prayed.

From that day, Grace was more cheerful, calmer, patient, and kind. Life began to return to its usual pattern. As she dresses in the morning, she looks effortlessly stylish in a long cardigan and a silver belt low over her print top, a dazzling red and white blouse. Her jeans cling tightly to her hips. She smiles as she glances at her image in the mirror.

Joe looked at Grace suspiciously. "Would you consider trying to have another child?"Joe asked.

She hesitated, "Let's clarify what you are proposing."

"You know what I want."

"Babies!" she made it sound like a heavenly word.

"Yes," he smiled a side smile. "A new beginning."

"I didn't realize there was anything else you wanted besides being transformed into a new man. I'm extremely curious how you came to this conclusion."

"Well, we both thought being parents was the best part of our life. I want it all back."

The surprise spoiled her carefully composed expression. Graced paused, staring at his hand in hers. She didn't know how to respond. She felt his eyes watching her, and she was afraid to look up. She bit her lip.

"Wait a little, I need some time to process this," she recommended.

"I will leave it in your hands," he wisely said.

At the end of June, on their twenty-fifth anniversary, Grace told Joe, "I think I'm ready."

Now that Joe and Grace understood things, they wanted to tell everyone in the entire world about their revelation. The kingdom had a process that must be learned if one wanted to flow in it. They both decreed that their lifestyle would now align with the word of God. Likewise, they would no longer tamper with what his word said to make it fit their own lifestyle or beliefs. You would hear them say, "I'm what the word says I am, and I can do what the word says I can do."

"Forces!" Forbodden shrieked, and fifty demons popped up through the roof of Joe's house with moans and grumbling. They launched themselves forward with the power of a wrecking ball. The force sent Lionel flying. Screams abruptly erupted, sending blasts at Michael.

"What brings you here?" Michael asked.

Enclosed by the demonic forces, Michael wanted a little more space. He yelled his command. The seething, hissing spirits backed off, landing in a disheveled pile in the corner. Their frenzied disappointment blazed in their eyes.

Now that he was more comfortable, he spoke. "What are you doing here? Didn't you hear Joe's prayer? Joe is now our charge!"

"Did you really think things would end that simply?" Forbodden protested.

"Forces!" they screamed, struggling to their feet, chanting hideous words at Michael.

Whoosh! The shield of the Lord's glory filled the air. Shredded particles of the demonic spirits fluttered and floated in all directions, trailing black smoke and dissolving into thin air. The remaining spirits froze. None of them were brazen enough to utter another word. They remained like statues, their eyes on the warrior. He remained motionless as well, watching them with his piercing blue eyes.

The demons spit sulfur into the air and, for a moment, looked as though they were planning one more attack. Fear, mustering all the courage he had, moved closer, hissing, spitting, and saying offensive words. Suddenly, Joel's hot words rested right between the demon's yellow fangs. He thought it best not to pronounce another word.

Forbodden began to curse Joel as his demon warriors became steadily braver. "Out! Begone you! This is our territory and none of your concern!"

Joel decided to push this hideous demon to his limits. "Oh, is that what you think?"

He made a move toward the ceiling, ready to pass through it and defend the territory they had just won.

"Attack!" Forboden cried, and every demon rushed forward with blazing words. "Away with him!"

Joel blasted skyward, drawing the horde after him. He stopped, spun, and faced them. His words became a continuous ribbon of light.

The first demon became two halves that passed by Joel on either side and then descended into oblivion. The second and third shouted words to deflect the onslaught. This fight was intense. Soon the demons and angels all joined in the scuffle.

"Yah!" Suddenly Michael, Joel, Gabriel, Raphael, Manuel, and Nigel yelled in unison, "Be gone!"

At that, the demons shot into the sky like rockets, retreating, totally surprised, and livid about it. They backed away higher and higher, trying to stay clear of the ear-piercing words. What horrible situation had they walked into?

Forbodden seemed to realize that he was on his own. He began to back away from Michael, turbulent disillusionment blazing in his eyes. He took one last agonized look at the angelic forces, and then he started to retreat faster. And then the fiery scuffle was over.

He lit the fire in the fireplace, hoping that it would be simmering red embers when Grace got home. He hoped that she would feel the warmth, and the love he had for her would simmer inside her heart. He could bask in it, stroking her hair, her skin, letting her surrender to him. Tonight she would be soothed by his hands and know the quiet glow of happiness. He'd made her favorite soup accompanied by strawberries dipped in chocolate.

Grace fumbled with her keys, and Joe opened the door and helped her carry in her packages. After placing them on the couch, Joe gently raised Grace's head slowly to meet his patient gaze. His expression was soft; his eyes were full of understanding. Joe recognized, and he supposed Grace did too, that their future would be forever altered if they proceeded to kiss. It was more than an everyday kiss. It was the meeting of two hearts, an admission of her openness and vulnerability. Love washed over them in sweeping waves.

Joe wasn't sure who moved first but chose to think of what followed as a mutual decision. As she reached for him, he wanted most to comfort her, to smooth out all her pain, and then lift her from it. No one else had ever reached that tenderness inside him; no one else had ever coaxed it out until he married her. Joe could give her that, the tenderness. And every soft sigh she offered back only enhanced his pleasure.

As he undressed her, his fingers brushed over her skin. The scent of his soap aroused her passion. To touch, to smell, to hold. Her fingers outlined his face and then slipped into his hair as her body arched to give and give. He touched her with care and patience, their lips met again and again with such sweetness.

Everything inside them went loose and liquid, and he could almost hear her purring with delight.

They fell into the deep magic abyss of love; their hearts fell with them, tumbling free. They couldn't stop the pleasure, couldn't catch their breath. Once again, Grace's senses reeled. The sheer pleasure of the caress scattered her thoughts, leaving her gasping and grasping for an anchor—something to hold her grounded. Whatever she had expected from him that night, this was more. Grace stared up at Joe, her emotions in such a rolling storm of passion and lust and ever-present love that she trembled. She felt lost in the ocean without a compass.

Love never fails.

They lay together entwined, as the night fluttered away and the embers died. When he felt her begin to drift off, he simply grabbed the throw on the back of the couch and pulled it over them. She cuddled in and murmured something. Beside her, he closed his eyes and smiled in the dark. "Thank you, Lord."

Then they slept a deep sleep filled with love.

The house was filled with visitors, no fewer than a hundred. Gabriel was there, along with Michael, recently returned from his surveillance of Manhattan Beach. Manuel and Raphael were already at Joel's side. And at their command was a formidable troop of warriors. Nigel was in attendance and overseeing the hedge of guards now surrounding the house. This home would be a safe haven, no longer invaded by marauding spirits.

The fact that Joe and Grace were now accompanied by several angelic forces helped keep things peaceful. "No more harassments for the rest of the week. I'm done with bringing railing accusation against Satan." Michael simply said, "God rebukes thee! It is time for Grace and Joe to heal from their heart wrenching past."

There was an eruption of sickly rancid vapors, one final shriek, and the flailing of withering Satanic creatures. Then there was nothing at all except the fading stench of sulfur and the angelic forces. The white light that surrounded them began to fade away, as their praises gently quieted. Fear was vanquished. Mercy would once again reign.

The next morning, they stood over the praying warrior in a circle, little by little, like a blossoming rose; white light began to flood the yard. Slowly the colors in the garden grew to intensity until the once plain and humble spot came alive with an extraordinary beauty. They placed their hands upon the shoulders of Joe and then—like a gracefully spreading canopy—lustrous, sparkling, nearly transparent wings began to unfurl from their backs and shoulders and rise to meet and overlap above their heads, gently fluttering in a spiritual wind. The angels ministered peace to Joe, and his time of tears and mourning had come to an end.

Joe finally understood the coming redemption, and his prayers would now be filled with a love that no longer feared an evil outcome. He knew that God was the loving God who gives and takes away. Now he understood that God took away evil and replaced it with blessing. It was Satan that stole and brought pain and suffering. Love would cover the multitude of sins his friends had committed. Love had taken away the fear. This time, when he prayed, he knew God would cover his friends with his amazing grace. God restored Joe's fortunes and gave him twice as much as he had before. All his brothers and sisters and everyone who had known him before came and celebrated his forty-eighth birthday with him in his house. They celebrated his new beginning.

Grace agreed that it would be nice to accompany Joe to the restaurant they'd gone to the first time they had a real date. She even felt a craving for one of their special dishes.

All the same, Joe sensed that Grace was still a little uncertain and struggling to find her footing. He was eager to find out exactly how things were going with Father Timothy.

"I've been wondering how your meetings with Father Timothy are going," he said.

"I'm all right. Father Timothy has helped so much. I feel as though a new chapter is opening in my life."

"I'm sorry all this happened. I never meant to put you through it."

"You shouldn't feel bad. After all it's not your fault."

He stared at her with an astonished grin. Her words were like medicine.

"Grace"—he put his arms around her shoulder—"You can't imagine how wonderful it is to hear you say that."

She didn't say anything for a moment, but she was weighing his words. "I'm glad I've made you happy. You have been so patient with me. So amazing."

He reached over and kissed her. "I love you."

She stared down at the table. After a pause, she picked up her glass of water, took a slow sip, and put it down on the table again.

"There's something else you should know," she hesitated and looked up into his eyes. Their eyes met, and she smiled the softest, sweetest smile. There was a moment of silence, and then Grace did something completely out of character. There in the middle of the restaurant, she did the salsa touchdown dance.

Then she yelled, "Touchdown, we're having a baby!"

When she finished, he grinned, enjoying the amusement in her voice. "I had no idea you were pregnant," he exclaimed.

"I know. Isn't it wonderful? I just found out from the doctor."

"Why didn't you tell me?"

"I don't know. I was anxious and nervous at first. I didn't want to get our hopes up before I was sure it was a strong pregnancy. The doctor says everything is the way it should be. I know it makes no sense to be fearful after what Father Timothy has taught us. But I'm still growing, learning, increasing my faith."

"Of course." He pulled her to him and held her closer. "You could have told me. You can trust me."

Grace nodded silently. She knew that now.

They talked quietly for a long time. It seemed to Joe that her mood was light and bright. She felt warm beside him.

After dinner, they walked down the Strand toward their house. Feeling light-hearted, Grace began to dance, her summer dress swaying with the rhythm of her body. Joe offered her his arm, and she put her hand through it. She liked walking with him like that. As they entered the gate in front of the house, Joe kissed Grace and she kissed him back. He hadn't planned it at all, but it felt so right—just like it used to.

He came into the kitchen carrying a load of tulips. His familiar husky voice sent a wave of yearning through Grace. "Are they still your favorite flowers?"

A thousand memories spun in her head, tangling together: his quirky smile, a mug of hot tea at her bedside, the deserted sandy seashore, his bagpipe lessons, a bag of popcorn they shared at the movies, and their honeymoon in Hawaii. She was homesick for all these things.

"Wow!" Her smile was luminous as she took them. "They are wonderful and beautiful and sweet. Like the rainbow after a really bad storm."

"Yes, a symbol that a hell of a storm has passed, and now it's time for rainbows. We will see all that God has promised us."

Joe took advantage of the moment. When Grace's face turned toward his with the slow movement of joy, he grabbed her in his arms till his lips reached hers. His hands seized her face, and he leaned over and gently kissed her cheek. "Is this really where you want to be?"

"Exactly where." Everything seemed crystal clear as she looked into his eyes. "Exactly where I want to be."

It was something that Joe had been waiting for. Something he knew that would happen again, as much as he wished it would. It would never end again, never!

He didn't stop kissing her. Grace was the one to break away, gasping for air. Even then, his lips did not leave her skin, they just moved down her neck. The thrill of victory was a strange high; it made him feel powerful. Loved.

Grace pulled his mouth back to hers, and she seemed just as eager as he was. Joe's hand still cupped her face; his other arm was tight around her waist, pulling her closer to him.

His lips were at her ear again, "Grace, if I asked you to do something, would you trust me?" Joe asked, an edge to his gentle voice.

Grace's pulse sped in response to his question, "That depends. What do you want me to do?"

Then came the pause and Grace's long expectant gaze.

"I want you to trust me that we are going to make this happen, you and me. Now that a baby is on its way, there is so much to be grateful for. Grace, we've been so blessed lately. I feel something beyond our imagination is on the horizon. I bet you are expecting twins."

Grace was lost in her own thoughts for a moment, and Joe wondered if she was thinking the same thing too. When she smiled at him, her expression suddenly triumphant, he knew that she already knew that his prayers had been answered.

God blessed the latter part of Joe's life more than the former part. Joe and Grace reconciled. Miraculously, she had a change of heart. Under Joel's and Father Timothy's watch and direction, she realized how much she had missed the fire in Joe's eyes and his loving touches. Some old pleasant feelings rose up within her, feelings she felt had been lost forever.

Joe had been reading Job every day now for the past month as his daily reading, and the more he read about Job and his struggles, the more he realized his limited knowledge about God. He needed to know the biblical characters who shook the world, the ones who today are remembered and would be his heroes forever.

You know what Joe noticed? Each and every one of these heroes, not only in the Bible, but throughout history, went through seasons of tremendous difficulties and trials. Some faced years. And yes, it continues being the pattern, which seems unfortunate for us; but if and when we overcome and endure that season, the end results are glorious.

Looking back, Joe remembered problems, situations, and circumstances that he struggled to get through because he was trying to rely on his own power and strength to change them. He had a lack of knowledge of the Word of God. Yes, he would pray here and there, but he really did not know what God's promises were and he didn't even know if his prayers were correct. It was almost like Joe was walking in total darkness. Joe finally realized that the things he was doing and saying were causing a lot of his problems and helping to sustain his problems. In other words, he was adding fuel to the fire, so to speak. The more problems he had, the more negative he became prophesying his own downfall. Joe was saying all the wrong things, and he said them long enough until he was fully persuaded that it would come to pass, and most of them did. At that point in his life he didn't know the full truth.

Finally, he received a revelation of the Word and how to apply the principles of the kingdom to his life. He began to learn and study these principles and build his faith in the Word of God. The change didn't come overnight. It was a learning process, and he practiced his faith and developed faith in the authority of God's Word. The change in his life was revolutionary when he began to say what God said about him in the Bible. He would still have battles to face, but now he would do it with God's power on his side. He would learn to stand on the Word of God and not waiver. He would walk by faith and not by sight. He would learn how to pray correctly so his prayers would be answered.

Joe felt that angels have appeared periodically throughout his life, and in the fall of 2010, even Jesus himself showed up in the guise of a young Southern California surfer dude. He helped save Joe from a fate not exactly worse than death, but close. He still has the binoculars sitting on the mantle above the fireplace. Examining the name on the front of them he smiled—TruVue. No wonder he saw everything in his life differently!

Joe 42:12

"Now the Lord blessed the latter days of Joe more than his beginning; for he had fourteen oil tankers, six thousand cattle, one hundred shares of Berkshire Hathaway stock, and three houses. He and Grace were blessed with two sets of twins: Michael (who is like God) and Jason (the healer), and Annelies (grace) and Tiffany (appearance of God). They were the most beautiful girls in California. After this, Joe lived to be one hundred twenty years old and saw his children, grandchildren, and great grandchildren for four generations. So Joe died, old, and full of days."

Epilogue

It's Your Choice!

In summary, Joe's word to Godly sufferers is that God marvels when he sees great faith in action. There isn't anything more sacred than using the words of God in prayer and manifesting spiritual success. Joe knows the great I am who was and is and is to come. Joe learned that praying in fear brought evil results by opening the door for Satan's persecution. Love and faith in an all-powerful God brought him success and blessings.

The reason many people don't understand what happened to Joe is that they believe God caused the evil that came upon him. But when you look at the book of Job the scriptures did not say God destroyed Job's family. It was the agents of Satan that performed these deeds. Satan knew that if he was to prevent the all-encompassing purpose of God, he must overcome the godly faith of human beings.

Like Job, Joe finally realized that there was no fear greater than his faith. There was only his complete and total trust in the promises of God. One's peace (*completeness, prosperity*, and *welfare)* are at stake in the titanic struggle between the adversary Satan and our great God.

People must learn to trust in God's promises and acknowledge, serve, and submit to an all powerful and all knowing Sovereign Lord, who has offered them a most amazing way of escape when they enter a spiritual conflict between the kingdom of God and the kingdom of Satan—between the kingdom of light and the kingdom of darkness.

It is a matter of Joe's understanding and acting on the authority of God's word. He used the word of God to defeat the purposes of the messengers of Satan. Joe submitted himself to

God, resisted the devil (He stopped fearing what would happen because he realized who God was), and the devil fled from him. Another way to look at it is: God couldn't if Joe didn't. God has offered Joe salvation, but if Joe refuses to accept, he will go to hell. It's just that simple. God will give us what he has promised in the Bible if we are willing to accept it as our own. Salvation is a free gift.

Joe also learned that it is Satan who gives evil and takes away blessings.

It has been my purpose since the beginning of this book to examine the subject of angels and demons. Having completed that, I must now ask, "What does all this mean for you? How will this affect your life?"

The first and most obvious step is to simply believe there are angels and demons. The words *angel* and *angels* are used 297 times in the Bible. In short, if one accepts the authority of the Bible, one must likewise accept the reality of angels and demons. They are attested to throughout it.

Even after more than three years of teaching by Jesus, the disciples still had to be rebuked for their unbelief and hardness of heart. This isn't because they could not understand, but because they chose not to believe. One may struggle at first to fully accept and realize that they are dealing with angels and demons every day. But, like a child, simply accept what God's word says.

If you do find yourself in dire straits, you can have confidence that when you pray, angels will be dispatched on your behalf. You may be one of the ones who have the privilege of seeing angels. But whether you see them or not, you must still be hospitable to strangers "for thereby some have entertained angels unawares."

If Joe had one last final word for you it would be, "Start confessing what you desire and stop confessing what you don't want in your life. Base your requests on the promises of God. It is as simple as that. If you read it in your Bible then God said it. Then it is up to you to use your faith to believe it and then it will be so. Take the word of God; meditate on it daily to build up your soul. Your soul can then connect with your born again spirit. It will transform your thoughts so that when you speak it out of your mouth things will change. Don't take hold of anything else until the spiritual word manifests in the physical realm—until you see the desired word come to pass." Joe wants you to know that rather than saying what you have, you should be speaking what God has promised you and receiving the desires of your heart.

Your future is in your faith!

About Gaelyn Whitley Keith

Writing in clear, understandable language, Keith introduced the concept of Christian self-talk and set the stage for the use of it in one's personal development.

Keith has enriched audiences with her enlightening, straight-forward presentations. An authority on the science of neuroplasticity and personal growth Keith presents an eye-opening and electrifying answer to each individual's search for both success and meaning.

In this exciting new book she brings the fields of neuroscience, Christianity, and personal growth together in a new and enlightened way.

We are presented with a Biblical truth that proves the human brain is designed to be physically rewired—throughout our lifetimes—based on the messages we give ourselves. We no longer need to reside in the Newtonian World—our new home is the Quantum.

Keith is a Certified Self-Talk Coach™ and a Certified Self-Talk Trainer™.

Books by Gaelyn Whitley Keith:
The Father of Hollywood

listen|imagine|view|experience

AUDIO BOOK DOWNLOAD INCLUDED WITH THIS BOOK!

In your hands you hold a complete digital entertainment package. In addition to the paper version, you receive a free download of the audio version of this book. Simply use the code listed below when visiting our website. Once downloaded to your computer, you can listen to the book through your computer's speakers, burn it to an audio CD or save the file to your portable music device (such as Apple's popular iPod) and listen on the go!

How to get your free audio book digital download:

1. Visit www.tatepublishing.com and click on the e|LIVE logo on the home page.
2. Enter the following coupon code:
   ac02-166a-d1e6-2e31-0dc1-a89e-2ec2-4ce7
3. Download the audio book from your e|LIVE digital locker and begin enjoying your new digital entertainment package today!